I0637427

Lights. Camera. Murder!

Published by Sanibel Press www.SanibelPress.com
318 E Orange Street, Altamonte Springs, Fl 32701

Second e-published by Sanibel Press March 2006
Second print publishing March 2006

Cover art by Sanibel Press, Inc.
Cover illustration Copyright © by Sanibel Press 2006

All rights reserved except for use in any review, the reproduction of
utilization of this work in whole in part in any form by an electronic,
mechanical or other means, now known or hereafter invented, including
xerography, photocopying and recording, or in any information storage
or retrieval systems is forbidden without the written permission of the
editorial office of Sanibel Press located at 318 E Orange Street, Altamonte
Springs, Fl 32701 U.S.A.

www.SanibelPress.com

This is a work of fiction. Names, characters, places, and incidents are the
product of the author's imagination. Any resemblance to persons living
or dead, business establishments, events or locals is entirely coincidental.
All characters in this book have no existence outside the imagination of
the author and have no relation whatsoever to anyone bearing the same
name or names.
Printed in the U.S.A.

Copyright © 2006 Linn Random
All rights reserved.
ISBN: 0-9776955-0-6

LINN
RANDOM

LIGHTS.
CAMERA.
MURDER!

2006

Lights. Camera. Murder!

LIGHTS, CAMERA. MURDER!
5 Stars, 5 Hearts, 5 Unicorns, 5 Cups of Coffee, 5 Angels

*M*s. *Random has delivered a story full of suspense. Sage is full of sass and Jon is the epitome of a hard-nosed, tough cop who demands things go his way-and if they do not? Well, find a place to hide while he roars. These two characters are the perfect complement to each other and a totally intriguing story. Coffee Time Romance*

On Location:

Just seventy miles north of Tampa, on Florida's Gulf Coast, St. Gabrielle offered McMasters Studio the perfect locale for this third in a series of reality "whodunits" that allowed the TV audience to follow along in week to week episodes. Isolated and surrounded by water on three sides, Sand Point Inn was attached to the mainland by a tiny piece of land that serves as a natural bridge. Dark foreboding cypress swamps stand as twin sentinels on either side of the roadway. The location supervisor had assured the Studio it's the perfect place for *MURDER!*

Sage McCall looked around the television production set and tried to focus her attention anywhere except at the dead man lying at her feet.

Long after midnight, the familiar shapes of television cameras, sound booms and dollies were obscured in the darkness. Their outlines took on strange silhouettes in the half-lit room.

Overhead lights hung from the dark shadows and the studio cameras pointed toward the empty set, which sat obscured in complete darkness. No actors, no contestants, no cheery host to startle the contestants with new surprises.

To her left, an empty director's chair sat surrounded by dark monitors. To her right, an odd assortment of heavy crates and boxes were stacked high.

It was all so quiet, too quiet.

Sage took a long breath and looked down at the lifeless body of the gaffer.

"He's dead," Double K said staring down at the corpse.

"I can see that," Sage replied in a voice void of emotion. She bent down and pressed her index and middle finger to the dead man's neck. No pulse, confirming what she already knew was true.

"He was shot with an arrow," Double K said as if she didn't notice the two foot arrow protruding out of the man's chest.

"Thanks," Sage said without humor, "I can see that too."

Ken Kendrick, 'Double K,' stood looking twice his 6'5" height. If he fashioned his hair into a Mohawk style, he could have easily passed for a younger Mr. T. He slowly folded his arms across his massive chest. "What are we going to do now?"

Sage slowly rose to her feet and took a backward step away from the corpse. A real life murder was not in the script of this latest reality television show.

"First, we are going to call the Police Chief," she said with a groan. She had already had two run-ins with him. Despite his movie star good looks, he had made it very clear that the film crew and cast of *Murder in Florida* were not welcome in his quiet resort town. She was still seething from their last encounter. What had he called her, Malibu Barbie? He was the last man she wanted to call; she punched in the numbers and braced herself for his reaction.

ALSO BY LINN RANDOM
Lights, Camera. Murder!

Your Cheatin' Hearts
Pirates in Paradise

Watch for these future best sellers from Linn Random
Black Waters
Haunted Hearts
Cold River Murders
Mourning Song

CHAPTER ONE

L ooking around the television production set, Sage tried to focus her attention anywhere except toward the dead man lying at her feet.

Long after midnight, the familiar shapes of television cameras, sound booms, and dollies were obscured in the darkness. Their outlines took on strange silhouettes in the half-lit room.

Overhead lights hung from the dark shadows and the studio cameras pointed toward the empty set, which sat obscured in complete darkness. No actors, no contestants, no cheery host to startle the contestants with new surprises.

To her left, an empty director's chair sat surrounded by dark monitors. To her right, an odd assortment of heavy crates and boxes were stacked high.

It was all so quiet, too quiet.

Sage took a long breath and stared down at the lifeless body of Evan Davis, the gaffer, the chief lighting technician for the production.

"He's dead," Double K said glancing down at the corpse.

"I can see that," Sage replied, her voice void of emotion. Bending down, she placed her index and middle finger to the dead man's neck. No pulse, confirming what she already knew was true.

"He was shot with an arrow," Double K said as if she didn't notice the two-foot arrow protruding out of the man's chest.

"Thanks," Sage said without humor, "I can see that too."

Ken Kendrick, 'Double K,' stood looking twice his six-foot-five height. If he fashioned his hair into a Mohawk style, he could have easily passed for a younger Mr. T. Sage knew him as a gentle black giant, who was both her protector and her friend. He slowly folded his arms across his massive chest. "What are we going to do now?"

Rising to her feet, Sage took a backward step away from the corpse, assessing the situation, and formulating a plan of action. A real life murder was not in the script of this latest reality television show. She found no humor in it.

"First, we are going to call the Police Chief," she said with a groan. She had already had two run-ins with him. Despite his movie star good looks, he had made it very clear that the film crew and cast of *Murder in Florida* were not welcome in his quiet resort town. She was still seething from their last encounter. What had he called her, Malibu Barbie? He was the last man she wanted to call this quiet, somber night.

The Chief of Police tolerated them because he had to. Fortunately for True West Production Company and McMasters Studios, the mayor of this hamlet was convinced *Murder in Florida* put his tiny coastal town, St. Gabrielle, on the map.

"After I alert the Police Chief," she continued, "we're going to partition off this entire area. No one is to come in or out. Speaking of…where the heck is Jamie Wolf? Wasn't he supposed to be here?"

Double K shook his head. "Haven't seen him."

Pressing her lips together, she looked around as if waiting for her second security guard to materialize from the darkness. This wasn't like Jamie. Despite his shaggy blonde California looks, he was hard working and didn't slack. With no immediate sense of urgency as she looked down at the corpse,

Jamie had probably made his last round about eleven and gone on to bed.

"Well," she said turning her attention back to Double K, "if this is a crime scene, we're going to have to keep the evidence, everything intact."

"Ah, Sage," Double K began matter-of-factly, "the man has got an arrow through the center of his chest. This is a crime scene."

Glaring at him, she said in a voice as cool as ice water, "Go get Hillary."

She groaned at the thought of waking Hillary. After years of struggling in the business, *Murder in Florida* was to be Hillary Kenyon's directorial debut. Though Sage considered Hillary a near psychopath, Sage admired Hillary's obsession to detail. She had no idea how Hillary would react and braced herself for either a facade of new age serenity or complete hysteria.

Watching Double K leave, she was painfully aware of being alone on the empty production set with the corpse.

The site location was actually St. Gabrielle, Florida; just seventy miles north of Tampa on the Gulf of Mexico. St. Gabrielle offered McMasters the perfect locale for this third in a series of reality "whodunits" that allowed the audience to follow along with week to week episodes.

Murder in Santa Barbara had been last summer's runaway hit. Its sequel in the winter *Murder in New England* hadn't fared as well. Despite the poor ratings in the last sequel, the producers believed *Murder in Florida* would rocket the series back to the top of the Nielsen chart. Though it was being filmed now for air play sometime next summer, the crew, the cast, the actors, and the contestants had assembled two weeks ago.

Most filming was set out of doors, but beginning and

closing segments were filmed in this room, a renovated restaurant known in its heyday as the Sand Point Inn.

The production set had been constructed months earlier in this abandoned restaurant. The adjacent hotel, also renovated by McMasters Studio, served as a backdrop for the make-believe TV murder, and also housing for the crew, cast, and contestants.

Isolated and surrounded by water on three sides, the Sand Point Inn was attached to the mainland by a tiny piece of land that served as a natural bridge. Dark foreboding cypress swamps stood as twin sentinels on either side of the roadway. A perfect murder indeed, Sage thought looking down at the corpse.

A light gray mist curled its silvery tongue at the windows, licking its moist breath and faint pungent smell from the sea, against the glass panes. Standing still Sage could hear the soft, steady pounding of the gulf waters, lapping against the restaurant's wooden deck. During the day the restaurant and outside deck provided a spectacular view of the Gulf of Mexico with brilliant multicolored sunsets.

Just before turning in for the night, Double K found Evan's body.

Evan lacked social grace and at times was downright rude, but Sage couldn't think of any reason anyone would have to kill him. She knew he had a drinking problem but she was sure Hillary, her AD, Assistant Director, Connard, and the crew's Associate Producer, Jeff Sanders, were all aware of Evan's frequent nips from 'the bottle.' Babysitting the crew wasn't her problem, security was.

Born the third daughter to Jack and Savannah McCall, she was Daddy's little girl and heir-apparent to her father's successful Los Angeles security firm. Neither sister would oppose her in this. Fallon, the oldest, was determined to follow in their beautiful mother's footsteps and become a movie star. Mallory, the youngest sister, denounced the superficial LA lifestyle and had taken her three dogs and a cat to the great woods of Northern California.

Though he loved his family dearly, Jack McCall considered her two sisters and their Mother certified flakes. He nevertheless indulged all of them in their every whim and gave each their heart's desire. He could afford to.

Once a stunt man, Jack McCall started his security firm shortly after the Tate-LaBianca Murders in '67. Today, McCall Security was one of the largest, most respected security firms in Los Angeles. Not only did it provide security and bodyguards to the movie stars and rock legends but also provided security to movie and television crews shooting in or out of LA.

Sage had grown up in this world and as a likable and lovely child had been embraced by both the famous and not so famous.

With a degree in criminal psychology, training in various types of martial arts, firearms, and special tactical training, Sage relished every aspect of the business, knowing one day she would be running it.

Murder in Florida was supposed to be just another assignment and not a very glamorous one at that. When asked by her father to oversee security on the location, she hadn't given it a second thought.

Now, less than a week into production, she had a corpse on her hands.

With two confrontations with the Chief of Police Jon Maddux under her belt in as many weeks, she was hardly eager for another one.

"I have to call Dad," Sage said aloud, pushing herself to action, "but I have to call Maddux first."

During their last meeting, while he split hairs with her about a traffic assistance permit, he had taken in every inch of her long blonde hair, her blue eyes, her full bust, small hips, and trim athletic body.

Gritting her teeth, she pulled her cell phone from her belt and bypassed the emergency operator to directly connect to the St. Gabrielle Police Department. The less people to know about this the better.

"This is Sage McCall, Security Chief for McMasters Production Company; I need to report a murder," she began in an even voice to the dispatcher, "on the set of *Murder in Florida.*"

"Hey Sage," a friendly male voice replied. "This is Billy Neville. Remember me? I work for you part time?"

"Hey, Billy," she replied wondering if he had heard her correctly, or perhaps, he thought she was having a bit of fun. She kept her voice clear and insistent as she said, "Look, I need you to get your Chief of Police and the Medical Examiner to the set. Double K found one of the production crew dead; he appears to have been shot."

"OK, geeze, look," came Billy's troubled reply. "Let me find the Chief right away. Stay on the line; I'll put you on through."

Before she could say, "no, you call him," Billy had already placed her on hold.

Fifteen long seconds later, she heard the clicking sounds that patched her though to Jon Maddux.

"A murder?" he snarled instantly.

Sage's heart sank; he was home and in bed. The call woke him up. This was getting better by the minute.

He didn't bother to hide his throaty yawn. "Are you sure?"

He sounded bored.

"Yes, I'm sure" she snapped.

The long exhausted sigh from the other end did little to soothe her temperament. Wishing she could hang up and apologize for disturbing his sleep, she stood still, her cell phone in hand. She wrapped her delicate little fingers about the cell the way she wished she could wrap them around Jon Maddux's neck.

"All right, all right," he said as though he were indulging a child frightened by the boogie man, "let me get dressed. I'll be there in twenty minutes."

He ended the call without the good manners to say goodbye.

Sage's lips formed an angry 'oh' before she snapped her cell phone into its casing.

"Jerk!" she said for no one to hear. Still incensed, she allowed her mind to drift to the tall, tanned, good looking Chief of Police. Dark brown eyes, short chestnut hair, and he had a chest that money couldn't buy. She imagined the long tanned legs sliding out from cool sheets. She followed the large hands as they reached for his pants, and then in her mind's eye followed the pants up the muscular calves and firm thighs to slip over the narrow hips to his trim waist. Indulging herself, she saw that tan police shirt being slid over each muscular arm to the broad shoulders before miraculously being buttoned over his broad chest.

He wouldn't bother to use a comb she mused, just unceremoniously rake his fingers his dark hair. Annoyed at the vivid images that sprang unexpectedly to her mind's eye and angry at herself for entertaining them, she banished the visions to the dark side of her soul. Clearly, she had more pressing issues to deal with than the handsome Chief of Police.

Glancing at her watch, she read 3:35 in LA. She hesitated about placing the call but knew she had to.

Her father answered. "Hello, Pumpkin. It's late, later for you. Anything wrong, sweet pea?"

Sage drew a soft breath. "Dad, there's been a murder on the set."

She heard her Dad chuckle.

"Very funny, now let your Mom and I go back to bed. You do the same."

"Dad," she said dropping her voice, "there has been a real murder on the set. Double K found the gaffer. He has been shot through the chest....with an arrow."

This time she had her father's full attention. She continued, "I have already called the Chief of Police. Double K has gone to wake Hillary."

"Do you want me to come out?" her father said slowly, "I'll fly out tonight."

"No Dad, I have it under control. I'll call you after Chief Maddux gets here."

She could almost hear her father thinking. "All right, honey, I'll need to call Nick McMasters. As studio head, he needs to know now. I'll call. No, I'll drive on over there. You say it was the gaffer? What's his name?"

"Evan Davis."

"Don't know him. Nick will want to know how this will affect the production. I'll find him. He'll either be at his house or the studio. Either way, I'll have my cell phone on. Call me when you know more."

The line went dead and Sage ended her connection. This

was going to be a long night in LA, Sage mused. This was going to be a long night in Florida as well.

Across town, Jon Maddux struggled to shake off sleep. The image of Sage McCall and all she represented flashed in his mind. He had fought hard to keep the television film crew away from his town. In the end, his voice was silenced by the city fathers eager for the tourist dollars that the show would bring. They didn't seem to realize with the fame and notoriety would come some big city problems. Problems he thought he had left behind in South Florida.

Glancing at the wall calendar, he read it was May twenty-second. Had he been here two years?

He tried to go back in his mind and remember a time when he was innocent of the cruelty man inflicted on his fellow man. He couldn't remember that far back.

He had come here to escape that world, to find peace, to find himself, and little Miss Sage McCall and company was on the verge of taking it all away...again.

This was not the life he'd planned. After college and a stint with the military, he had joined the DEA, being assigned to his hometown, Miami. He grimaced, remembering that once he actually believed he could make a difference in the drug war in South Florida. For every drug felon down, for every murder, for every good cop gone bad, a hundred more rose in their place. In the end, his efforts were hardly a drop in the proverbial bucket.

Frustrated, he left the DEA, his partner's untimely death for which he felt responsible and a string of mediocre relationships, to move to the small town of St. Gabrielle. The change had been good for him and he liked the feeling of keeping peace in the small town. Somewhere in the back of his mind he was even beginning to hope he could have what other men had: a wife, family, kids. Hell, he wanted it all.

His world was about to turn inside out and he resented it. He resented the damn TV show that came to town and he resented her!

Sliding into his pants, he muttered a silent oath under his breath at the Mayor and his group of small town cohorts who, when they had heard the TV studio was going to lease the old Sand Point Inn, had rushed in and purchased the property for a song cheating a widow from her due.

He jerked his shirt off the chair where he had thrown it the night before, and with it came the haunting image of beautiful Sage McCall.

She had walked into his office the first time regarding one of the location's shooting permits. He had been unprepared for their initial meeting and recalled quickly the image she had left.

Her manner had been crisp and straightforward. Transfixed by the tempting, sensuous way her full lips moved as she spoke in a soft, melodious voice, it was her sapphire eyes, the color of the shimmering turquoise waters of the Florida Keys, that held him the most.

Her lips were the color of a pink hyacinth and promised to be every bit as sweet.

He had let her talk while he took the time to examine the soft curves of her trim, athletic body as she moved about his office.

The wealth of blonde hair pulled back in a ponytail gave the impression it had been spun from pure gold. She was a natural blonde with luxurious strands of wheat gleaming with honeyed highlights, perfected by the golden California sun. He wondered at the time if it would also be as soft to touch.

She reminded him of an actress he had seen on TV recently, but couldn't place the name. Besides, wasn't everyone in Hollywood just waiting to be a star? He was sure this seductive little beauty, despite her wholesome good looks, was no exception.

Though he would hardly qualify as an expert on women's makeup, she wore little. He did, however, like the way she accented her perfectly shaped oval face with just a touch of dusty rose at her high cheeks. It suited her and appealed to him.

He had admired her tight, hard little body. She was athletic, with slim hips curving to firm thighs, and well-defined calves. Her arms were small but shapely and suggested a weight-training regimen. Overall, she was exquisite and pleasing to the eye.

He had originally guessed that she was some rent-a-cop who had little to do but walk the set and look good. Then he realized she was Sage McCall, Jack McCall's little girl. Even he had heard of the legendary McCall Security Firm whose bodyguards and security details kept watch over Hollywood's most affluent and prestigious palaces.

Ignoring his attraction to her, he was under strict orders to ensure her wishes were followed. My job, he thought, tightening his belt, is to uphold the law, not cater to the whims and fancies of Sage McCall.

On her second visit, he had argued with her and had been pleasantly surprised to find that when attacked she could turn into a little wolverine who held her ground.

Now she was claiming a real murder had happened. He swore under his breath. Given the nature of the TV show's theme, the news media was going to have a field day. What he thought would stay under wraps until the show aired would now be on the cover of every new tabloid in the country.

At the moment, however, he wasn't all that certain that there had been a murder. There was only one way to find out.

He glanced at his watch. He would be at the Sand Point Inn in less than twenty minutes. Strangely, he found himself interested not only in this alleged murder but also seeing Ms. McCall again, Hollywood rent-a-cop or not.

Sage turned just in time to see the show's director, Hillary Kenyon, standing at the doorway. Though Sage and Double K were her only audience, she slumped dramatically. She cried out, "Oh my God!"

Noting Hillary's momentous pause at the doorway, Sage frowned.

Assured she had Sage and Double K's attention, Hillary's beautiful features relaxed a bit. With her hands flaying wildly in the air, she rushed across the room, her white silk housecoat open to reveal a matching ankle-length gown. At least she was clothed, Sage thought with gratitude.

"Oh my God! Oh my God! Oh my God!" Hillary cried. Rushing toward Sage, Hillary dodged cameras and moved as quickly as a Monday night running back, ducking about lighting equipment, around the dolly, and almost leaping over electrical wiring. She stopped abruptly at Sage's side and stared down at the dead man propped up against a long wooden crate.

Staring at the corpse, she blinked and turned to Double K. Hillary's lovely face twisted. With an exasperated sigh, she spat. "You didn't tell me it was the gaffer. You made it sound like someone important!"

Double K's expression didn't change. Sage knew he was pleased he had annoyed her. No one liked Hillary, least of all Double K.

Hillary looked back to Sage. "Is he really dead?"

"Well, yes, he's dead," Sage said pointedly, "Notice that arrow sticking out of his chest?"

Looking down at the corpse, Hillary glared at Sage.

"Is this going to affect tomorrow's shoot? I can't allow this production to fall behind schedule," Hillary hissed.

Shaking her head, Sage glanced at Double K. She was beginning to feel sorry for Evan Davis. Surly or not, the man deserved some semblance of respect.

"Hillary," Sage began as if talking to a child. "This man has been shot. Law enforcement is going to close this area as a crime scene. Until they release it, we won't be able to breathe in here."

"They can't do that," Hillary protested.

"They can and they will," Sage assured her.

"Well, you're the Security Chief, do something!"

"I can't, Hillary," Sage argued, annoyed that she had to. "You're going to have to deal with this problem; shoot around it."

For a moment, Hillary was lost in thought.

"I suppose I could," she said, her mouth curling into a thin-lipped smile. "You get this cleared up as quickly as possible."

"I'll do my best," Sage promised with a glance at Double K. Hillary appeared momentarily satisfied.

"Hillary," Sage said softly, "the Chief of Police is due here anytime, and I'm sure the local TV crews will be right behind him. You'll probably want to..."

"Oh my God," Hillary said, bringing her hand to her face. "You're right! I will put on some makeup and come right back. Something like this is bound to be on *Extra!* I might even be interviewed on *E!*"

Hillary looked at Sage and smiled. Then without warning,

Hillary's face became expressionless. She sneered at Sage, "I don't know why I am telling you this. Just do whatever it is you do."

With that said, she ran from the set.

"That was mean," Double K said under his breath. "It will take the nearest TV crew hours to get here."

Feeling her tight expression relax into a smile, Sage didn't bother to hide her snicker. "I know that and so do you. Hillary will figure it out sometime tomorrow."

"One thing is for sure, this is gonna mess up filming," he said with a long sigh.

"It sure will," Sage agreed, "I doubt if the police here will be as accommodating as they are in Los Angeles."

Double K rocked back on his heels and his dark eyebrows arched as Jon Maddux walked into the set. Under his breath, he asked, "Called your Dad?"

Sage gave Double K a quick nod and shouted out to the Police Chief, "Over here."

Like Hillary, Jon had little choice but to maneuver his way about the camera, wires and studio equipment scattered throughout the set.

With his velvet brown gaze steady and affixed to the body, he cursed as he approached the body.

"What happened?" He asked without looking at either Double K or Sage.

Double K answered. "He's dead."

At six foot three inches, Jon Maddux was almost as tall as Double K but he hardly appeared to be intimated by the former Hollywood cop turned bodyguard turn security enforcer. Double K's pleasure increased in equal proportion to the Police Chief's growing animosity.

"Double K found the body about two thirty," Sage interjected.

Jon's attention was on the corpse. "Who is he?"

"His name is Evan Davis. He is or I should say was the gaffer," Sage replied. Deciding she should explain, she added, "A gaffer is the chief electrician on the set who oversees the lights, all power sources from supplying the equipment to shutting down the set at the end of production."

Jon didn't bother to thank her for this bit of information.

"Have either of you touched anything? Disturbed the body in anyway?"

Sage resented the implication but answered with a simple, "No."

"All right," Jon said firmly, "I'm going to ask you both to leave. I can't have this crime scene contaminated any more than it already is. I'll have a lot of questions so don't go far."

"Excuse me," Sage responded sharply, abandoning all pretense of civility, "but I'm not leaving."

"You don't understand Ms. McCall," Jon said looking straight at her for the first time. "This is my crime scene."

His glare was hard, unflinching, but Sage had no intention of moving one inch.

"And you don't understand, Chief Maddux, this is my production set!" Sage said her small feet firmly planted on the floor. She met his accusing eyes without flinching and for good measure added, "I'm going nowhere."

Behind her, Double K folded his arms emphasizing their immobility.

Jon Maddux glared at her and Sage guessed more often than not, he was used to having his own way.

Holding her emotions in check, Sage said, "Look, we know how to stay out of your way. Double K was with the

LAPD, and I have experience in the field. We won't hamper your investigation."

Jon grunted. He didn't appear convinced.

"Who'd shoot this guy with a bow and arrow?" He asked aloud, turning his attention away from Sage and back to Evan Davis.

"The arrow didn't kill him," Sage pointed out. "Look, there is minimal blood around the entry wound."

Jon bent on one knee and examined the wound on Evan Davis chest.

"You're right," he said with grudging respect. "So, he was shot post mortem. Why?"

Sage shook her head. "He wasn't the most likable guy on the set."

"The medical examiner is on his way," Jon said, the response holding a heavy note of impatience. His voice was cold as he turned to her. "Look, can you to keep your people out of here until our men go through the scene?"

It was at that moment that Hillary Kenyon returned sweeping through the set as if she were on her way to a Hollywood premiere.

"I'm in charge here," she announced, her arms flaying dramatically as she rushed toward them. "I'm in charge here!"

"Who the hell is she?" Jon asked under his breath.

"The director," Sage replied, keeping her voice low.

"Look," Hillary said as she came near, "I have a heavy day of shooting, so do what you need to do and get him off my set. Thank you."

"This is a crime scene, Miss..."

"Kenyon," Sage supplied him.

"Ms. Kenyon," Jon continued, "no one is filming anything in here until I say you can!"

"Sage," Hillary demanded.

"Chief Maddux, how long do you think this will take?" Sage asked, already knowing the answer. She wasn't about to tell Hillary this could take anywhere from a few days to several weeks.

Jon Maddux shook his head. In a voice that was barely civil, he said, "Until I have a forensic team in here, I'm not making any promises."

Hillary sniffed indignantly and glared at the corpse. "I'm sorry but that simply won't do."

Noting the flash of anger in Jon's eyes, Sage interjected, "Double K, would you see if you can help Ms. Kenyon get organized? We're going to have a Crime Scene Unit and more cops here shortly. Perhaps the two of you could get Oz or someone in Craft Services up to fix coffee and..."

She stopped and allowed her mouth to twist into what she hoped was a tantalizing smile. Looking at Jon, she couldn't resist adding, "And make sure we have plenty of donuts."

His gaze caught and held hers. Amusement flickered in his eyes, and then they grew dark and unfathomable, compelling and magnetic.

Sage was unnerved.

Hillary's soft cry stole her attention. Sage watched in horror as Hillary placed the back of her hand on her forehead. Oh please, Sage thought, not now, Hillary!

"This is too much," Hillary whimpered. "I'm going to lie down. I don't know how I will tell Nick McMasters."

"My father is probably with him by now, Hillary," Sage announced, fearing this would evoke another hysterical response. It did.

Hillary's mouth dropped open in surprise.

"What! I should have been the one who called him!" She

wailed, "You can't begin to know how inconvenient this is! It's going to send costs sky high!"

"Think about the ratings, Hillary," Sage said under her breath and was rewarded with an instant smile.

"Yes, yes, you are right!" Hillary said, her eyes glowing with sudden fire. "The ratings will go right through the roof."

Hillary stopped and looked at Double K.

"If you don't mind, Mr. Kendrick, Sage is right. Do go and wake up the Craft Service people. I have to go and call Nick McMasters."

Double K stared long and hard at Hillary. Sage knew he hated being treated like a go-fer. He turned back to Sage.

"Well, I was getting hungry anyway," Double K said with a yawn. "I'll see what I can do about some coffee."

Jon looked at Sage as Hillary left with Double K in tow.

"Do you always control everyone around you with such diplomacy, Ms. McCall?"

"In this business," Sage replied, offering him a soft smile, "you have to."

"What do you know about this guy? You say he was an electrician?"

Sage nodded. "Apparently in his day, one of the best."

"Any idea why someone would shoot him after he was dead?"

Sage shook her head.

Jon stared at her. She looked away, trying to avoid his inquisitive brown eyes.

"Any other vices, especially ones that would get him murdered?"

"Not that I know of," Sage replied, "I'll ask the crew. The Best Boy knows him better than anyone else. He may have some answers."

"The Best Boy?"

"His assistant," Sage explained. She boldly met his eyes.

"I've noticed those positions at the end of a movie but never quite knew what they were or did," Jon replied with a half yawn, he hardly sounded interested.

"Look, I know you don't like us in your town," Sage began.

"You got that right, Miss McCall," Jon interrupted her, making no attempt to hide his disdain. His comment sent her temper soaring.

Her shock at his ill manners turned to rage but she knew full well she could not afford the luxury of anger. In a cool voice, she replied, "Nevertheless, we are here. I think it would behoove us both to work together."

Jon remained motionless.

"The sooner we get to shoot the show, the sooner we get out of your town, Chief."

Jon's dark brown eyes turned black with anger. The silence between them was unbearable.

"We may look like a backwater Florida town to you, Miss McCall, but unfortunately this isn't our first homicide."

"Nor mine," Sage lied evenly.

"Look," Jon said his angry gaze sweeping over her, "just stay out of my way!"

This was neither the time nor the place to bicker with him. Deciding she would choose the next battle and battleground, she gave him a terse nod. Whether she wanted to or not, she had to work with this man or more likely work around him.

"And just so I make myself perfectly clear in this, Miss Hollywood, if it were up to me, you wouldn't even be in my town."

Giving him a cold smile, Sage said pointedly, "Well fortunately for us, it's not up to you, is it?"

Whatever he was about to say was lost as the bright red flashing lights of a rescue squad heralded the arrival of the Levy County EMS.

Jon scarcely looked at her as he walked outside to greet the new arrivals. Sage stood for a moment debating whether to follow or not.

Moments later two EMS technicians and a disheveled older man in a Hawaiian shirt, presumably the Medical Examiner, and a police officer walked into the set. They followed Jon Maddux's lead to where she was standing.

The four men stood looking wide eyed at the cameras and the television production set before gazing down at the corpse.

No one spoke.

At last, the ME bent down and looked at Evan, taking care to look at both sides of his face.

"He's been dead for a while," the doctor said rising to his feet. He looked at Sage, "Any idea what happened here, young lady?"

"Sage McCall," Sage said offering her hand, "I'm Security Chief for the production company. One of my men found the body around two thirty."

The doctor accepted her hand and shook it firmly. "Dr. Edwards. Nice to meet you."

Sage continued, "We wrapped taping early last evening. To my knowledge the set was empty for the most part after that time."

"Isn't that your responsibility?" Jon asked, his voice dripping with accusation.

"No," Sage matched his cool remark, "that is not my

responsibility. My responsibility is to keep outsiders off the set, not the production crew who are free to come and go as they like."

"When I first saw you, I thought you might be an actress," Dr. Edwards interjected in an effort to defuse the open hostility between the Chief or Police and the Studio's Security Chief. Dr. Edwards added in a soft tone to Sage, "You are certainly pretty enough."

"Thank you," Sage said to the Doctor without ever taking her eyes from Jon.

Double K returned and gave Sage a quick nod. She smiled in return knowing coffee and an elaborate array of ham biscuits, croissants, and pastries would be available for everyone shortly.

Jon turned to his men, who were both donning latex gloves. One reached in the black bag and retrieved a 35 mm camera.

The second officer pulled out a video camera. Sage knew he would be panning the entire crime scene and giving viewers of the tape a realistic look at the production set, the body and details of the crime scene that the officer's note pad couldn't capture.

"Take plenty of photos." Jon snapped. Turning back to Sage he asked, "Can we get more light on in here?"

"I'll see what I can do," Sage offered, giving Jon a long and hard look before she turned to the still dark far corner of the production set.

Cursing her way through the darkness, she bumped twice into some heavy camera equipment. Almost over to the fuse box, she fell over a large, strangely soft object lying across her path. She hit the floor hard but was not hurt.

Thinking she had fallen over a piece of rolled carpet, she

turned over, pressing the palms of her hands onto the cool wood floor.

As she righted herself, she heard Jon Maddux and Double K call out her name. Their voices were distant. She could hear the men moving toward her.

She focused instead on the mound that was beginning to take shape in the darkness. She felt the stickiness on the palms of hands. Too late she noticed what seemed to be a tiny puddle of dark liquid seeping, with a life of its own, running, and filling in the places between her fingertips. Her eyes adjusted to the faint light coming toward her from the other the side of the production set. She looked back to the heavy swell lying across her path. It seemed out of place even on a busy production set.

The taste of horror rose within her. Icy fingers raced across the hair on the nape of her neck. She held her next breath. The dark outline shifted in the dim light and took on human shape.

She had fallen over a second body.

CHAPTER TWO

Choking back an electrified cry, Sage felt her heart jumping in her chest.

"Oh my God, Double K! K! Get over here, quick!"

As her eyes adjusted to the shadows, tall boxy shapes became the familiar shapes of sound, lighting and camera equipment. She had not fallen through the looking glass. She was on the dark side of a television production set.

Across from her, the mound shifted and she heard a muffled groan. Dim light seeped in between the equipment and she slowly recognized the long gangly legs of her missing security guard. Scanning the body, she took in the muscular arms and long dusty tuffs of shaggy, blonde hair. Jamie Wolfe's outline became more distinguishable. He lay, seemingly lifeless, across from her. Uncontrollable fear swept through her. Scrambling to his side, she tried to shake the fearful image building in her. Turning his body over, gratitude washed over her as she heard him groan in protest. In the darkness she could see the weak rise and fall of his chest and heard shallow breathing.

Behind her, she heard the sounds of Double K pushing and knocking over equipment in his charge to her side.

"It's Jamie," she cried looking up to him. "Doctor Edwards! Over here! Quickly!"

Jon Maddux and the paramedics collected behind her as Jamie Wolfe's eyes fluttered, then slowly opened. Jamie's blue eyes focused on her face and a thin smile spread across his lips. In a voice barely above a whisper, he said, "Sage, I saw an angel."

"Don't talk," Sage cautioned him. For Jamie's sake she forced her lips to part in a smile and forbade herself to tremble. Tenderly she ran her fingers across his forehead brushing long strands of blond hair from his face.

Dr. Edwards maneuvered his way to Jamie's other side.

As the paramedics flanked Dr. Edwards, Sage reluctantly released Jamie's hand and moved toward his feet to allow the medical team to care for him.

Opening his eyes one last time, Jamie looked at Sage and smiled. His expression almost peaceful, he slowly closed his eyes. His head dropped to the side.

"Is he dead?" Jon asked. His voice was emotionless and she felt the sound of it hit her stomach hard.

"No, but he is pretty bad shape," Doctor Edwards responded without taking his eyes off Jamie.

Finding her breath, she stared at Jamie willing him to live. Reluctantly she pushed herself away from Jamie. As she struggled to rise, she felt the strong hand of Jon Maddux just under her elbow as he helped her rise to her feet.

She rose, holding her raw emotions in check.

Doctor Edwards continued to check Jamie's vital signs. One of the EMS technicians skirted his way through the set to retrieve the gurney.

With the assistance of the second EMS technician, Doctor Edwards started an IV. Jon, Double K, and the two officers shoved equipment aside to clear a path for the gurney. The paramedics quickly brought the unit into place and snapped the locks in place. With Dr. Edwards's approval, they bent to Jamie's side and on the count of three, lifted Jamie onto the stretcher. They immediately began to roll him out.

There was nothing more she could do but follow them to the EMS Rescue Vehicle.

She touched Dr. Edwards' sleeve as he entered the rescue vehicle. "Please, do whatever you can for him."

Doctor Edwards smiled and patted her hand gently.

"Don't you worry, Miss McCall, he'll be just fine," he said climbing into the vehicle.

"Double K," Sage said, her mouth dry, her hands shaking. "Go with him. Call me and let me know he is okay."

Double K's deep brown eyes were full of strength and shining with a steadfast resolve. "Don't worry, Sage, we won't let anything happen to him."

Sage clenched her jaw to kill the sob in her throat. Guilt threatened to overwhelm her. Could she have prevented this?

She couldn't think about it now, she would think about this tomorrow. Tonight, she couldn't afford the luxury of a single misstep. Double K was right. Jamie was strong. He would, in the end, be all right.

Drawing her shoulders back, she reclaimed her self-control. Weakness was not an option.

Double K vanished into the thick fog that surrounded the Sand Point Inn and minutes later she heard his rented KIA come to life, its bright headlights casting two long shafts of light into the smoky mist.

With the dual slam of the rescue vehicle's doors, the lights atop the vehicle began to whirl, illuminating the silvery ground fog. Grinding the loose rocks under its wheels, the rescue vehicle spun away from her. Across the parking lot, Double K's small SUV raced in its wake.

Watching them speed into the night, she thought of Evan and the broken body of Jamie Wolfe.

Swallowing hard, she lifted her chin in defiance. Fury

replaced fear, and her eyes narrowed as she scanned the darkness, demanding an enemy come out from the shadows. Her thoughts were racing dangerously and she knew she was capable of harm.

"He'll be fine," Jon said behind her, his voice was rich in soft undertones. "Your guy looks pretty tough and it was just a bad bump to the head."

Sage stood silent, feeling the vaguely sensuous light pass between them. Her breath quickened and her cheeks became warm. She accepted his kindness gratefully.

"How long has he worked for you?" The question seemed more to set a distraction than an investigative inquiry.

Sage cleared her throat. "Jamie has been with McCall Security for about six months. He's a good worker. I hand picked him for this assignment."

Though her voice sounded cool, Jon witnessed the mix of emotions that danced across her brow.

His gaze remained steady. In the last few hours, he'd seen her change from a cool professional, to a defiant little minx who had no hesitation in challenging him, to a soft vulnerable woman whose tenderness was disquieting. Her softness fell like a shadow across the loneliness of his soul. He had watched her china blue eyes widen with fear and her delicate hands tremble as she had stroked Jamie Wolfe's hair from his face. Seeing her hurt had left him shaken with the powerful need to keep her safe.

Unable to dismiss the feeling, he knew he was being unreasonable. It grated on him to realize he hadn't even given this beautiful woman a chance. He had let his own prejudice over who she was override any sense of fairness. That was unlike him.

He hadn't wanted to be attracted to her and yet he was

from the minute she had walked into his office. He had been too long without a woman, and this blond pixy from California fit the bill but she was not for him, no matter how damn beautiful she was.

Still, in the light mist of the fog, her skin was damp and her shirt clung to her like a second skin, sensually emphasizing the soft outline of her shoulders, molding itself to her like a lover's touch across her full up-tilted breasts to the soft, slender curved hips.

Perspiration wet her porcelain skin, and illuminated a lovely sparkle in her sapphire eyes. Her mouth was seductively inviting. The look she gave him raced across his heart and he tried to turn away, knowing his expression was full of hunger.

She's not for you, pal, he reminded himself. In a matter of weeks, she would be drinking margaritas or whatever was popular at a trendy LA nightclub before he could say, "Look, I know we got off on the wrong foot." Besides, like it or not, there was a murder to solve, and at this moment everyone was under suspicion, including the seductive Ms. Sage McCall.

The silence between them was haunting and lonely. A spray of gray mist danced around them like a siren willing them to darker passions.

Sage felt uncomfortable under the scrutiny of his dark brown eyes.

What did he see? What did he suspect? What did he know?

She knew there was no getting around him. She had to work with him. She needed to find some common ground. Arguing with him would get her nowhere.

Jon's eyes darted back toward the building. "I need to get back to ..."

"Mind if I join you?" She asked prepared for yet another argument. He surprised her with a nod of his head.

"Yes," Jon said evenly, "we may need your help."

With her mind on Jamie Wolfe, she followed Jon Maddux back to the production set.

The entire room was now bathed in dazzling light. Sage blinked at the sudden change and her eyes quickly adjusted to the blanched intensity.

Across the room, the two officers worked diligently on their respective tasks and were oblivious to their return. One was busy taking photos of Evan. The other, wearing latex gloves, was painstakingly writing down details of the scene now including the spot where she had found Jamie.

"How many people do you have with you, Miss McCall?" Jon asked.

"There are around eighty-five people all total. The LA production crews totals sixty-five, eight actors, and twelve contestants," she added, "and please, call me Sage."

"Sage," he repeated with a chuckle he didn't bother to hide. "Is that one of those California names?"

His tone was again sullen. Sage was instantly annoyed for even thinking she could let her defenses down around him. She had been wrong to trust him. Sage shot him a withering stare which he appeared to dismiss without notice.

"Well, since we don't even know if the assailant was from your group, I can also throw in the two thousand two hundred and twenty-seven people who live in St. Gabrielle. That hardly narrows the list of potential suspects. Anyone have a grudge against Evan?"

Sage gave him a slight shrug and shook her head. "The contestants were selected months ago in a casting call as were the actors. They arrived here a little over a week ago. The production crew arrived here earlier. Most of the crew works directly for the studio, as does the security staff. We were here over a year ago for this assignment. I have two full-time security personnel working for me."

"What can you tell me about the victim?"

"Not much. No known enemies to my knowledge. Evan kept to himself. I will request their full employment histories from the studio in the morning."

Jon nodded and continued to look about the room.

"Does this area stay open all the time?" Jon asked moving a step away from her. "Who would have a reason to be here?"

"Everyone except for the contestants. Most of the production crew would have access to the set at all times," Sage explained. "My security team keeps everyone else out of the production area."

"This stage," Sage continued, "is used for the beginning and closing scenes of each episode. A camera crew follows contestants when they are outdoors."

"When I knew you were coming," Jon said, a chill hanging on each edge of his words, "I made it a point to watch both *Murder in New England* and *Murder in Santa Barbara*."

"Hope you enjoyed them," Sage snapped. It would have been delicious to ask if he had learned anything.

Jon's grin unsettled her; she crossed her arms and pointedly looked away, annoyed. He seemed to enjoy taunting her. Damn, she hated that he was so good looking. Masking her inner turmoil with deceptive calmness, she looked back at him prepared for yet another critical comment but his eyes were filled with what appeared to be genuine concern.

"I hope your man pulls through quickly," Jon said his voice softer again, "he may have seen something or someone."

Sage wasn't sure if he was making a passing comment or

trying to appease her. Without giving him quarter, she reached for her cell phone, "I need to make a few calls."

Jon smiled at her and raked his long fingers through his cropped hair. He turned giving her a breathless profile of his features. With a nod, he walked over to the area where they had found Jamie and began speaking in low voices to the officer who was examining a corner of a heavy piece of sound equipment.

As she punched in the numbers on her cell, she wondered if Hillary had had a chance to call Nick McMasters. She was no longer concerned with protocol, Nick and her father had to know about Jamie Wolfe.

"Sage," her father answered, then paused. She could hear Nick McMasters in the background.

Without preamble, Sage quickly told him about finding Jamie.

At her conclusion her father said, "I'll call the hospital and keep a check on him. You said Double K is with him?"

Her father paused but then picked up the conversation before she could respond. "Sage, we're also concerned about what happened to Evan. You said he was shot with a bow and arrow, but you don't think it was murder?"

"I think he was shot post mortem, Dad, but we don't know the cause of death," came Sage's quick reply. "We're just as baffled as you. The Chief of Police of St. Gabrielle is here."

"We realize it's a bit early to speculate but Nick wants to know if you feel we should close down the production."

Sage was profoundly aware of the expense, manpower, and large amounts of money already invested in this production. She did not want this responsibility, but it was hers. "At this moment, I believe it would be premature. For all we know, Evan may have died of natural causes and the arrow some sort of twisted prank. Until we get the autopsy results back, we have to also assume this could be murder. We need time."

Her father relayed her comments to Nick, and she could almost hear his audible sigh. Though Nick's reply was muffled, Sage heard his concern for the safety of the production crew.

Her father's voice came back clear and strong. "All right, we'll follow your lead for the moment. Sage, is there anything you need?"

"I don't think the few off-duty cops I have hired are going to give us the manpower we need, especially when word of this leaks to the press."

"Say no more," her father interrupted her. "I'll send Cowboy Bob and Reese out tonight. Will you need more men?"

"If we do, I'll pick up additional guards from a local security firm, but Reese and Cowboy Bob would be a big help."

Satisfied for the moment, she changed the subject. "You said Hillary called?"

"Yes," her father replied, from the sound of his voice, she knew intuitively he didn't want to say more just yet. "She's with Jeff Sanders."

Despite herself, she smiled. Jeff Sanders, the associate producer, had his hands full with Hillary at the moment.

"Who's this Chief of Police?" Jack McCall asked his daughter.

Looking across the room, Sage eyes found him. His head was bent slightly and she watched his muscular frame. His attention was focused on something his officer was telling him, and his gaze was steadfast and intent.

"He seems competent enough," Sage said turning away. "I know he didn't want us in, and I quote, 'his town'. His name is Jon Maddux. I would like to run a background check on him.

I would like to understand a bit more about who I'm dealing with here."

"I'll take care of it. What's next?"

"They're making their preliminary findings at the crime scene now. It's going on five o'clock here. I'm sure Chief Maddux is not going to let anyone touch the production set until he is through. I suspect it will be days before the company can get back on schedule."

She took a breath, "I'm going to have to make an announcement in the morning. I'll make sure Jeff and Hillary are both there. The cast and crew will want to know what happened, and I think Jon Maddux will have a few questions of his own. I'll keep you informed."

"You're doing a great job, honey. Look, I will probably be with Nick for a few more hours. Try to get some sleep. Call me when you hear anything."

"I will," Sage promised just before she turned off her cell.

The night before dawn was quiet.

Through the heavy gray haze, Sage looked up and could see the soft glow of distant stars twinkling in the early morning sky.

She should have been tired, but she was wide awake.

There shouldn't have been a dead body on the set, and yet poor Evan Davis lay dead twenty-five feet away from her.

In a little over an hour the cast and crew would be waking up. She could only imagine the impact of finding Evan's corpse with an arrow struck though it would have on the ensemble. She had a couple of hours to figure how to soften its impact. Unanswered questions hung in the night sky as the hazy silver moon broke through the clouds. Swallowing hard, she lifted her chin, and returned to the set. She had to solve this with or without Jon Maddux's help.

Jon stood in the middle of the room commanding a powerful presence. His massive shoulders completely filled out the tan shirt he wore, muscles rippling under the cotton cloth. She was acutely aware of his tall athletic physique and his chiseled male body the closer she came to him.

He turned to face her. His bronzed skin glistened with drops of moisture from the night's steamy heat and darkened his deep brown eyes. She could feel the scent of male virility as his eyes swept over her. He made no attempt at turning away from her adding to his sheer animal-like sensuality. She was determined to hold her ground

"Find anything?" She refused to flinch.

He shook his head and turned away.

"The crew is going to be getting up shortly," she said still feeling too annoyed to give him anything but an icy remark. "I need to tell them what's going on before they read it in this morning's paper."

"I'd like to be there when you do," Jon voiced, looking down at her. She knew he would. He continued in a voice rich with command, "Someone may have seen something. We'll need to get statements."

Sage gave him a slight nod.

Over the next several hours, Sage had little more to do than watch Jon and his officers examine and take endless photos of the crime scene but watch them she did.

At almost five o'clock, Jeff Saunders, the Associate Producer, walked onto the production set, stopping a few feet from the entrance.

Jeff was Nick's right hand man, overseeing all production as well as maintaining the shooting schedule and finances.

By nature, he was mild mannered and was content for the most part to let Hillary run the show while he remained undisturbed in his trailer happily pouring over reams of financial paperwork.

Standing almost six feet tall, with salt and pepper hair, he was trim and always looked like he was ready for a round of golf.

Sage liked Jeff and walked to where he was standing.

"Anything I can do?" He said with a bit of hesitation, looking past her toward the center of the set.

Sage shook her head. "The police are conducting their investigation now."

"Poor Evan," Jeff said casting his eyes down. "Hillary said the police think its murder."

"They don't know. Can you tell me anything about Evan?"

Jeff took a deep breath. "We have used Evan off and on for several years. He was in charge of lighting for both previous productions. Always did a good job. We all knew about the alcohol thing, but he never allowed it to effect his work."

"I've asked my Dad to send out employee files on everyone," Sage said softly.

Jeff nodded. "Have you have talked to Nick?"

"Yes, I did. Understandably he's pretty upset. For obvious reasons, he wants to keep this as quiet as possible."

Sage had already anticipated the media frenzy that would follow the minute word leaked to the press. "I understand. We'll try to get as many answers as we can before the media medley begins. My Dad will be sending out more security staff to help out."

Jeff shifted. Sage knew he was uncomfortable.

"If you could join me in the tent around seven thirty, I thought we would inform the cast and crew. The Chief has already said he would like to question everyone as soon as possible. I'd like you and Hillary to be present."

"I'll be there." Jeff promised.

"Speaking of Hillary, where is she?"

"I left her asleep on the couch in my motor home. She was understandably extremely upset about Evan."

Remembering Hillary's irritation that Evan's death would interfere with her production schedule, Sage had little sympathy for the Director. At least she had the good sense to demonstrate a consolatory show of grief for Jeff's sake, if not for Evan. Maybe, Sage thought, Hillary was a better actress than she thought.

"I'd better get back to her," Jeff said. "She was a bit hysterical."

Unconvinced that Hillary cared for anyone but herself, Sage gave Jeff a wave goodbye.

"Who was that?" Jon said joining her.

"Jeff Saunders," she replied, "the Associate Producer. He's in charge of finances and the day-to-day operations of the production."

Jon shook his head. "I came over here to let you know the Medical Examiner is on his way back here. Your man has a pretty bad concussion but is in stable condition."

"That is good news," Sage said, "I'll go over and find out what is going on with Craft Services and have them bring some coffee over here."

"Coffee would be nice," Jon said with a yawn. With that he walked over to direct his police photographer to an angle five feet away from Evan.

Outside thick layers of mist clung to the ground and obscured the beautiful view of the Gulf of Mexico. Seeing a dim light from the kitchen, Sage hurried in that direction.

In a few hours the Sand Point Inn would be bustling with rushed activity, but now only a few vehicles cluttered the parking lot.

Nick McMasters couldn't have chosen a more ideal backdrop for *Murder in Florida*. Abandoned in the early nineties, the location offered the studio a spectacular view of the Gulf of Mexico. Across the parking lot, a small hundred-room hotel provided residence for the cast and crew. At the far end, three rather lavish motor homes half-circled the parking lot. Three semi-trailers housing the props and additional production equipment were on the other side of the motor homes.

Sage and Double K had each chosen one of the outside motel units and while not as spacious as newer hotel, their rooms, like most of the hotel, had been refurbished by McMasters Studio as part of his lucrative lease agreement.

Sage knew Nick had leased the property for a song. She had heard from the realtor that a small group of investors had bought the long-abandoned property anticipating the financial windfall tourists would bring once *Murder in Florida* aired.

The stretch of shoreline offered only a little splinter of sandy beach before it curled back into the land giving the water a small natural harbor.

Two old gas and diesel pumps stood like sentries at the end of a long wooden dock reminding any beachgoers who dared to trespass that this was boating country.

The hotel even boasted a small commercial kitchen. As the studio used the restaurant as the set and the hotel had no conference or meeting room, a large event tent complete with tables and chairs had been rented to serve meals.

Oz, Oswald Anderson, a family friend, oversaw Craft Services. His small team prepared breakfast and lunch in the small commercial kitchen; dinner was usually catered by any number of local restaurants. Oz kept the Craft Services table laden with sandwiches, lavish deserts, and an assortment of gourmet chips, as well as keeping a storehouse of aspirin, toiletries, and any other need imaginable.

The kitchen light was shining like a tiny beacon, as Sage made her way around the outside of the hotel toward the brightly lit kitchen.

Opening the screen door, she found slabs of ham, bacon, chopped potatoes and a large stainless steel bowl of eggs positioned across the counter. Breakfast preparation was under way.

Oz stood in his kitchen, his uniform and apron draped over his forty-four inch waist. Just barely topping five inches over her five-foot-five frame, Oz's once light brown hair was thinning in direct proportion to his thickening body mass. His eyes lit at the sight of her, and his apple cheeks curled into a welcoming smile.

"Hey Sweetie," he said, laugh lines gently deepening around his mouth and the corners of his eyes. Bullnecked, overweight, he was nevertheless light on his feet as he moved about the kitchen. "Grab yourself a cup of coffee."

He moved away from the sink, and tossed a dishtowel on the counter. "What's going on? Double K came in and asked coffee to be sent over to the set. What's this about a rescue squad? Two police cars outside? Was someone hurt? Something get stolen?"

There was no easy way to tell him.

"Double K found Evan Davis dead this morning. Jamie Wolfe was injured and is in the hospital now."

For a moment, Oz stood motionless. "Are you serious? Evan's dead? What the heck happened?"

Sage poured herself a cup of coffee. "We don't know. The St. Gabrielle Police Chief is here. It could be murder."

Oz looked visibly shaken. "Does the studio know?"

Sage nodded.

"Oh my god. Are they going to close down the production?"

"We have no idea. It's premature to speculate at the moment. Look, Oz, do me a favor, until we make a formal announcement, don't mention this to anyone, okay? We are going to tell everyone just after breakfast."

Oz nodded, his gray eyes growing dark with concern. "You got it. How's Jamie? I would be sorry to hear anything's happened to him."

Sage struggled to keep her emotions steady.

"Look," Oz said as if attempting to brighten her mood, "Let me fix you something to eat. I'll have Manuel take coffee to the set right away."

Sage smiled. "I'm not hungry but thanks. And just have him set it up in the catering tent. The production set is closed."

Placing her empty coffee cup on the counter, she added, though she knew he needed no reminding, "I appreciate you keeping quiet about this until we have a chance to formally tell everyone."

She was halfway across the parking lot when she saw Hillary rushing toward her. With a firm grip on her small white poodle, Hillary was dressed in a beige pair of perfectly tailored *Versace* slacks and white long-sleeve cotton crew neck sweater bearing the *Versace* logo across the bodice.

"Oh there you are," Hillary said sounding very annoyed. "Don't you answer your page? For heavens sake, I have been trying to reach you."

Sage looked at her pager. In the turmoil of events, she hadn't turned it on. She did so now. Scanning the numbers, she recognized Hillary's number.

"I thought you were resting in Jeff's motor home."

"I was but then I went back over to the set looking for you, but that good-looking Police Chief said you had gone. He wouldn't let me on my own damn set. And, would you believe, Nick McMasters is already thinking he might have to close the production. Oh! This is all so horrible!"

Sage stared at Hillary. Like so many who came to Hollywood, Hillary had hoped to become an actress. She had never quite made it beyond bit parts. Refusing to give up her dream of stardom, one way or the other, she had gotten behind the cameras. Hillary was assistant director on the last two whodunits, and when the previous director bowed out for a movie commitment, Nick McMasters had given Hillary the opportunity to direct this production.

Hillary stood in front of her, glaring. "You have to do something quickly, Sage. I'm counting on you."

"I'll do what I can, Hillary," she promised, "but I am not God and Jon Maddux is not the LAPD. I can't manage this guy, Hillary."

"Here he comes now," Hillary said, watching Jon approach. "Do something."

"Do me one single favor, Hillary," Sage said quietly. "This guy wants us out of his town. He has the power to make this more difficult for us. Take care what you say, Hillary, or we could all wind up back in LA out of work."

For once Hillary looked genuinely flabbergasted. Under her breath, she hissed, "We can't close down. This is my first big break to direct. We simply can't close down!"

Jon was now upon them and Sage had no opportunity

to give Hillary any assurance on way or the other. She hoped Hillary had the good sense to keep her mouth shut.

"Find anything?" Sage asked Jon.

He shook his head. "I thought I would let you know we're going to remove the body now."

Sage looked across the parking lot. A newly arrived EMS vehicle had backed up to the door of the restaurant. The two technicians pushed a gurney with a body bag resting on top of it toward the ambulance's open doors. There was no need to hurry. Jon, Sage and Hillary watched as they slammed the doors shut. The metallic clang of the door rang was deafening and final in the quiet of an early sunrise. The technicians waved as they passed by them. The lights atop the vehicle were still.

"Good," Hillary said, watching the EMS vehicle drive down toward the entrance. She turned to Jon, "We can resume shooting now. Thank you for getting this taken care of so quickly."

"Not so fast, Miss Kenyon," Jon interrupted, "We're still considering this a crime scene. Until my men are through, this area is off limits."

Hillary was about to protest, but the glare from Sage stopped her.

Turning back to Sage, Jon said, "I want to talk to anyone who might have seen him last evening."

"You'll have your chance," Sage said watching the crew start to filter past them. "The cast, crew and Production Company will be coming in for shortly for breakfast. It will be our best chance to speak to everyone."

Jon nodded.

Hillary stiffened and glared at both Jon and Sage. "You cannot imagine how inconvenient all this is and I see neither one of you helping me. I'm going back to see Jeff Saunders. I'm sure he'll be able to do something!"

With that said she whirled about and headed back toward the motor homes.

"Jeff Saunders?" Jon asked turning back to Sage.

"He was in earlier, "Sage reminded him. "Jeff is the Associate Producer."

"Another unbalanced personality?"

Had he meant to be funny? Sage frowned. "No, Jeff is the most level-headed guy I know."

Jon looked at her and an easy smile played at the corners of his mouth. He looked as if he were going to say more, but two police officers approached him.

Stopping only long enough to drop off a black leather bag into one of the patrol cars, they joined Jon and Sage.

Jon turned to the younger officer, "Matt, head back to town and get started on the paperwork. I want all the evidence logged as soon as possible." Turning to the taller officer, he said, "Chris, you'll stay with me and question potential witnesses. Someone must have seen something. We need to find out who?"

Without comment, the men departed to their assigned tasks.

"Now what?" she asked, aware of his smoldering brown gaze upon her.

"Now we wait," Jon replied, "The crime scene is telling us nothing. Until we know more, there's nothing more we can do. Now, I distinctly remember you mentioning something about a cup of coffee."

"Come on," Sage said without waiting for him to follow, "coffee should be waiting for us in the event tent."

As promised, on one end of the table inside the tent, Sage

and Jon found a polished commercial size coffee machine. Pouring Jon a cup of coffee, she then helped herself adding more sugar than usual. They sat silently looking at each other and their coffee while they waited for time to pass.

Right on schedule, members of the crew and cast began to stumble in. They were followed by the actors and contestants. Though clearly most of the contestants considered this a vacation, one lucky contestant would walk away with half a million dollars, not bad for three weeks work.

Jon and Sage said little and didn't bother to exchange pleasantries. She tried to ignore the curious stares in their direction.

Everyone was aware of the police cars in the parking lot and the uniformed officers standing guard outside the production set.

On three separate occasions, designated leaders from one group or another came over to speak to Sage. She acknowledged there would be an announcement but nothing more.

Double K called twice, the first time to let her know the Doctor was with Jamie and the second to tell her Jamie was in critical but stable condition.

Jon had gone back to the production set. It was almost seven before he returned and they both worked their way toward a podium.

As if on cue, Jeff Saunders walked into the large tent. He was supporting Hillary. Hillary floundered twice and leaned on Jeff to help her cross the room. Her dramatic entrance fooled no one, least of all Sage.

Sage glanced at Jon. His exhausted expression told her Hillary's theatrics were wearing thin.

Sage and Jon joined Jeff and Hillary at the podium.

"I'll be all right," Hillary assured Jeff in a low voice that was still loud enough for those near to hear.

The four turned to face the production company. All eyes were riveted on Hillary and Sage.

Fumbling with the microphone, Hillary at last managed to turn it on.

"Could we have everyone's attention," she stammered. "Today we lost one of our own. Early this morning we found the body of Evan Davis on the set."

A loud groan swept across the dining room. Those who did not know Evan were looking at each other mouthing, 'Who?'

"Was he murdered?" a voice shouted above the fray.

Before Sage could soften the truth, Hillary looked tragically out into the crowd.

"Yes," she announced with crisp clarity, "Evan Davis was murdered."

CHAPTER THREE

Sharp gasps and cries of alarm rippled through the crowd like a wave breaking against a sandy shore. Several shot to their feet but were pulled back into their seats by their companions. Their voices rose in dazed outcry of shock and anger.

Sage glared at Hillary with burning reproach. With her hammering heart and her breathing ragged, Sage stepped in front of the microphone, forcing Hillary away from the podium.

Hillary managed to look wounded under Sage's thunderous scowl, but Sage had no time to deal with her. She fumbled with the microphone, knowing her next words would either calm or add to frenzy.

"Everyone, please stay calm," Sage said in a strong even voice, "there's no need to panic. We don't know there has been a murder. Evan Davis was found dead on the set early this morning. His death could have occurred by natural causes."

The startling image of the arrow buried deep in Evan's chest flashed through her mind but now was not the moment to share that bit of information. Keeping her tone monotone, she projected each word in a cool composed delivery. "I realize what you heard was disturbing, but I am going to ask you to remain calm. Evan Davis was found dead this morning but until we have the medical examiner's report, there is no need to jump to any conclusions. The circumstances of Evan's death are considered suspicious. Police Chief Jon Maddux of the St. Gabrielle Police Department will be conducting the investigation. I want to stress that no one is in danger as far as we know."

"Was he murdered, Sage?" The Script Supervisor challenged her as the group began to quiet.

"As I said, we don't know the cause of death." Sage replied, and her voice carried with it the ring of truth. "The Studio is sending in an additional security team. There's no need to panic or be concerned for your personal safety. I promise to keep you all informed."

An uneasy stillness settled on the assembly. Sage managed a smile to the group; grateful hysteria had been diverted at least for the moment.

"This is Chief of Police, Jon Maddux," Sage said in way of introduction. "Chief Maddux has some questions. I am going to ask everyone on behalf of the studio to cooperate."

Jon stepped to the podium. His leg and thigh brushed hers. His proximity to her caused her to swallow hard. She could taste his rugged masculinity and hated that she noted his breath, his each and every movement.

Jon cleared his throat. "What I need to find out is who saw Evan Davis last evening and if any of you saw anything suspicious last night."

"I saw Evan headed to the set about quarter after six, "the lanky boom operator said, rising to his feet. With nothing more to add, he sat back in his metal chair.

"Yeah," the two stunt men sitting next to him agreed, "we went out for a beer. He was headed for the set."

"Good. I need the three of you to meet with my officer and give him a statement," Jon said as he pointed one of the officers who had just arrived and was standing at the back of the room.

"Anyone else?" Sage called out but except for a few low mummers, no one spoke up.

"Are we in danger?" One of the contestants called out, fearfully looking about the room.

Sage wasn't sure how to answer. She was relieved to heard Jon respond.

"Today, we're asking for your cooperation. If any of you saw something, no matter how small, please give your statement to the officer."

"Hey," the Construction Set Foreman asked, "Are we going to work today?"

Hillary took the microphone. "Out of respect for our fallen colleague, there will be no work today; however, I'd like to talk to the actors around eleven. I will meet with the contestants around two o'clock. The rest of you relax. I urge you all to look into your own hearts, think about those you love and how truly, truly precious life can be. Thank you all."

The contestants looked wide-eyed at the director. The cast and the crew traded glances barely able to conceal their smirks. It was evident to those who knew her best that Hillary's move behind the cameras had been a good one.

With one tragic sweep of her eyes across the room, Hillary grimaced and snapped off the microphone. She turned to Sage and Jon and gave them a brilliant smile.

"Well, that went well," she said brightly.

Sage could barely stand looking at the woman. She knew her eyes were flat, hard, and passionless as she sarcastically agreed, "Yeah that went well."

Hillary sniffed and managed to look offended. She twisted her sculptured hands, and looked back to Jeff for support.

Jeff took a long breath; expressing in a single sigh the exasperation no one dared mention out loud.

"I need to get away from her," Sage said in a whisper to Jon.

Without waiting for his reply, she made her way around the back of the room. Jon followed instantly without comment.

Jon's officer took the statement of the three men who had seen Evan go into the production set. They had nothing more to add to their previous comment.

Evan, it seemed from their statements, vanished into the production set to never to be seen alive again.

As his officer wrote down their names, Sage thanked both for their assistance and reminded them that if they thought of anything more to get in touch with either Chief Maddux or herself.

"Well, that's not much to go on. I was hoping someone heard something, saw something," Jon said to Sage outside the in front of the tent. Careful to keep his voice low, Jon watched as members of the production company wandered out in groups. The cast and crew were careful to keep their voices low and their suspicions to themselves.

Sage's cell phone rang. She recognized her father's phone number and answered.

"Better brace yourself, pumpkin," Jack McCall warned her. "The word has gotten out to the press. This thing is about to blow up into a media nightmare."

Sage closed her eyes briefly and looked over at Jon. Feeling her mouth go dry, she said, "Thanks for the heads up. Anything else I should be aware of?"

"Cowboy Bob and Reese left last night. They're flying into Tampa and will be driving the rest of the way. Expect them early afternoon."

"Thanks, Dad," Sage said, grateful for two of McCall Security's most respected employees.

"How's the Police Chief?" Her father asked. "Friend or foe?"

"Jury's still out."

"OK. Keep me posted."

"Will do," Sage said ending the call. She looked at Jon. There was no easy way to tell him. She began slowly, "Look, the press has found out about the death. There's going to be an all out feeding frenzy."

Jon just stared at her. His brow wrinkled and she knew he was angry. "Your production was supposed to be a secret. This is exactly what I didn't want to happen."

Sage laughed. "We'd like to think so, but trust me, the groupies and fans of this show know we are here in Florida shooting. Good grief, *Survivor* fans somehow got their hands on satellite photos while it was still filming in Africa a few years back. The secret in the movie business is there are no secrets. At least not any more.

"Speaking of reality TV fans," Sage continued "both *Murder in Santa Barbara* and *Murder in New England* have their own web sites and chat rooms. Information about this sequel is readily available to fans who want it. Between the Internet, the fan clubs, and reality TV devotees, they know we're here. So, the person or persons unknown could be anyone."

"I don't think so," Jon disagreed. "Whoever shot Evan Davis and hurt Jamie Wolfe knew his or her way around the set."

"Thanks for not being gender specific," Sage said feeling the chill on her breath. "That narrows it down to eighty-five people plus the caterers we bring in nightly."

"Doesn't your man Oz take care of that sort of thing?"

Sage shook her head. "The kitchen facilities here are small but Oz and his staff cook breakfast and lunch, which usually consists of sandwiches or something easy to prepare. On occasion, he'll grill out steak, hamburgers, and hotdogs something simple but for the most part, meals, especially dinners, are catered by a local restaurant. Someone is always working on a movie or television set, so the Craft Service table has some sort of food on it all the time."

The beginning of a smile tipped the corners of his mouth, and Sage realized this very practical man was amused by the impracticality of the movie industry.

"As you're not shooting a western, where exactly would you find a bow and arrow lying around?" Jon asked with his tongue heavy with sarcasm and ridicule. His dark sensual eyes were tolerant, impatient, barely concealing the veiled innuendo that she would be unable to give him a straight answer.

"Follow me," Sage said taking his dare. She started walking to the trailers and motor homes parked at the far end of the lot.

"Where are we going?" Jon asked though he willingly followed.

"To the prop trailer," she said pointing to one of the unhitched semis at the far end of the lot. Three motor homes formed a semicircle at the opposite end of the property.

Sage stopped before the first semi and turned to Jon. "I wasn't aware of any bows or arrows in the script, but you never know what you will find."

"It's locked," Jon said as he yanked at the bolted door. His voice, though slightly more courteous, was still patronizing. "So who would have a key?"

"The prop master," Sage replied, and then added pulling

out a key ring with an assortment of shiny keys, "and, of course, the head of security."

She found the master key. It fit the lock and in one snap and sprang open.

Sliding the heavy metal door up, the prop trailer was dark and cluttered. It was filled to the top with plastic plants, wigs, lamps, furniture, as well as an odd collection of household items, clothing, and candelabras. Wedged in the far corner were funeral wreaths, a signature part of the script, but no weaponry or archery targets.

"Nothing seems disturbed," Sage said glancing about the clutter.

"How can you tell?" Jon's low voice was cool and broke with huskiness.

Watching his eyes roam about the jumble, she smiled feeling pleased she had caught him off balance.

"I'll ask the prop master if he has archery equipment. As I said, I don't recall reading about a bow and arrow in the script but I wasn't looking for one then."

The metallic door scraped as she and Jon rolled it shut. Locking it and testing the bolt, together they turned and began the long trek across the parking lot.

Her cell phone rang. The caller ID displayed a local area code and a Florida phone number.

"Our boy's gonna be okay," Double K announced in a deep voice not bothering to hide his exuberance. "He woke up about fifteen minutes ago."

The guilt she had been trying to hide was instantly replaced by a wave of relief. All she could manage was a soft, "Thank God."

"The local yokel standing by wants to question him,"

Double K said, his voice a protective growl. "I told him not to talk to the police until you get here."

"Good," Sage said pleased, "I'm on my way."

She got off the phone and looked at Jon. "That was Double K. Jamie Wolfe is awake."

"We need to talk to him," Jon's voice rang with authority. She noticed his supple muscles tense as he wheeled and felt the sheer power that coiled within him in every step he took. Though he had hardly invited her, she was hell bent to go.

"Get in," he said without ceremony when they reached the Ford. His voice was raw and husky with a sensuality she was trying to ignore.

She brushed past him to the passenger seat, her thigh touching his firm leg. Staring straight ahead, she tried to ignore the electrifying heat of his skin.

She couldn't help noticing the alluring scent of musk fragrance and felt her face flush. She waited for him to close the door, but he stood poised, his dark eyes raking over her, casually dropping from her shoulders before resting on her full breasts, her small hips, and well-toned legs. His eyes were dark and she was overly aware of this handsome and deadly man.

Jon had been impatient for her to get in the Explorer and the last thing he wanted to do was touch her. She had brushed too close to him; her tight little body with full breasts touched his arm and chest. Now he was supposed to drive?

Swearing under his breath, he could still feel the satin softness of her skin riveting through him with subtle waves of desire.

He hadn't meant to be drawn in by the inviting eagerness of her beautiful blue eyes, the sweet, sensual, softness of her full lips and flower fragrance of her golden hair. Hell, he was only a man, and he half-excused himself as he took in the swell of her breasts and sensual curves of her small waist.

Walking around his highly equipped police Ford Explorer, he recalled how she looked when the rescue squad drove away. For just a moment, she stood looking vulnerable and ethereal in the dim light. He'd had the overwhelming urge to hold her and protect her.

He opened the door and slid behind the steering wheel, jamming the key into the ignition.

Just in hand's reach, he took in her beautifully shaped calves and firm thighs. He was acting like a dog but damn it, he'd been too long without a woman.

Sage brushed a strand of hair from her face, and he couldn't help following her small elegant fingers as they slid the strand across her high delicate cheekbones before gliding to her slender white neck.

His throat went dry as he gripped the steering wheel. His hands needed something to do besides touch her.

Shifting too hard, he glanced over at her once more. As her gaze met his, his body tensed in desire.

Her smile taunted him. A flush that prettily colored her cheeks only made his body ache for her touch.

Across from him, Sage could feel her heart pounding inside of her. She hadn't missed his bold examination. She had recognized the hunger in his eyes and was both flattered and angered by his interest.

Trying to focus on the road ahead, an unwelcome blush ran over her cheeks like a shadow of a southern pine. She tried to quell the blood pounding in her veins, tormented by a confusing rush of mixed emotions. Damm it, she hadn't asked for his interest, yet she was exhilarated by it.

As they left Sand Point, she dared not look in his direction.

The silence was unbearable, but she could think of nothing to say.

Each lost in conflicting emotions; they remained quiet on the twenty-minute trip to St. Gabrielle. The warm Florida sunshine did little to brighten the mood in the police cruiser.

"Hospital is a few blocks from here," Jon said when they reached the edge of town.

A few short turns later, he pulled into the hospital's emergency room entrance and parked the Explorer in the space reserved for police vehicles.

Without waiting for him to open the door for her, Sage got out of the Ford and hurried toward the emergency room entrance.

The oversized double doors opened on cue, and an orderly waved them onto the elevator.

"This way Chief," he said to Jon and gave Sage an appreciative glance.

As soon as the elevator doors slid open, Sage saw Double K standing in front of a closed door, arms crossed, barring the officer's way into the room.

"Sir, he won't let me in," the younger officer protested. With a quick glance in Double K's direction he grimaced.

Double K stood, his arms folded. He offered Jon a broad grin.

"Its okay," Jon said to the officer. Looking to Double K, Jon frowned. "Is he awake?"

"He came to about forty-five minutes ago," Double K explained, but he made no attempt to step aside. Looking at Sage, Double K added, "Doctor says he was hit pretty hard. He has a pretty bad concussion, but he's okay."

"Have you talked to him?" Sage asked, "Does he have any idea who hit him?"

At that moment, the doctor emerged from the room. In her late forties, she looked more a librarian than a medical doctor. She held her clipboard close and regarded Jon with guarded hostility.

"How is he?" Jon asked. "We need to talk to him as soon as possible."

"No," came the doctor's sharp reply. "I gave him a sedative. He needs to rest."

"I need to talk to him now," Jon stated without emotion.

"You mean interrogate him," the Doctor snapped. Her angry glare told Sage she wasn't the first female to have had a run in with the handsome Chief of Police. Clutching the clipboard, the doctor finished, "I realize you want to get the details while they are fresh, but this time you'll have to wait, Jon. He's my patient and he needs the rest."

"I'm Sage McCall," Sage introduced herself. "Jamie Wolfe works for our company. I appreciate your care of him."

The doctor smiled at her. Sage handed her a business card. "Doctor, if he needs anything, please call."

"When will he be able to talk to us, Doctor?" Jon growled.

The doctor frowned in Jon's direction. "I'll call you when he wakes up."

"Do that," Jon grumbled, "but I am leaving a man here. I want to talk to him the minute he's conscious."

The doctor gave Sage a slight nod, Jon another glare then hurried down the hallway toward the nurses' station.

Jon turned to Double K and Sage, "Excuse me; I need to talk with my officer."

As Jon took the young officer aside, Sage leaned closer to Double K. "Did Jamie say anything on the way here?"

Double K grunted. "Yeah, but it made no sense. He said he saw an angel."

"What? Did he recognize you?"

"Yeah, he recognized me, but he kept telling me he saw an angel."

Sage looked down at the floor then back to Double K. "He said that to me when I first found him. I wonder if his angel is real or imagined."

Double K shrugged. "I've seen stars a time or two but no angel."

Sage silenced him with her eyes as Jon returned to her side.

Jon held his gaze steady on her.

"There's nothing more to do here at the moment," he said in a low southern drawl. "I have to get back to the office. I'm leaving my man here to keep an eye on Jamie. Can I give you a ride back to the..."

"I'll take her back," Double K interrupted.

With a sharp turn of his head, Jon seemed ready to challenge the large black man. Double K's body stiffened.

"I won't hold you up, Jon," Sage said in a rush of words.

Though Jon's expression remained somber, he didn't object, though his silence left her with little doubt he wanted her. He stood aloof, cool, his dark brown eyes shrouding the fire that flashed for a moment across his aristocratic face.

With a shrug, he said, "Suit yourself. Call me if you learn anything new."

With barely another glance at Double K or Sage, he turned toward the elevator.

Sage stood silently. Why wasn't she glad she had rid herself of him? She felt her flesh color and tried to hide it from her companion.

Double K chuckled.

"You like him." He grinned.

Sage whirled upon him, clenching her jaw so as not to reveal herself.

"Don't be ridiculous," she snapped. She tossed her hair across her shoulder and firmly placed her small fists defiantly upon the soft curve of her hips. "He's is obnoxious, rude, and..."

Double K chuckled. "And you like him."

Sage stiffened. "I'm not going to dignify that with an answer."

Double K laughed again. "He likes you too."

Shock flew through her. She was barely able to control her gasp of astonishment. "That's nonsense!"

"Besides," she said, ignoring the drop in her own voice. "I'm sure I am not his type."

Double K regarded her with an amused stare. "You're his type."

Before she could protest, he changed the subject, "There's nothing more we can do here. Let's get back to the set."

"You are totally off-base, Double K," Sage protested, not willing to let his comment about Jon Maddux slide, but Double K had already started to walk away from her.

"No, I'm not," he insisted as he turned and headed toward the elevators. "Come on, let's go."

Still annoyed with Double K as they reached the elevator, Sage hit the down button too hard. The door opened immediately.

"This proves to me," Sage said as they stepped into the elevator, "that you know nothing about women."

Double K stepped in behind her and made no attempt to hide his laughter.

"This proves to me," he said, his whole body rocking in titillation, "that you know nothing about men."

Sage frowned as the elevator door closed. It wasn't until they were outside the hospital before she spoke.

"My Dad is sending out Cowboy Bob and Reese."

Double K grunted his approval. Pointing to the rental car, he added, "I don't like leaving Jamie alone."

"Me either," Sage agreed, "but we have no choice. We have to get back to the set. With that guard outside his door, Jamie will be safe enough for now. As soon as Cowboy Bob and Reese arrive, I want one of them back here."

"You got it."

On the ride back to the Inn, Sage called McCall Security.

She reached her father's secretary and quickly recounted what happened the night before. Concluding her update, she requested a private duty nurse be hired for Jamie.

There was no need to advise everyone be tight-lipped; everyone at McCall Security knew a single word leaked to the media about any of their high profile clients or projects was grounds for immediate dismissal.

Before ending the call, she requested she be sent background information on everyone involved with the production.

The call absorbed most of the ride back to Sand Point Inn. Sage leaned back in the seat, satisfied, at least for the moment, she could do no more.

At the set, the production crew had clearly taken the day off. Though a few of the stunt men were gathered about the back end of a pickup truck, most of the company was either cloistered in the event tent or in their rooms.

Jon had left a lone police guard in front of the production set. Sage gave the officer a weak smile knowing he would prove little resistance should Hillary decide she needed or wanted to get back on the set.

"Go get some sleep," Double K said. Sage started to protest, but Double K raised his hand to silence her. "I slept a couple of hours at the hospital. You need some rest if you're going to be good for anyone."

Sage was simply too tired to resist.

In her room, she barely glanced at her clothes, papers, and personal effects lying undisturbed and scattered across the dresser, desk, and in the open closet. Hanging the "Do Not Disturb Sign" on the door, she closed it and bolted the lock. She snapped the wall switch and plunged the room into cool darkness. The queen size bed was only two steps from the door. She fell into it without bothering to undress or turn back the cover. Her eyelids burned and physical exhaustion weighted each limb. With her eyelids heavy, she fell into a deep, restless sleep.

Somewhere between a dream and reality she heard pounding on her door. Annoyed, she frowned trying to shake the sleep from her body. Convinced she'd just closed she eyes less only minutes ago, she was surprised to find the red digital numbers on her alarm clock change from twelve thirty-one to twelve thirty-two. She had slept two and a-half hours. Her body was damp and aching.

The pounding continued. She muttered a response but her throat was dry and was lost in the rattle and hum of the air conditioner. She rose and stumbled to the door, hitting her leg on a chair before she reached the door opening. Cursing under her breath, she was grateful to find Double K standing before her room.

His eyes were dark with thunder, his brows gathered and his full lips taunt and twisted in anger. "It's Hillary. She and the Mayor are holding a press conference. I think every television station in Florida has sent in a team, and we've got some foreign paparazzi here as well. Your Dad and Nick McMasters are gonna have a cow."

Sage cursed under her breath. Glancing at her wrinkled blouse and shorts, she stammered, "Give me a few minutes to change. I'll be right out."

Double K nodded and respectfully took a couple steps away from the door as she closed it.

Less than five minutes later, she emerged; her hair combed with a clean McCall Security Uniform and touch of fresh makeup.

Crossing the parking lot to the makeshift press conference, Sage spewed expletives at Hillary who was practically preening in front of the news media.

Hillary turned and pointed toward the production set as gracefully as Vanna White would have turned a letter. Whirring camera motors and flashing lights followed her every gesture and magnanimous smile.

Sage and Double K almost ran into two reporters trying to connect a live feed.

Hillary looked very pleased to be the center of attention. St. Gabrielle's portly Mayor and Hillary's first AD, Assistant Director, Connard, flanked her.

Connard clutched Hillary's snowy white poodle, Pepe, who squirmed nervously in his arms.

Overdressed in gray Armani dress trousers with a navy Burberry polo, Connard looked uncomfortable, but then he always did. The Mayor's meaty face flushed as he raised his hand in an attempt to draw some of the attention from Hillary.

"Where's Jon Maddux?" Sage hissed as they reached the throng of news reporters. "He should be here."

"Is the murder victim one of the cast, or contestants?" shouted one reporter.

"How was he killed, Ms. Kenyon?" cried another.

"Is McMasters Studio accepting blame for this murder?" a third called out.

Used to fielding questions about designer clothes and Hollywood gossip, Hillary was beginning to struggle. She was rapidly losing control of the situation. What had a moment earlier seemed so promising was turning ugly. Hillary was out of her league with top investigative reporters and she knew it. Her gaze crisscrossed the group and rested on Sage. Relief visibly washed over her, and she pointed to the back of the throng to where Sage and Double K stood.

"Here comes our Security Chief, Sage McCall. Sage will answer your questions."

Sage watched the lights, cameras, and handheld microphones spin in her direction. She didn't have time to react to Hillary's announcement before the attention was instantly upon her.

"Let's have it," a dark voice rang out above the crowd. "Was the murderer a member of the cast or crew?"

Sage drew to her full height; she could feel Double K's strength and massive power behind her. She made her way through the crowd with little resistance.

"I hate to disappoint you, " she said evenly as she took a place next to Hillary. "But we're not even sure there has been a murder."

"Surely," a man's angry voice challenged, "The man didn't commit suicide by falling on an arrow."

Sage cursed under her breath. How did they know about the arrow? She threw an angry glare at Hillary, who squirmed and recoiled under her glare. Both the Mayor and Connard had the good grace to look away.

"Until we get an autopsy report," Sage said forcing her voice to remain cool, "any comments are mere speculation. Now, on behalf of McMasters Studio, I'm going to ask you all to leave."

"Is this going to halt production?" a familiar reporter from *Inside Edition* called out.

Double K raised his hand. "You heard the lady. This news conference is over!"

As a group they were hardly rebuffed but Sage's demeanor left little room for doubt. Ignoring the angry stares and low whispers, Sage turned to Hillary who was positively shrinking under her glare.

"Come on," one former actor turned television host pleaded, "can't you tell us any more?"

The paparazzi and television reporters stood frozen, waiting for her next response. Sage took a long breath.

She knew better than to annihilate the Hollywood news media. "As soon as the autopsy is complete, I'm sure the studio will issue a statement. Until then, we have no further comment."

Sage turned toward Hillary, who clutched Pepe for defense. Before Sage could say a word, her cell phone rang.

"Good job," Her father said, "the conference was live. Glad you ended it. Nick is furious. How did it get started?"

Sage answered simply, "Hillary."

"Well, she's done it this time," her father replied. "Nick is livid. She had no business calling a news conference."

"Well, it won't happen again," Sage assured him.

"No kidding! Nick is sending out a publicist to handle the press."

"He'd better send a bulldog. I think Hillary sees this as her golden opportunity to promote herself any way she can."

Her Dad chuckled, "She'll be lucky to find another job in Hollywood if she doesn't stop. Keep an eye on her."

"Is Nick still thinking of closing production?" Sage asked in a low silvery voice.

"Not yet. He wants to see which way the wind blows, but I can tell it's on his mind. This series has already gotten way too much negative publicity. Too much more and the network will cancel the series. Nick may have no choice."

Sage looked at Hillary and shook her head, exhausted with her antics.

Her dad continued, "Sweetie, you are doing a great job. By the way you looked great on TV. Your entire interview was live in LA. Your sister is going to be jealous of your exposure."

Though half a continent away, Sage gave her father a half smile as she replied, "Fallon is welcome to my share of the spotlight. I hope that's the last time I'm ever on the news."

Sage kept a steady eye on Hillary, who was speaking in low tones to the Mayor and Connard. Whatever frustration she had felt before introducing Sage was fast turning into righteous indignation. Some of the reporters were purposely hanging back. Sage had to ring off with her father.

"I'll be in touch," she said signing off.

"About time you got here," Hillary said sounding very annoyed. She sniffed and stroked Pepe's snowy coiffure. The toy poodle barred his lips warning Sage to stay away from his mistress.

Sage ignored the poodle. "You shouldn't have called a press conference."

"I didn't," Hillary whimpered, clutching Pepe close.

Sage frowned. "Hillary, you are a poor liar. Nick wants this quiet."

"Nonsense," Hillary spat. "He'll love the publicity."

"Don't pull this again, Hillary. You gained nothing and you may have cost yourself your job."

"I'll have you fired!" Hillary said loud enough to garner the attention of the reporters still gathering their gear. She stood toe to toe to Sage. "You and your security team."

Sage almost laughed in her face. She didn't bother to hide her smile, knowing Hillary's threat was as empty as it sounded. "There are a lot of things you can do Hillary but firing McCall Security is not one of them."

"Are you threatening me?" Hillary demanded, "I will not be threatened Ms. McCall. That sounded like a threat."

"Hillary, you're compromising a police investigation and causing unwarranted spotlight on the studio. Know when to keep your mouth shut."

Red-faced Jeff Sanders raced across the parking lot. Sage could only guess he had just gotten off the phone with Nick McMasters. Pleased that Hillary was going to receive a well-deserved tongue lashing, Sage tugged at Double K's shirt sleeve and moved away from Hillary and her poodle.

Connard was already slinking away.

The Mayor hurried up to catch up with her. Good manners dictated she wait for him.

"I'm sorry we brought this to your town," Sage said in apology.

"You know what they say," the Mayor said brightly, watching the reporters load their vans, "any publicity is good. We'll have every hotel filled with news crews by nightfall. This murder has put our little town on the map."

He licked his thick lips in anticipation of the storm of

notoriety that would surely follow this news story. Sage looked at him. This man was going to be useless.

Before she could reply, Jon Maddux's heavy Ford Explorer barreled down the drive to Sand Point, dodging press vans and vehicles.

A lone reporter called out the Mayor's name. The Mayor turned without so much as a goodbye to Sage and carried his great body over to speak to the reporter.

Sage turned to give her full attention to Jon's Explorer. Watching it come toward her, she felt a rush of excitement. With no time to understand her reaction, she wrapped her silken emotions in a cocoon and buried them deep inside her heart. She took a quick breath. She was impatient for him to reach her. With her eyes totally focused on the driver of the Explorer, she struggled to gain some semblance of composure.

He brought the Explorer to her side. She felt her face burn just knowing he was near.

The automatic window slid down.

"Looks like everything is under control," His words were distant, but his eyes were focused solely upon her. He casually rested his left arm upon the SUV's door. Sage tried to look away from his muscular arms, his mouth, and his eyes. She failed.

"I take it your director called this fiasco."

Sage noted the rich distaste in his voice and grinned. "She did and she is not my director. And your Mayor was here as well."

Jon chuckled. "He's not my Mayor."

Sage smiled. For once she and the Chief of Police were on the same side.

"I just got a call from the Medical Examiner. His

preliminary findings are ready. I'm gong to see him now. Would you like to join me?"

Damn, why did he have to be so good looking? Without waiting for her to reply, he reached over to the passenger door and opened it. This was hardly the romantic invitation a girl would want, but Sage was admittedly interested in what the M.E. would say. Without hesitation, she climbed in the Explorer.

Catching Double K's attention, she waved a quick goodbye.

Next to her Jon grinned, and then turned his attention to navigating the vehicle through the parking lot.

Masking her inner turmoil with deceptive calmness, she looked out the window and brushed a long blonde curl from her face. Her hands shook and she clasped them together in the hope he would not notice.

The worlds of Hollywood make-believe had irrevocably collided with the real world, a simple realm that was filled with suddenly complex questions. She was swimming through a sea of haze, unexplored direction and staggering desire. Strange and disquieting thoughts raced through her mind.

She looked at the man sitting beside her and was surprised to find his eyes upon her.

At this moment, she could be sure of nothing.

A figure stood in the shadows of the old hotel, watching the SUV carrying Jon Maddux and Sage McCall drive away. Half hidden by the side of the building, standing among overgrown shrubbery, no one had seen the figure and if they had, they would have hardly taken note. Why should they?

No one would ever suspect this was just the beginning.

This had worked out so much better than planned. Now that, the Hollywood Press Corps had been mobilized, the eyes of the nation would be glued to this tiny town. Perfect.

The heady sense of victory was imminent. All that was left to do was to get rid of pretty Sage McCall. They would hardly be prepared for what would come next.

CHAPTER FOUR

J on gave his full attention to the road ahead. Whatever he was thinking or feeling, he kept to himself.

The quiet was awkward for Sage; it seemed for both of them. Like it or not, she was going to have to find a common ground with this private man if she was going to make headway in this investigation.

"Are you from St. Gabrielle?" Sage asked breaking the silence between them. Her voice broke miserably and for several moments he said nothing. His fingers remained firm on the steering wheel, and his eyes steady on the road.

Sage slumped back against the seat, annoyed with herself. Why had she bothered?

Looking out the window, she instantly regretted her attempt at small talk. This man had no intention of letting anyone close to him, least of all her. Well, no matter, she thought, shifting in her seat; she had at least tried to break though his cool exterior. It wouldn't have hurt him to give her a polite response.

"I was born and raised in Miami," he said unexpectedly.

She had almost jumped at the sound of his velvety smooth voice.

"What brought you here?" She asked, giving him a sidelong glance. She wasn't sure he would answer but he turned to her as if he wanted her to know.

"Moved here a few years ago, after a stint with the DEA in South Florida."

Sage sat silent across from him allowing him to tell her more.

"I came here because I needed the quiet. I needed to feel like I could make a difference."

Sage nodded.

"And, I lost a good friend," he volunteered after a moment's pause.

"I'm sorry," Sage offered softly understanding this enigmatic man just a bit more.

Sage smiled. However small, he had given her a glimpse of himself she guessed he rarely shared. She cast her eyes downward hoping he would say more. She wanted him to continue. She wanted to know him and to understand. She wanted to soothe him, comfort him as only a woman can. She sat quietly allowing him have whatever time was needed to resume speaking.

"After Sid's death, I needed to make a difference. I thought I could do it here." His voice faded, was almost apologetic.

Sage took a deep breath feeling the door that was ever so slightly opened was once again closed.

Jon stopped. He swallowed hard and lifted his chin, startled at his own words.

Why was he giving this woman information about himself? Why did he want her to know and understand? Being a good cop, he had always been careful to keep his emotions in check and here, in less than two minutes, he had shared with her the long buried guilt and the secret anguish he carried inside him that he let no one see.

Why would this woman care, he scoffed. She comes from an ultra-rich society with a luxurious lifestyle. Why would she be concerned about him or his town? She and her company were just passing through. He would have to deal with the aftermath but for now he needed an in with the movie crowd, and unfortunately she was it.

He would know soon enough if he was dealing with an actual murder or a bizarre prank. Either way, he couldn't shake the feeling that something sinister was going on and this was only the tip of the iceberg.

The moment she pointed out the pattern of the bloodstain, he knew she had guessed right. The man had been shot post mortem. Why?

Gritting his teeth, he tried to concentrate on the drive but he was too conscious of the woman beside him.

In the tight confines of the Explorer, the soft scent of her perfume was intoxicating. Her body too near. Clutching the wheel, he tried not to think of her, yet, her presence was overwhelming, assaulting, and tantalizing his every sense.

He wanted to taste the sweetness of her lips; instead, he focused on the turn he was about to make and the body laying in the county morgue.

At the moment, he had more questions than answers and he drew a long breath as he struggled to gain control of his thoughts and his senses.

Hardening his heart, he reminded himself, as he had told her only minutes earlier; he had come here to St. Gabrielle to find peace, but the peace he was hoping to find was slipping through his fingers.

As they reached the outskirts of town, Jon slowed behind traffic. He was glad to be back on familiar ground.

Weaving through a matrix of residential streets, Sage sensed he was taking a shorter route to the hospital and sat quietly enjoying the distinctively tropical landscape and the southern charm of its stately homes.

The streets of St. Gabrielle were made of brick and still echoed with the sounds of horse drawn carriages.

St. Gabrielle was as it seemed a typical southern town found along the Florida coast. Its cobblestone streets were lined with a mixture of elegant, white-framed houses with immaculate gardens, and classic Victorian architecture.

Thick green ferns hung from spacious porches and enormous oaks lined the streets. The bright cheery sunlight added to the peaceful friendly atmosphere.

St. Gabrielle was a quiet little Florida town. She could see why Jon wanted to keep it that way.

With its five stories, the county hospital rose like a skyscraper around the last turn. The hospital that served St. Gabrielle also housed the county morgue. She relaxed hoping the Medical Examiner would answer some of their questions.

Jon, again, pulled into a parking space reserved for police vehicles, and turned off the engine.

"I'd like to check on Jamie before we leave," she said exiting the Explorer.

Jon gave her a quick nod as he followed her to the double set of sliding glass doors.

The two white-haired volunteers greeted Jon as they entered the building and smiled at Sage as they passed them.

Knowing his way to the county medical examiner's office, Jon weaved his way down a long corridor of administrative offices, past a door marked bio-labs, and a down a series of nondescript hallways before reaching their destination.

Reaching for the doorknob, he opened it and allowed Sage to pass.

A single secretary-receptionist sat behind an antiquated computer that should have been replaced years ago. Behind her, the cabinets were cluttered with mounds of file folders that needed to be sorted and put away.

Before she could greet them, Dr. Edwards appeared wearing a lab coat over his flowered Hawaiian shirt and slacks. He motioned them to come into his office.

"Saw you on TV," he said to Sage, showing her to one of the two chairs, "looked like a three ring circus out there."

Dr. Edwards's voice was courteous and without reproach.

She wrinkled her brow. "It was."

Dr. Edwards grunted. Settling comfortably in his cast-off leather chair, he sorted through several file folders before opening one. He took a moment to read over his finding.

"Well, I had to send a blood and tissue sample to the state lab for analysis but my preliminary findings indicated that Mr. Davis didn't die from that arrow as you surmised, Ms. McCall," Dr. Edwards said in a slow southern drawl. "Mr. Davis died of a heart attack. The arrow was then shot into him post-mortem."

Jon and Sage sat motionless.

Dr. Edwards continued, "No evidence of a struggle. His blood alcohol level was high, over three-point-o. I suspect he was passed out drunk when he had his heart attack and didn't know what hit him."

Jon shifted in his chair. His voice was soft as he asked, "The body was shot post-mortem?"

Dr. Edwards gave him a quick nod and flipped over several pages of notes.

"My men found no signs of a struggle."

"That would be consistent with my findings. No defensive wounds."

Sage leaned forward in her seat. "Any idea when he died?"

The coroner looked at Sage and drew a breath before he answered.

"Evan Davis was still in the early states of rigor. The body, Ms. McCall, doesn't go into full rigor mortis until twelve hours. Now, don't hold me to this because I'm still waiting on my toxicology report and some other lab work to come in, but, I would venture to say Mr. Davis' died around nine P.M. last night."

Jon glanced at his watch before he looked back at the Medical Examiner. "So he had been dead approximately five to six hours before his body was discovered."

Dr. Edwards gave him a nod. "That would be my guess, but as I said, these are preliminary findings. I'll know more when I get the lab work back."

"Now, to answer your next question," Dr. Edwards said as if anticipating Jon's next concern. "I extracted the arrow and have sent it to state crime lab for analysis and prints. Don't hold your breath; I doubt it we'll find anything that will help."

As he finished his last comment, the Medical Examiner closed the file and laid it directly in front of him. Turning to Sage he asked in a somewhat brighter tone, "How's your young security fellow? Any better?"

Sage smiled. She appreciated him asking. "We are going to go see him next."

Glancing at the silver Timex watch on his wrist, Dr. Edwards said with a weary yawn, "Well, it's been a long night and day. I think I'm going home to have some dinner and check with the Mrs. You're both welcome to join me."

"Thank you," Jon answered for both of them, "but we really need to check on the security guard."

"You know, my wife is a big fan of your show," Dr. Edwards

said with a twinkle in his eye. "I don't suppose when all this is over, she could..."

Sage rose and offered her hand to Dr. Edwards. Shaking his hand firmly, she was pleased to say, "Doctor, as soon as we resume production, why don't you and your wife come out to the set. You would both be welcome to have lunch with the cast and crew. I would be happy to introduce you to everyone."

Dr. Edwards looked pleased and instantly rewarded Sage with a radiant and quick smile. "Miss McCall, my wife is such a huge fan of the show; she's going to be very excited."

Sage smiled. "You both are most welcome."

As she and Jon turned to leave his office, Dr. Edwards's face clouded once again. "I almost forgot, what about the body?"

"The studio will be in touch. Evan has a sister in Kansas, so when you release the body, call us. The studio will make all the necessary arrangements."

Doc acknowledged her with a grim smile and escorted them out of the office.

Outside the Medical Examiner's office, Jon and Sage silently made their way back through the labyrinth of corridors until they reached a set of elevators and rode one to the second floor.

A fresh St. Gabrielle police officer was seated outside the door of Jamie's room. He rose as he saw Jon. The magazine he was reading fluttered to the floor.

Without waiting for the guard to speak, Sage pushed the door open slightly to find a pretty young nurse hovering over Jamie.

The nurse put her finger to her lips and motioned for Sage to remain quiet.

"He's sleeping but doing much better," she offered with a smile.

Sage nodded with gratitude and gently closed the door just in time to hear the officer say, "He woke briefly but the Doctor sedated him."

Jon looked toward the closed door.

"Call me if there is any change," Jon instructed him. Looking to Sage, he said softly, "There is nothing more we can do here. It's after three. Why don't I buy you some lunch?"

"All right," Sage agreed a bit surprised by the offer, "lunch sounds good."

"Good," Jon replied with a casual grin, "I know just the place."

Outside the hospital, Sage reached for her cell phone and called the Sand Point Inn.

"Everything is pretty quiet, Sage." Double K assured her, "How's Jamie?"

"He's better. He's sleeping now. The Doctor has him sedated."

Sage heard Double K's sigh of relief. "Oh, Cowboy Bob and Reese arrived from LA about thirty minutes ago. I have Cowboy Bob at the gate and Reese is on his way in to the hospital to be with Jamie."

"Good," Sage said feeling momentarily relived. She knew she was going to need more help but at least she had two more men she knew could depend on. This was good news. "Okay, I'll see you later then."

With that she turned back to Jon. "Two more McCall Security men have arrived to assist us."

Jon eased the SUV out of the parking space. "Good. You'll probably need the additional manpower."

Less than two minutes later, they were driving out of the hospital parking lot and headed toward the south edge of town.

Jon wasted little time in driving to a rustic restaurant. The parking lot was oversized and even mid-afternoon was almost completely filled with cars and pickup trucks.

Sage read the sign 'Buddy's Bodacious Barbeque' affixed to a long tin roof that covered the structure. Bright neon signs lit the windows and offered patrons a variety of domestic beer.

The heady, sweet smell of smoked ribs assaulted Sage as she opened the door of the Explorer.

She looked at Jon and he smiled. As they headed for the restaurant, she was sure she wasn't going to be disappointed... about anything.

Jon made a special attempt to reach the restaurant door before her, and then gallantly allowed her to pass.

"Thank you," she said in a voice so low she wasn't sure he had even heard her but his smile was as close as a stolen kiss. His eyes were warming and she felt the heat from his gaze rise from deep within her causing her face to burn in a feverish blush.

She turned her attention to the restaurants interior hoping he hadn't noticed his affect on her.

The restaurant itself was divided into two distinct sections, a long lacquered wooden bar with tall bar stools and tables at one end and on the other four or five long lines of wooden restaurant booths.

Country music softly filled the air and mingled with the heavenly scent of barbeque and hush puppies. A group of construction workers and fishermen filled the bar. At the sight of Sage and Jon waiting by the hostess station, their conversation stopped.

Both Sage and Jon took immediate notice of the appreciative stares directed toward Sage.

Jon's raised his eyebrow a fraction and his jaw line tensed

betrayed his irritation. Raising his hand into the air, he impatiently motioned for a waitress to show them to a table.

"Man," Sage overheard one of the men whispering to his companions, "That's one good looking woman."

Jon touched the small of her back in a brief but clearly possessive caress. She tried to hide her grin as shock waves from his fingers spread across her back, electrifying her entire body. Her pulse skyrocketed and she was sure he could hear the sound of her thundering heart.

"Must be one of those movie stars," a second male voice offered after noting Sage and Jon by the door. The men, well into their cups, were making no attempt to conceal their comments.

The hostess with a plastic pitcher of iced tea hurried toward Jon and Sage and waved them to follow her. Sliding two menus under the crook of her elbow, she deftly maneuvered her way through the restaurant to a clean booth.

"Your waitress will take your order," she said before leaving to deposit the pitcher of tea at a table at the far end of the room.

"I'm not the only one who thinks you're a movie star," Jon whispered in her ear as she slid into the booth. The low husky sound of his whisper reverberated through her body like the electric sounds of a steel guitar.

Sliding into the seat across from her, she tried to stay her eyes from the rich outline of his shoulders that seemed to strain against the fabric of his tan police uniform.

Jon didn't bother to pick up the menu; instead, he made a quick glance around the room before turning his full attention on her. His humor restored, an easy smile danced at the corners of his mouth.

"Hey Chief," the waitress greeted Jon. Reaching in her apron for a pale green order pad, she said, "Ready to order?"

"How about a pitcher of beer," Jon asked, looking to Sage for her unspoken consent.

She nodded. A cold beer sounded good.

With the precision of a West Point cadet, the waitress spun about and headed for the kitchen with their order.

"Thought cops didn't drink on duty?" Sage said with teasing reproach, as she picked up the menu.

Jon kept his eyes steady on her as he replied, "I just went off duty."

Sage formed a perfect 'oh' with her mouth, and opened the oversized menu. Realizing she hadn't eaten since early morning, she was simply too hungry to give the colorful menu the attention it deserved. Everything looked good.

Folding the menu, she laid it to one side. Looking at Jon and finding him watching her, she asked, "What do you recommend?"

"I'm getting a sliced beef barbeque plate with fries and slaw."

"Sounds good," Sage agreed

The waitress returned with a small pitcher of beer. She deposited the pitcher and two frosty mugs on the slick wood tabletop. Apparently, it wasn't her job to pour. Taking a step away from the table, she touched the tip of her pencil with her tongue and poised it ready to write down their order.

"Two barbeque plates, Rachel," Jon ordered while pouring the beer into the mugs. He offered one to Sage, and took a hearty drink of his own.

Rachel diligently wrote down their order and with a slight bob of her head, hurried over to help two truck drivers who had just been seated.

"You could have ordered gator." Jon informed her. She heard the soft chuckle behind his sensuous voice. His lips curled into a seductive smile.

"You're joking?" Sage replied with a soft laugh. "Are you serious, real alligator?"

Jon nodded.

"I thought they were endangered."

"They were," Jon informed her, "but the conservationists have done such a great job, they've come back with a vengeance. Trust me; if it's a lake, river, or pond in Florida, it's probably got a gator in it."

He seemed a bit satisfied his comment had brought a visible shiver of complete surprise and soft gasp from her. Sage didn't take offense; she guessed he enjoyed imparting this bit of local lore to every unsuspecting tourist.

"Buddy gets his gator meat from a farm."

"A gator farm?" Sage repeated, taking a sip of the icy cold beer. "I suppose you're going to tell me it tastes like chicken."

"No, it tastes like gator," Jon replied from obvious experience.

Raising his hand, he caught the attention of their waitress. "Hey Rachel, bring us a gator appetizer with some ranch sauce."

Sage physically shuttered and looked out the window to avoid his grin.

"So tell me about the people in your television crew."

"All right," Sage said, glad she had something to think about besides eating a reptile for the next few moments. With a fresh breath, she answered him. "You can categorize the cast and crew into three groups, the film and production crew, the professional actors, and the contestants."

"Any big names?"

"No, thank God! Just actors and actresses with solid experience who haven't made it yet. The Studio Head prefers, at least for this series, to use unknowns. It adds to the show's credibility. I've already ordered background information on everyone. When it arrives, you're welcome to take a look at it."

"Did Davis have any friends here? Or for that matter, enemies?"

"Evan was social with Gray Morrison, the Best Boy, and Steve Wilder, one of the prop men." She paused and tried to remember any incident of conflict. She couldn't recall anyone who might have had a grudge with Evan. "He was known to be rude on occasion and at times downright obnoxious, but I don't recall anyone who stands out."

"Is there anyone at the moment who does stand out as someone who would do this?"

Sage shook her head. "No."

Whatever Jon was about to say was lost as the waitress appeared with a large platter of what looked like golden fried chicken nuggets. She deposited the platter along with a small bowl of white ranch sauce and two plates, one before Jon and the other in front of Sage.

"Bon-a-petite." Rachel drawled in a heavy southern accent. Satisfied with her delivery of the delicacy, she hurried off to wait on a group of tourists.

Sage just sat and stared at the crispy tidbits. She did not recall ever being served alligator at any of social gatherings she had attended on the west coast. She wasn't sure what to do with them and wasn't sure she wanted to know.

Jon was enjoying her discomfort too much. He lifted a piece and dipped it into the sauce. "Try one."

Though said quietly with a soft smile on his lips, he had nevertheless thrown the gauntlet, in the form of a gator appetizer, before her. Trying not to grimace, she lifted one and placed it on her plastic plate before spooning out a small bit of spiced sauce.

Jon had stopped eating and held his beer mug in his hand waiting for her to taste the delicacy.

Delaying as long she dared, she bared her little teeth then took a small bite.

The meat was tender and stringy. It was distinctively chewy and did not taste like chicken, it tasted like reptile.

She looked at Jon. With a deep, unsteady breath she said between chews, "Humm…gator—the other white meat."

Jon's laugh was instantaneous and came from deep within him. His dark eyes were sparkling with approval. Sage took another bite somehow knowing she had unwittingly passed another of his unspoken challenges.

He returned to his beer and dipped a golden strip into the sauce.

Sage tried not to notice the way his lips wrapped around the tasty morsel or the steady movement of seductive pleasure his jaw made as he chewed. His body though slightly curved was powerful. His skin glistened beneath his shirt and she was acutely conscious of his athletic physique. She smiled remembering the touch of his fingertips and the protective way he had urged her from unwarranted stares from other men at the bar. Whether he meant to or not, he gave her a sense of protection and strength.

Trying to ignore the distinctly reptilian delicacy, he didn't seem to notice she had nibbled at only one.

"I've had better," Jon said, his eye twinkling with a touch of humor.

Sage made no attempt to hide her sarcasm. "Oh yeah, me too"

She felt the ripple of his laughter and was pleased to hear him laugh.

"So, Sage, how did you get into the movie security business?"

"My dad, as you must be aware, owns his own security firm, McCall Security. We do all sorts of work in and around the industry. Everything from security patrols to bodyguards and security on the sets of movie and television productions, both in and out of LA."

"You're very modest, Sage," Jon interjected. "McCall Security is one of the most recognized security firms in the United States. I know because I checked into it when I heard McCall would be doing security for this project."

He was thorough, she thought, pleased with this bit of new information.

"Why don't you like us being here in St. Gabrielle?" Sage asked bluntly. "We have got to be good for business."

"As I have told you before," he said, his voice soft and serious, "we have a small quiet town. Despite how the Mayor and Town Board may have presented this town to your studio people, there are a lot of people here who like the quiet lifestyle. I'm one of them."

"You find us disruptive?"

"To say the least, and I'm also concerned with the aftermath of people flooding into the town to see where your TV show was shot."

"It'll blow over," Sage assured him.

"Yes, how long?" Jon replied refilling her mug before topping off his own. "You Hollywood people come in, do your filming and leave. Those of us who live here are going to have to deal with the problems that follow."

"I would hardly think the minor traffic problems and

influx of tourist dollars would be an inconvenience. Most towns welcome our, what did you call it, intrusion."

Rachel chose that moment to return and expected both Sage and Jon to clear the table in front of them. They complied and were rewarded with two plates teeming with steaming beef, thick Texas fries that spilled off the plate, and a goodly portion of creamy cold slaw.

"I'll be back," Rachel said sweeping away.

"Your opinion probably doesn't sit well with Mayor Frederick. He is excited we are here."

Slicing a large bite of beef, his mouth tightened. "It may surprise you to know the Sand Point Inn has sat vacant for years. When the Mayor learned that McMasters Studio had selected that location for the show, Frederick and his cronies put a substantial down payment on the property. They have plans to turn it into some kind of tourist attraction."

"And you don't like that either, do you?" Sage asked knowing the passionate response it would no doubt bring.

"No," Jon answered with an honesty that bit at her core. He stopped speaking and regarded her softly. His eyes grew gentle, soft and rich in their warm gaze. "Let's eat."

Without a word of protest, Sage lifted her fork and began to eat the mouthwatering smoked meat. The long slices tasted succulent and sweet in the rich red specialty sauce. The fries were lightly seasoned and the coleslaw was smooth and cool to her lips and mouth. Sage and Jon hardly spoke while they each ate their meal.

Rachel stopped by twice. First, to bring a plastic basket filled with hushpuppies, and a second time to remove their plates.

Sage wiped her mouth and took a final sip of beer.

"I have to admit, that's the best meal I've had since arriving in Florida. I will have to tell Oz."

Jon sat back, his powerful shoulders hitting the back of this seat. "Oz?"

Then his eyes lit with recognition. "The head guy of Craft Services for the Studio? You introduced him to me this morning. Seems like a nice guy."

"He is," Sage said softly, "but he lost his wife and daughter some years back. I'm not sure he's gotten over it."

"They have great Key Lime pie here," Jon offered, while signaling Rachel for the check.

Sage shook her head and pushed her plate away from her. Seeing Rachel approach with their ticket, she reached for her small billfold tucked in the pocket of her black shorts. "No thanks, I couldn't eat another bite."

"This is on me," Jon said reaching for his wallet from his hip pocket.

"The studio will cover this." Sage assured him.

His square jaw visibly tensed and his brown eyes grew dark. A warning cloud settled on his handsome features.

"I didn't take the movie studio out, Miss McCall," he said smoothly with cool reproach, "I took you."

Sage froze and remained absolutely motionless for a moment. His eyes met her blue ones and held her suspended in his dark emotion.

Looking down at her, his expression softened slightly. He hadn't meant to sound so gruff. Realizing he had won the day, his smile was radiant.

Sage felt a flutter of pleasure as he smiled. She tried to ignore it.

Why did everything about him make her body throb with distraction? She stood, wrenching herself away from her ridiculous preoccupation of his every move. As she turned to leave, a heavy-set man in a stained barbeque apron approached them.

With thinning hair and a ready smile, the man offered his hand to Sage even before he reached her. She accepted his handshake, liking this big gregarious man before he even spoke.

"Hey Chief," the man said reaching past Jon to pick up their dinner check, "who have you got here, one of those movie stars?"

Sage felt her face burn red.

"I'm not a movie star," she managed to say still feeling a bit embarrassed by his attention. "I'm Sage McCall. I'm in charge of security."

"No, no," the man protested. He was adamant and had no intention of being swayed. "I know I saw you in a movie the other night. It was you!"

"By the way, if you haven't guessed, Sage, this is Buddy. Sage, Buddy introduce yourselves," Jon interjected.

Sage smiled. "You must have seen my sister, Fallon. She has been in any number of movies and television shows."

Buddy stood rocking back on his heels. He looked confused as though sure he was talking to the ravishing actress he had seen on TV. Sage wasn't certain she could convince him otherwise. The McCall daughters bore a striking resemblance to one another.

Buddy shook his head in disbelief. "Are you sure it wasn't you? Looked like you! Jon, you've got to admit she's a mighty pretty one."

Jon turned to Sage. His eyes caressed the soft curve of her brows, her small nose, the lift of her chin, her mouth before he said "I think she's beautiful."

The heavy lashes that shadowed her face flew up in surprise. She looked at him remembering the hostility between them but she could find no lie in his dark brown eyes. Instead, his eyes were shining in natural unabashed desire.

In an intense but private expression he turned back to Buddy as she felt her flesh color to crimson.

The pounding rhythm of her heart was so loud she missed much of the jumble of words Buddy said as he continued to shake her hand.

Buddy paused suddenly, waiting for her to respond.

"I'm so sorry," Sage stammered, "what did you say?"

"He said," Jon replied in a slightly patronizing tone, "that he'd like to do some catering for the television show."

"Absolutely," Sage promised giving her full attention to Buddy, adding quickly, "I'll make sure I tell Oz about you. Oz is in charge of catering for the production. I'm sure he'll be in touch."

Jon reached back for the check but Buddy grabbed it.

"This is on me, Chief," Buddy said firmly.

Jon gave Buddy an appreciative nod and pulled out a few dollars for the waitress.

"Ms. McCall, you won't forget," Buddy shouted out to them as they made their way though the crowded restaurant.

"I won't forget," Sage promised.

Though sunset was still a few hours away, a cool steady breeze was already blowing in from the Gulf of Mexico. It played with a strand of blond hair about her cheek and caressed her lips like a lover's kiss.

Jon had taken the lead ahead of her. Watching him walk purposely ahead of her, she realized his long leggy strides were becoming familiar to her. His short, dark brown hair was glistening in the afternoon sun and she was mesmerized by the way his massive shoulders moved in perfect symmetry with the gentle sway of his trim hips. The muscles of his thighs rippled to his calves as he purposely walked his way to the SUV.

For a moment, Sage thought to look away but walking behind him, he would hardly know she was watching. There was a restless energy about him and she tried, with no avail, to anticipate his thoughts.

Reaching the car, he stopped and looked at her. His strong features held a certain sensuality. His eyes grew dark as she closed the few steps between them.

He pulled out the keys from his pocket, unlocked the door and before depositing the keys in his right front pocket. His movements had been slow, deliberate, and strangely sensual.

Instead of opening the door, he turned; his massive arms circled her body and pressed her back into the side of the car door. With his eyes intently upon her, his long cool fingers cupped her face, and lifted her chin.

She was imprisoned with no place to run, move, or breathe as his powerful body covered her. His massive chest pushed against her soft breasts.

In one fluid movement, a muscular thigh easily parted her legs. The electric shock of his skin raced through her. Helpless but to give herself to him, her body sensually arched to his. Her arms rose from her side to his finely sculptured back. Her soft, supple body molded perfectly into his hard, muscular frame. She fit into him as through she belonged there.

His lips, soft and intoxicating, covered hers hungrily demanding her mouth open. His tongue sent quivers of desire racing through her as it explored the soft recess of her mouth.

Sage welcomed his savage need of her as sweet spirals of desire, one after the other, raced through her to meet the liquid fire that rose within her.

From a place of lost abandonment, she clung to him; her senses clouded, separated from all sense of time and reason. As her soul yielded in surrender, the world spun in sweet blackness. She was swept back through the ages to a singular moment when in the darkness of a primeval forest woman first yielded to primal man. She was lost to him and her submission was total.

Without warning, he abruptly stepped back before again brushing her lips with a second long tender kiss. From the dark recesses of her soul, she felt the pull of her body hurtling her back to earth. Still feeling his breath, savory soft and sensually sweet upon her, she opened her eyes as he brushed his powerful jaw against the hollow of her cheek. She stood suspended.

Turning her slightly toward him, he buried his head into her neck, as his hands hungrily tangled his fingers into her thick blonde hair. It was an act of possession.

Sage felt the ache of his body for her and his warm breath sending shock waves down to the small of her back. Her arms locked around his waist as a soft moan escaped his lips. For one breathless moment, they stood engulfed in a web that surpassed need and desire. Her heart was hammering in her chest and her breath was ragged.

With her lips still soft and moist from his mouth, she looked up at him. Their eyes met and Sage was startled as she heard his deep husky voice say without excuse or regret, "I wanted to do that the moment I first saw you."

With that, he took two steps back, flung the passenger door open and left her standing, stunned and shaken, by the door. The taste of his lips lingered on her mouth and the musk smell of his cologne was clinging to her like a second skin.

With her knees weak, she slid into the passenger seat and they slammed the doors in unison.

Instead of reaching for the steering wheel, he cupped her heart-shaped face into his left hand and pulled her to him.

This time the kiss was soft. Once again, she offered no resistance. In a series of slow, shivering kisses, she felt the sensual pleasure of his lips on her mouth, her brow, the tip of her nose before claiming her forehead. Her lips parted and waited impatiently for the satin pleasure of his kiss.

With every bit of self-restraint he could muster, he broke free of her. With a heavy breath, he tried to focus his attention back to the moment. His hand was trembling with desire for her as he turned the key into the ignition. The Explorer's engine roared.

"I want to know you better, Sage McCall," Jon said gazing into her eyes.

"My boyfriend won't like this," Sage replied unable to hide her wicked grin.

"You don't have a boyfriend," Jon said evenly.

She blinked and tried to hold back a grin as she asked smartly, "And, just how do you know that?"

"Because if you had a boyfriend. You wouldn't have let me kiss you like that."

Sage's eyes flew open. How could he know her so well, or was he simply guessing? The cocky look he gave her sent her passions rising, robbing her brain of any quick or clever comeback.

At last she found her tongue, and gave it to him sharply.

"Well, next time your hormones kick in," Sage began but Jon interrupted her.

"My hormones, Miss McCall, are just fine and in good working order," Jon said with an easy laugh, "May I suggest, the next time you start something with a man, you'd better be prepared to finish it."

Without apology, his gaze traveled over her taking in each soft curve of her body.

God, she was beautiful. He tried to tell himself he hadn't meant to kiss her but in his heart he knew that was a lie. He had wanted to ravage her honeyed mouth since the moment he had seen those beautiful lips. He half-expected her to taste like any other woman, and if she had, it would've made his life easier by dispelling the sexual fantasy he was building around her. But she tasted like no other woman had or ever would again.

A delicious shudder heated his body when he brought her to him. She had felt weightless in his arms, soft, warm, which left him with the aching need to keep her sweet body in his arms where he could always keep her safe.

She had offered little resistance and the velvet warmth of her lips, with its promise of complete surrender, only inflamed him with hot desire. He had felt the blood surge from his fingertips to fire him with searing need of her.

His pleasure in her was pure and explosive. At the moment he was about to lose himself in her, he forced himself to stop. What the hell was the matter with him? He thought angrily.

He should apologize but he didn't feel one damn bit remorseful. For one brazen moment, he thought to take her in his arms again. The need to feel the warmth of her soft body was overwhelming. He resisted just a bit too long.

Instead, he stood looking at her, drinking her soul. If he touched her again, he wasn't sure he would be able to stop himself from taking her right here, right now. She deserved better, better than him.

Sage sat frozen unable to face his mocking smile.

"I didn't start anything," she spat, "it was you!"

He was wicked, she knew that now.

Jon chuckled and moved the vehicle into the flow of traffic.

"You started it," he said evenly. "You start it the moment you walk into a room, Sage. You start it every time I'm near you."

Sage folded her arms and looked out the passenger side window. She wasn't sure if she should be angry or pleased.

"Don't expect me to apologize. I liked kissing you, Sage McCall." Jon said with a smile. His voice was rich in warmth and velvet sweetness. "I think you liked kissing me back."

"Don't be ridiculous!" Sage replied trying to quail her anger, "Are you this forward with all women?"

"No, and you are not all women, are you?"

Sage's cell phone rang before he could finish the sentence. It was Double K.

Alarmed, Sage asked, "What's wrong?"

"Not sure," Double K stammered, "the paramedics are on the way out."

Sage looked at Jon. At that moment, Jon's dispatcher called for him on the police radio.

"Chief, there's an emergency at the Sand Point Inn."

"What?" He demanded then answered the call, "I'm headed there now with their Security Chief."

"Double K, "Sage continued over Jon's voice, "what is going on? Why have you have called the paramedics. For what?

"I don't know Sage, everybody is sick. Very sick."

"I don't understand."

Double K grew quiet before he answered. "I think someone poisoned the food."

"Poisoned the food?" Sage cried.

Jon reached to the dashboard and hit a switch. A siren

squealed in pulsating rhythm. Flashing blue lights atop the light bar illuminated the bright afternoon with color.

"We're on the way there now," Sage said into the cell as Jon downshifted and passed several cars that had pulled off the road before him.

"Gotta go," Double K said into the phone as he ended the call.

"What is it?" Jon asked. "Someone is poisoned?"

"Not someone," she said evenly, "*Everyone!*"

"I don't understand." his quiet voice had an ominous quality with his eyes on the road as he flew past an old station wagon. "How could everyone be sick?"

"Food poisoning," Sage replied grimly.

Jon picked up the mic. With his left hand steady on the wheel, he called the police dispatcher. "Contact Levy County, there are eighty-five people out there. They're going to need all the help we can give!"

Sage sent Jon a grateful look.

With the siren screaming, Jon hurled the Explorer toward the Sand Point Inn.

Reaching the driveway of the shooting location, the Explorer almost jumped from the main highway onto the sandy drive careening toward the front gate.

Faces of the crew, the cast, the actors, and the contestants flashed through her mind.

Sage looked helplessly at Jon. She was scared.

With her voice shaking, she barely heard herself ask, "Why would anyone poison the entire crew?"

CHAPTER FIVE

Sage grabbed the armrest as the Explorer charged toward the closed gate.

Jon's eyes were cold and hard. His fingers were tight around the steering wheel. His muscles were tense, his full focus on the road.

Just ahead of them, a tall lanky man with a McCall Security shirt, well-worn jeans and cowboy hat was signaling them to stop.

Sage recognized Cowboy Bob and was suddenly glad to know he and Reese must have arrived.

With a weathered face and steely eyes, his lips were tight as he motioned for the police vehicle to come to a complete stop.

A small contingency of reporters camped along the highway froze as they watched the massive SUV barrel its way toward the entrance. Discarding coffee cups, and papers they were holding, the reporters ran with cameramen in tow, toward Jon and Sage.

"Is this guy deaf?" Jon spat over the siren as he slammed on the brakes and silenced the alarm.

Seeing Sage in the Explorer, Cowboy Bob had already began swinging open the heavy metal gate to allow the police unit room to pass but his eyes were focused on the reporters scurrying his way.

Sage couldn't resist a smile. Cowboy Bob, like all McCall Security men, were hardly intimidated by the law.

"What have you heard?" Sage called out as they passed him hoping for more information.

Cowboy Bob shook his head. "Don't know. Half the crew is sick, don't know why."

As the Explorer cleared the entrance, Cowboy Bob closed the gate behind them quickly shutting off reporters.

Turning slightly in her seat, Sage watched Cowboy Bob wave the army of reporters away. In a matter of moments, they reached the parking lot.

Jon brought the vehicle to a full halt at the center of the parking lot.

Members of the cast, crew, and production staff mingled in front of the event tent. Their faces reflected their confusion and fear.

Double K, looking more green than black, had watched them stop. His eyes were watery and growing a sick yellow. Sage couldn't get to his side fast enough.

"What's wrong?" She asked trying to keep alarm from her voice.

"Wish the hell I knew," Double K said clutching his abdomen.

"When did you get sick?"

"About three this afternoon," was his barbed reply.

Jon moved to her side. "Symptoms?"

"Abdomen pains, diarrhea, vomiting." Double K answered the Chief. "Some are complaining about headaches, some had pains throughout their bodies. When I found out I wasn't the only one, I called you and 911."

"EMS is on the way."

"I've been thinking, it must have been something bad in the food?" Double K growled looking as if he was going to collapse.

"Where's Oz?" Sage asked looking around. "How about Reese?"

Double K groaned. "I sent Reese to the hospital the minute he and Cowboy Bob arrived. I don't think either one of them ate anything here."

Sage caught the eye of one of the production assistants leaning against a light pole. She called out to him. "Find Oz and bring him here."

With a nod, the PA hurried off looking happy to oblige.

Directing her attention back to Jon and Double K, she tried to keep panic out of her voice as she said, "EMS will be here shortly. K, let's get you seated somewhere."

Together Jon and Sage helped Double K toward the tent.

When they reached the tent, Oz, his face pale, his hands clutching his abdomen, was headed toward them. Manuel his assistant was following him. Though worried about his employer, Manuel showed no signs of illness.

"What's your name, son," Jon asked as Manuel lowered Oz into a chair.

In a thick Mexican accent, he answered, "Manuel."

"All right, Manuel, can you do us a favor," Jon said as he and Sage helped Double K to his chair. "EMS is going to be here shortly. I need you to locate everyone who is sick and bring them here to the main tent. Okay?"

Jon turned to Sage, "We're going to need some cots in here?"

Manuel's face brightened. "Sir, I can go and get some beds."

"Get some of the PAs to help you," Sage called out to him as he left the tent. He nodded and she could hear him calling out to others in the parking lot. Good, she thought, it would give them something to do.

Turning her attention to Oz, she said softly, "I guess you're sick, too."

"Yeah, sick as a dog," Oz stammered, "I think we all might have food poisoning. But Sage, I don't know how, I mean, I have never..."

"It's all right," Sage replied in a soothing tone, ""we just need to get to the bottom of this as soon as possible."

Oz nodded and looked across the table to Double K. "You dead?"

Double K didn't bother to raise his head. "Not yet."

"What did you serve for lunch?" Jon asked.

"I didn't." Oz answered in short gasps, "Since there wasn't any filming today, I ordered out from one of the local pizza delivery services. He brought out pizza, pastas, salad, spaghetti—the usual."

"Do you remember the name?"

"Yeah, of course," Oz replied. "It was *The Pizza Guy* in St. Gabrielle. I used him before."

His voice was laden with guilt as he looked at Sage. His face was weary and filled with anguish. Sage knew he felt he was responsible. He coughed nervously. "Last time I heard of a crew getting food poisoning was on a set in Mexico. The chef had prepared Chilean Sea Bass, everybody got sick. But I've never had any problems. Ever! I used this guy a week or so ago, no problem."

There was no consoling him at the moment, and Sage could only look at Oz and smile hoping he knew she understood.

"You two wait here," Jon said to Double K and Oz as if either men could move away from the table. He looked at Sage. "Manuel and the men helping him should be back any minute. I'm going to help shift some of these tables around."

"I can help," Sage said rising to follow him. She couldn't just sit idly by.

Without argument from Jon, they worked silently clearing space in the immense tent.

Even before Sage and Jon could lift and move a single table, they were joined by others who made quick work of moving the round tables to the back of the tent creating ample space for the beds

Six production assistants returned with folding cots and mattresses found in a storage room back behind the small hotel. The beds, despite their age, were sturdy and in good condition.

The hotel maid service, hired by the studio, began making the beds with clean sheets and pillows as fast as the men were positioning the cots around the tent.

As the beds were readied, suffering members of the production crew, four of the twelve contestants and two of the actors staggered in, practically falling into the freshly made beds.

The final count was twenty-eight, almost one-third of the company.

Fear and anger knotted inside Sage. A flicker of apprehension swept through her. Was this coincidence or intentional? Working feverishly with Jon to ready the room had kept her mind occupied.

Hearing the EMS vehicles arrive, Sage rushed outside and quickly directed them to the helpless victims inside the tent.

After a quick word with Jon, paramedics went to work checking blood pressures, heart and pulse rates, and questioned the stricken crew members about their symptoms.

Sage and Jon could do little but watch the medical personnel work.

Though so many were moaning in pain, no one was dying, Sage thought with no small measure of comfort.

Surveying the activity, Jon took a deep breath. As a man used to taking control, at the moment there was nothing he could do except watch a very experienced EMS Team do their job.

Holding his emotions in check, he heard Sage's jagged breath beside him. It had only been a short time ago he had held her, kissed her in the carefree sunny Florida afternoon? The contrast to this moment was dramatic. He needed to cradle her in his arms again.

Why had he ever thought her a helpless creature when at every turn she had done nothing but prove herself a consummate professional, an equal who didn't flinch under any circumstances? She bore each new development and twist with a courage and intelligence he couldn't help but admire.

And yet, he had seen the quick flashes of anguish in her eyes and sensed her helplessness. It was those moments when he wanted to touch her, bring her into his arms and tell her he was going to make everything okay.

The California beauty should be on the beach in Malibu, playing volleyball surrounded by a group of admirers; instead, she was here in the trenches of life not caring whether she broke a fingernail or not.

She was every bit a woman and he wanted her. And, he liked the way she made him feel as a man by just being with her.

His need to be close to her was overwhelming and filled with both desire and anxious need just to have her close. Her very presence was soothing to him and each glance from her left him aching for that which he didn't even know he needed.

Standing next to her, longing for her in every way a man

longs for a woman, he vowed even though he could never have her, he would make everything all right for her.

Hearing a sharp cry from one of the victims brought him his attention back to the moment.

Had Sage not been with him, she could be suffering. Watching her, he asked God to forgive the man who would ever dare harm this perfect beauty for in his heart he knew he never would!

Sage had seen his eyes darken with unreadable emotion as they flickered ever watchful of her. She guessed he was asking the same question she had. Was this coincidence or intentional?

They waited in silence for answers. They didn't have to wait long.

One of the paramedics walked over to them. In his late thirties, his face spoke of strong German descent.

"We have more medical personal on their way here," he explained in a hushed tone. His light blue eyes were strained and troubled. He spoke in clear tones. "The symptoms we are finding are pretty consistent with a mild case of food poisoning: nausea, vomiting, abdominal cramping, and diarrhea. The doctor will have to be the one to give you an official diagnosis, but, off the record, it looks like a mild form of food poisoning."

"Mild?" Sage repeated looking at the faces of those tormented. It looked anything but mild.

The paramedic gave a backward glance at the triage. Wiping his large hand across his forehead, he said discreetly "Oz, the catering guy, has the leftovers of the foods that were served for lunch. We're going to have to send them out for analysis."

Jon spoke first. "Any idea what could have caused this?"

The paramedic shook his head. "Right now, everything points to the local catering service that served lunch. The Health Department has been notified. I'm sure they'll be making a move to shut down the restaurant right away."

He continued, "As you are probably aware, the majority of food poisonings comes from mishandling of food like mayonnaise, spoiled meat or poultry, any number of things."

"Are you going to transport everyone to the hospital?" Sage asked, looking across the room to the suffering members of the production company.

The paramedic shook his head no. "I suspect the doctor will let the majority of people stay here and let the irritants work out of the body. The decision will be up to the doctor on call. He should be arriving any minute."

Taking a deep steady breath, Sage shifted impatiently. "I understand."

"Look, I know everyone is anxious," the paramedic said with a glance at the crew members gathered at the tent's opening, "but if you could help move some of the people out of here, it would help us to do our job."

"Of course," Sage answered. With Jon at her side, they went to the center of the group.

"Everyone, please," she called out in a voice that commanded attention, "the paramedics believe there has been a mild case of food poisoning. The doctor is on the way."

Her statement brought a soft murmur that rippled through the crowd. Jon stepped protectively closer.

"What about Evan Davis?" A strong male voice called out from the back of the group.

Sage looked at Jon and asked in a whisper, "You or me?"

Jon looked down at her. His handsome face was somber.

Yet, she saw a softness radiating in his warm velvet brown eyes. He trusted her.

"Go ahead," Jon said in a husky voice that was low and smoothing, "You've got the floor."

Sage turned back to the crew. "Evan Davis passed away from a heart attack. For those of you who knew him, the studio is making arrangements to have him sent back to his family."

"Sage," a female voice argued, "we heard that he had been shot with an arrow. Is that true?"

Sage dropped her voice slightly, "The Medical Examiner has confirmed Evan Davis died from a heart attack. We don't know how or why anything else happened. I'm not going to speculate further at this time. McCall Security has brought in additional staff and we are bringing in more personnel. You're helping us by remaining calm.

"Tonight, we will have additional help on patrol beginning this evening, speaking on behalf of McMasters Studios and McCall Security; we have every intention of keeping you all safe. Thank you for your understanding and for your cooperation."

With that she turned to Jon.

"You did great," he said softly as she watched the play on emotion on his face.

With a sharp breath, she said to him, "I'm going to need additional help, fast. Do you know any security firms you would recommend?"

"Sure," he replied his sharp eyes scanning the parameter of the Sand Point Inn. "I'll give you their phone numbers."

"Do you think this was intentional?" She asked barely above a whisper.

Jon's eyes frowned. "The thought did run through my mind and for now, I think we had best keep this between ourselves."

"Where do we begin?" She asked in a soft voice.

"We need to find out what made everyone sick," came Jon's quick reply.

"By the way," Sage said looking about alarmed. "Where's Hillary and Jeff Sanders?"

It was unlike Hillary to have missed the fray.

"We need to check on them," Sage said with a sharp intake of breath.

Almost leaving Jon, she went outside and began walking abruptly toward the motor homes. He was instantly at her side. "You know, it's hard to believe that the movie studio would just come in here, lease the property, do thousands of dollars in improvements, and then just walk away."

"Trust me, it's not that big a deal and it happens more than you can imagine. They consider it part of the cost of doing business. Besides they will make millions off this show."

Nearing the motor homes, Sage heard Pepe's incessant barking which did little to soothe her nerves. She could see no movement in either vehicle.

"That's Jeff's motor home," she said sending Jon to check on him.

Sage heard Pepe's sharp little bark as she jerked open the door, grateful it was not locked. Useless animal, Sage thought, glaring down at the poodle.

Pepe snarled at her and scrambled on top of Hillary who was lying prone on the white leather sofa. She looked dead. She wasn't.

Hillary raised her head slightly and lifted a designer icepack from her brow.

"Oh thank God you're here," she moaned. "Be a dear and bring me some water."

"Hillary," was all Sage could manage, grateful she had not found the director dead, "you're alive."

"Of course, I'm alive," Hillary snapped, "but you're going to have to do something. I think someone is trying to poison me."

Sage took another step into the living area as Jon joined her.

"There was no answer at Jeff's."

At Jon's appearance, Pepe bared his little teeth and gave Jon several warning barks from under Hillary's arm.

"Oh for Pete's sake, hush, Pepe!" Hillary wailed, "I'm dying! Why can't I die in peace?"

Seeing Jon, Hillary narrowed her eyes on him. "Jeff Sanders left before lunch, some sort of business in Tampa."

Hillary turned back to Sage and sniffed impatiently, "Water, please. And bring me a cold cloth, dear."

With that Hillary fell back against the couch and moaned.

Feeling almost sorry for the woman, Sage obliged her. She went into the bathroom, she opened a small cupboard, pulled out a cotton washcloth, and she placed it on Hillary's forehead.

"Thank you," Hillary groaned, "I'm in absolutely excruciating pain. You're going to have to take me to the emergency room. I refuse to die this far from Beverly Hills."

"You are not dying," Sage assured her. "We have three EMS vehicles outside the main tent and some doctors are on the way. The EMS technician tells us you and other members of the company are experiencing a mild case of food poisoning."

Hillary sniffed indignantly, "And I suppose all of you were just going to let me die alone."

Sage hid her smile and looked at Jon. "Hillary, can you

walk over to the tent, you need to be examined and where's Connard?"

Hilary threw the cold rag across the floor and brought herself up.

"Connard went down to pick up my dry cleaning, and for heavens sake, would one or both of you please bring me a glass of water. My God, what do I have to do to get a glass of water around here?" Hillary whined looking perfectly capable of getting her own water and making her way to the paramedics.

"I can get your water," Jon offered looking ill-fit for domestic service.

Wide-eyed Hillary watched him head to the kitchen. She straightened her clothes as if remembering herself. Pulling Sage close to her, she said in a whisper, "He's handsome in an odd sort of way but clearly too macho for me. More your type, isn't he, Sage?"

"I hadn't noticed," Sage lied.

"Well, he's good looking," Hillary said softly as the door of the motor home abruptly opened.

"Oh thank God you're all right," Connard said rushing in.

Connard in his late twenties was dressed in black Armani slacks and a stylish, silk floral shirt. His chestnut hair was freshly cropped in the latest rage. Looking exasperated, he stood motionless allowing Sage, Jon, and Hillary to take in his abrupt entrance. Pursing his lips together, he placed a hand on his hips and with a distinctly feminine sway hurried to the center of the room.

He was breathless as he began, "First that brut of a security guard wouldn't let me through, then there are hundreds of emergency vehicles here. What in the Sam's hill is going on?"

Without giving her a chance to respond, Connard rushed to Hillary's side and lifted her hand. "Are you all right, my dearest? You look dreadful."

"Where have you been?" Jon asked bringing a glass of water to Hillary.

Connard gave Jon a withering stare. "Like it's any of your business!"

"It is, Connard," Sage reminded him, "in case you have forgotten Jon Maddux, Chief of Police."

While Sage had no personal opinion of Connard's sexual preferences, she was annoyed that he perpetuated the stereotype of gays with his exaggerated mannerisms. It always seemed more a role for him than a lifestyle.

"Oh, for heavens sake!" Connard replied disgusted that he had to tell. "If you must know, I had to go and pick up Hillary's dry cleaning in that place you call a town."

He turned his attention back to Hillary and cooed, "You poor thing. I'm back now, honey, I'll take care of you."

"I'm going to die," Hillary mewed taking Connard's hand.

"Your man didn't put ice in my water." Hillary said impatiently passing her glass back to Sage. "I have to have ice in my water."

Sage stood a moment debating if she should leave the glass on the table but then decided to oblige. With Connard here, she and Jon would be free to leave. The sooner the better.

Sage made quick work of adding a few ice cubes. Adding more water to the glass, she noticed Hillary's half eaten plate of spaghetti lay sideways in the sink.

Only a few long strands to pasta remained, but on one side, Hillary had pushed aside a handful of what looked like uncooked mushrooms. Sage examined the mushrooms and other than the fact they looked raw, she could only surmise Hillary Kenyon did not like mushrooms raw or not.

Hearing Hillary call out her name, she returned to the living room and handed the director her glass of water.

"Since Connard is here to help you," Sage said evenly, "I've got to call my father and the studio to report this."

"Oh must you?" Hillary whined. "Well, do tell Nick someone is trying to poison me."

Sage had no intention of telling Nick McMasters any such thing.

She gave Hillary a nod and left Connard to deal with her.

Walking back across the parking lot, she dialed McCall Security and was patched through to her father. Giving her the chance to speak to her father in private, Jon walked on ahead.

Her father sounded shaken. "Sage, honey, what happened? We're getting reports of food poisoning. Do you need me to come out?"

"For the moment everything is under control. I'm going to bring in some additional security immediately."

"Good," her father agreed from McCall Security corporate headquarters high atop Sunset Blvd. "This could be just a coincidence, but I doubt it. What ever you need, Sage, I have confidence in you, Sweetie."

"I'll keep you posted," she promised.

Just as she was ending the call, Jon returned to her side.

"I spoke to the Doctor," he began giving her a bold appraisal and liked what he saw. "He feels there is no need to transport anyone. He has a medical staff on their way. The food poisoning is acute but not serious. He's going to stay for a while longer and is planning on keeping several paramedics here throughout the night. Right now, they are giving everyone plenty of liquids and keeping an eye on them. It just has to work out their systems."

Nervously she ran her fingers through her hair. She was keenly aware of his interest. This was no college, wet-behind-the-ears, frat boy but a very strong and sensual man.

She took a step away; trying to focus on his words and not on the dark eyes holding a seductive flame. She could still taste his hungry lips on hers and feel his hard muscular body as a second skin.

"Is there anything more we can do, I can do?" Sage asked trying hard not to notice him. She moistened her dry lips with her jab of her tongue and saw his mouth curve into a sensual smile.

His gaze raked her body, caressing each line of her silken skin from the soft lines of her slender waist to her hips before resting deliciously on the soft cleavage of her full breasts. He focused his attention on the top button of her shirt and with his eyes cupped the shapely beauty of her nipples pressing hard against her shirt. Her breathing was shallow and her knees weak.

He made no attempt to neither hide his brazen desire nor apologize for it. He thrilled and frightened her and made it all the more impossible to steady her erratic heartbeats. She struggled to maintain fragile control.

"At the moment, Sage, there's not a damn thing we can do here." he said his voice with staid calmness, "I did get an update from the hospital. Jamie Wolf has regained consciousness and will be available to us within the hour. We need to talk to him and to the caterer."

Beyond Jon, the sky was already rich in soft pastel colors of a breathtaking sunset.

Sage pushed back a blond strand of hair from her face and

raised her hand to shelter her growing urgency of him. Sage realized he did not know his effect on her and she had to keep it that way for both their sakes. Yet, an open hunger loomed between them like a heavy mist that threatened more simple desire.

"Let's get back to town," Sage agreed in short, sharp breaths, willing her body back to a sane reality.

Together they returned to the police car. She was conscious of his every movement, his every breath.

Jon opened the door for her and quickly closed it behind her. Sage watched him move around the vehicle and get in the driver's side.

He's arrogant, egotistical, and way too sure of himself, she thought and she was more attracted to him than she had been to any man in her life. Get over it, she warned herself, fearing her warning had come too late

Watching them leave, he smiled. They would know soon enough that the food had been deliberately poisoned. What? Did they think this was an accident, coming on the heels of the arrow he had carefully shot into Evan Davis' chest?

Fools!

He had wanted the press to know; hell, he wanted the world to know. He hated dealing with incompetence!

His eyes narrowed, he was going to up the ante. After all, he was the last person they would suspect and there had been no real murder...yet!

Reporters were already pressing around the entrance gate as Sage and Jon approached it.

Though Cowboy Bob was trying to push them away, there was very little he could do.

Jon kept a firm grip on the wheel and inched through the

reporters who were screaming out questions until he had an open path to speed away.

"This is exactly why I did not want your studio in my town," he spat in a voice rancid in uncontrollable fury.

His lips thinned with anger, and he flashed her a look of utter disdain. She watched his handsome features harden. He stared angrily at her for just a moment, before turning his sardonic expression back to the road.

Looking down at her lap, Sage could only imagine the impact the production was bringing to St. Gabrielle. In a whisper, she said, "I'm sorry we brought this to your town."

His angry gaze swung over her and she colored fiercely.

As quickly as his anger had surfaced, it dulled into remorse.

"Look, I'm sorry, too," he said, slumping into his seat as regret washed over his face like a shadow. "I didn't mean to take it out on you. I'm not sorry you're here."

Sage floundered and bit her lip.

"I just didn't want to see St. Gabrielle spread all over some grocery store rag," Jon said, struggling with an explanation. "By the time they get through with us little green men will figure in somehow. I don't know how you Hollywood types handle it."

"We don't have to," Sage said not trying to be funny, "we have publicists. By the way, my father said Nick McMasters was sending one tomorrow to deal with the reporters."

Jon tilted his head. "I thought Hillary took care of that stuff."

"Hillary's too sick to manipulate the reporters as much as I know she would like to be in the spotlight."

Drawing a deep breath, she looked out the window. "I'm

concerned Nick might pull the plug on this anyway. It would be disappointing to the contestants and the crew."

Jon looked strangely at her before he turned his full attention to the road ahead of them.

After a few moments of silence, he said," Maybe this will blow over and everyone will be able to stay a while longer."

Giving him a sidelong glance, she bit her lower lip to keep the smile from touching her face. He wasn't talking about everyone. He was talking about her.

Passing St. Gabrielle's Welcome sign, Jon shifted uneasily

A half-mile down the road, Jon pulled into a small strip center. "If you don't mind," he began, "I want to talk to the caterer first."

A large red and white sign said closed in front of the small Italian restaurant. It was after six o'clock and the *Super Dollar Store,* the strip center's main anchor, was closed. The stores on either side of the pizzeria were also closed up for the day.

Only the tiny Italian restaurant showed activity.

Two men were standing in front, arguing. One looked angry as if he was trying to pick up an order. The other in a white chef's outfit was wildly flinging his arms about. As the first man noticed the police cruiser, he abruptly turned and walked away.

"Hey Tony," Jon said hailing the cook. Sage made the quick assumption that the stocky man with classic Sicilian features was the owner of *The Pizza Guy Restaurant.*

"Chief, Chief," Tony answered in a heavy Italian accent. "What is this they are tryin' to say? I have-a made pizza and spaghetti for all my life! Not one time, not one time, anyone complained or is sick. Is not right! Come into my kitchen, you see, we gotta 'A,' is good an 'A' we always getta 'A'. Good food, very clean, you know eh, Chief?"

"I know Tony," Jon began, then introduced Sage. "This is Sage McCall, security chief for the TV show."

Tony immediately turns his attention to Sage. "You tella everyone, you come in my kitchen and tella everyone. There is no need to close my restaurant."

"Let's go in," Jon said and with Sage followed Tony into the small café.

"Come in and sit down. Have a seat? Want a Coke, soda, Miss?" Tony stammered his worries reflective in his friendly black eyes. "Chief, this is very upsetting to me. My business is gone for the day. I don't know what I a-gonna do? Are you gonna close me down, Chief?"

Tony waived his hands and motioned for them to follow him back to the kitchen.

"Here, I give you a Coke, no charge, *Okay?*" Tony stammered in a heavy Italian accent.

"I don't understand," Tony continued not taking a breath as he pulled out two gold plastic glasses from the shelf. He filled them with Coke and gave Jon and Sage each a glass.

"Chief, I mean I have-a been in business for twenty-five years. Twenty-five years, no ever get a bad rating."

"It's going to be okay," Jon interrupted trying to soothe the highly aggravated restaurateur. "Can you tell me if anything's different that you did with the food?"

"No, the man called me about ten. He said I should deliver some pizza and spaghetti for the TV people. I say sure, sure, and took it out about one."

"Tony, your ingredients?" Jon asked.

"Everything fresh, you know me Chief, I go to the farmers market and everything is fresh. It's-a always good!"

Jon and Sage looked at each other.

"How about the meats?" Sage said turning back to Tony.

"No problem," Tony assured her. "I always buy them from Wright's Meat Company direct. Sometime I go to the wholesale club, if I am short of ingredients."

"You brought out pizza," Sage said slowly, "and subs and spaghetti, right?"

"Always the best, number one spaghetti sauce, fresh onions, peppers, garlic, seasonings, tomatoes. I buy the tomatoes fresh at the farmers market."

"What about the mushrooms?" Sage asked softly remembering the mushrooms left on Hillary's plate. He didn't mention the mushrooms.

Tony looked at her and shook his head.

"Oh no, I don't use mushrooms in the spaghetti no more. Mushrooms are so expensive, if you know what I mean. So I stopped. Nobody notices, nobody complains, so I don't use them no more. Twenty-five years, nobody complains, everybody is happy with *The* Pizza *Guy*. Everyone happy with Tony."

"What about the subs?" Jon asked but Sage touched his arm. He looked at her then to Tony.

"Excuse me," Sage interrupted, "Did you say you didn't use mushrooms in the sauce?"

Tony stopped and looked at Sage. He frowned and impatiently repeated, "No mushrooms. Nobody notices. On the pizza pie, sure, when they ask but I buy them precooked from the wholesale store."

Sage looked at Jon. "There were mushrooms in the spaghetti sauce. I saw a plate of spaghetti in Hillary's motor home, it was loaded with mushrooms."

"Are you sure?"

"Of course I am," came her quick reply.

"Look, see," Tony said retrieving a small container of red spaghetti sauce from the walk in cooler. "See, this is the same sauce, onions, peppers, meat, tomatoes. No mushrooms!"

In the background, Tony continued to ramble in short, thickly accented sentences. Sage felt fear rise from deep within her and course through her veins like molten lava. Her heart was pounding and she felt the color drain from her face as she realized the mushrooms must have been added to the sauce once it reached the Sand Point Inn.

Jon's hawk-like eyes grew dark and savage. Tense lines formed around his face.

Sage closed her eyes and tried to steady her world, willing the truth to leave her in innocence. It was too late. The act had been deliberate. Her stomach clenched as fearful images were being played out in her mind. Twenty-eight people violently ill! This was no accident. This was a crime!

"Tony," Jon interrupted without apology. His voice was quiet, yet held an undertone of unwavering authority. "I want to take a sample of the sauce with me. I would normally need a warrant to..."

"No, no, I put some in a nice clean container for you, all fresh."

"Tony," Jon began to apologize but the smaller man interrupted him with a wave of his hand.

"No, no, you test this. Do it quick, okay? Okay! I need to open my restaurant. Everything will be all right, you want I should sign something, I will sign something. I deliver good food, Chief."

Jon nodded accepting the container.

Sage knew as Jon did Tony was harmless and the real danger lay hidden in the shadows of the Sand Point Inn.

With a quick departure, Jon drove toward the station and asked Sage to wait while he dropped off the sauce.

"One of my guys is going to take it to the lab for analysis. I'd like to see Tony open as soon as possible."

Sage said nothing.

"We still need to speak to Jamie Wolf. He's conscious; maybe he can shed some light on this."

A starry night had descended on St. Gabrielle. The quiet darkness was deceptive and frightening.

They took the drive to the hospital in silence.

Relief flooded Sage at the sight of Jamie sitting up.

He returned her smile and pointed to the bandage wrapped around his head. An IV was attached to his forearm. Jamie's grin was contagious and his blue eyes sparkled at the sight of her.

Reese, the other security guard from LA rose when she entered the room and acknowledged her with a smile.

"I guess you thought I was a goner," Jamie said in smug delight.

"Naw," Sage teased him, "I knew it would take more than a hit to that hard head to stop you."

Jamie chuckled as Sage reached out to squeeze his hand.

"Jamie," she said, "this is Jon Maddux, Chief of Police. Can you tell us anything about what happened? Do you remember anything?"

"I knew Evan was in there fiddling with some lightening equipment. I went in there to make sure he wasn't passed out drunk or something. It was dark when I went in. I never saw Evan. Someone hit me on the back of my head. That's about it, Sage."

"Anything else?" Sage asked softly.

"Just one thing but promise you won't laugh. I remember thinking I was dying because I saw an angel, a beautiful white angel standing over me."

CHAPTER SIX

A heavy set nurse in her late thirties suddenly appeared at the doorway. Wearing little makeup, her arms folded across her chest, Sage watched as her hazel eyes narrowed in Jon's direction. Her commanding presence bore no quarter.

"That will be enough for tonight," she huffed, walking into the room. "The man needs to rest. Doctor's orders."

'We just arrived," Jon protested.

"I need to check his vitals," she snapped, pushing Jon and Sage aside with the sway of her broad hips. "Come back in the morning. No more tonight. Doctor's orders."

"Look here..." Jon argued. "I just need to...."

"Not tonight," the nurse scolded him. "Now, everyone out! That includes you, Chief Maddux. Out! Out! Out!"

Jon looked at Sage for a bit of moral support, but she barely managed to hide a smile that threatened to curl the tips of her mouth. Whatever more they could learn from Jamie would have to wait until morning.

"I don't remember anything else anyway," Jamie offered, earning him a hard glare from the nurse as she lifted his wrist to check his pulse. She silenced him with a hard glare.

Knowing he'd met his match, Reese was the first to comply with her mandate. Sage followed.

For a brief moment, Jon stood looking as though he had no intention of leaving Jamie's side but a scowl from the nurse sent him to the hallway.

"You want me to stay with him?" Reese asked. Sage knew he wanted to stay. McCall Security took great care of their clients but McCall Security also took care of their own.

Sage nodded. "Call me if there is any change but what about you? Don't you need a break?"

"I'll grab a quick bite at the cafeteria and that chair," Reese said pointing at the cushioned chair outside Jamie's door, "looks as good as any."

Sage gave him a nod and made a note to include a bonus on his next check.

Jon and Sage moved wordlessly to the elevator. He waited until they were alone in the lift before speaking.

"An angel? He saw an angel?" Jon asked Sage. "Do you think he saw a woman?"

Had there been a woman there? Could their prime suspect be a woman? Sage asked herself before angrily adding, "If someone was actually there, why didn't they help Jamie?"

"You were the one who found Jamie," Jon pointed out, "Do you suppose he was speaking about you?"

Sage laughed. "Me? It will be the first time I have been mistaken for an angel."

"Not really," Jon said in a soft voice as the elevator stopped with a hiss.

The dual doors opened onto the first floor.

Sage looked at Jon expecting to find a mocking gaze; instead, she found a warm luminous look in his eyes. Her heart jumped inside her and she held her breath. A warm glow of emotion rose, titillating her senses with pleasure. Why should his opinion matter?

Nervous, she moistened her lips. His hungry eyes followed her small tongue around her mouth. He was standing close, too close. As their eyes met, she felt a shock run through her.

Sage stood motionless. She had dated Hollywood actors, producers, men of power, and yet, this man and only this man disarmed her at every turn. Her heart was pounding. She couldn't turn away. Standing so near to him, she could feel the hammering of his heart within her.

At that moment, an elderly woman assisted by her middle-aged daughter stepped onto the elevator bringing her back to the world of sight and sound, back to reality.

With a nod to the women, Jon grabbed the side of the door to keep it from shutting, and allowed Sage to pass to the ground floor.

He followed her into the busy corridor and out into the hospital parking lot.

The palms of her hands were clammy by the time they reached the Explorer. She was grateful the interior was dark while she steadied her emotions.

When Jon joined her, he sat quiet for several moments in the stillness of the night, his dominating frame outlined against a distant street light.

His voice was husky and raw as he said, "If I knew you better, I wouldn't be taking you home."

Sage laughed. "And would I be getting much sleep?"

As her vision adjusted to the dim light, she could easily see Jon's smile.

"You little brazen hussy," he said in a voice that was sweet and intoxicating and it captivated her and washed through her like a shot of warm whiskey. "But to answer your question, you minx, no, I don't think we'd be getting a wink of sleep."

His grin was contagious. The beginning of a smile tipped the corners of her mouth.

"I like to see you smile," Jon said softly as he backed out of the parking space.

Sage turned to stare out of the window, wrapped in a silken cocoon of pleasure. Why did everything about this man affect her so?

"I would offer to let you lean against my shoulder," he teased, "but my shotgun would be in the way."

Sage felt a shiver of happiness ripple though her and her heart was dancing in places it shouldn't go. To her complete astonishment, she wanted with all her heart for him to find her desirable. Her pulse quickened. Her heart was hammering in her ears, as she turned away willing herself to snap out from his spell.

On the drive back to the Sand Point Inn, Jon gave Sage a quick history of St. Gabrielle. Established in the 1920s, its favorite son was John Weathers, a poet of some notoriety.

The light narrative gave way to the hush stillness of the night, with only the constant humming of the Ford's engine and the occasional sound of communication on the police radio breaking the background of silence.

A security guard in crisp uniform was at the gate of the Sand Point Inn. The news vans had left for the night.

Sage shifted uneasily knowing full well the circus atmosphere would return with the morning.

Jon slowed for the guard in his late twenties and the guard tipped his baseball hat toward him.

"Chief," the security guard said in a friendly, familiar tone to Jon, "all quiet."

"I'm Sage McCall, McCall Security," Sage introduced herself, "thanks for being here."

"Hey, it's pretty exciting," the guard replied with a grin. He pushed his cap back away from his face, "we usually just do security checks for homes. First time on a real television set."

Sage gave him a soft smile. "If you need anything, call us."

The guard held up his thermos. "All set, ma'am. Nice to meet you."

"Thanks," she said waving him goodbye.

"Seems very nice," Sage said to Jon, "thanks for recommending the security firm."

"Good group of guys. Mostly made up of retired law enforcement."

Cowboy Bob was waiting for them by the time they reached the Inn.

"Is the Doctor still here?" Sage asked him, exiting the vehicle.

Cowboy Bob shook his head. "No, he left hours ago, but a paramedic is still hanging around. Everyone has gone back to their room except for three people. They look like they are going back to their rooms shortly. It's been a rough night."

"Nobody died," Sage said with just a hint of irony. She was immensely grateful all were well.

Cowboy Bob grinned and shifted slightly, "Yeah, nobody died."

"What about Hillary and more importantly, how's Double K?"

"Hillary went back to her trailer around seven and I don't think she was as sick as she was letting on," Cowboy Bob answered quickly. "Double K said to wake him up if you needed him but the big guy looks okay."

With a yawn, he pointed over to the set. "We have a rent-a-cop stationed by the set and two more are making the rounds. Everyone has settled down quite a bit."

"Good, now go get some rest, Cowboy," she instructed him.

Cowboy Bob yawned and with a grateful nod, vanished quickly into the night.

He was exhausted, they all were.

Sage turned to Jon. "I think I'm gong to make one last round myself, care to join me?"

Before he could answer, she stammered, "I'm sorry, it's been a long day, if you want to go home, I'm perfectly capable of handling this on my own."

"I'll stay with you," he said moving sensually in her direction.

Offering him a grateful smile, her pulse quickened as he neared. Her every sense was intoxicated by his presence. She brushed a stray strand of hair from her face and tried to ignore the sensual look in his eyes.

She was tired and knew it was making her vulnerable but she selfishly wanted him here though he must be exhausted.

As they began walking around the perimeter, Sage let her errant thoughts wander.

He would never come to Los Angeles and she had too many obligations to ever remain here in Florida. There was no chance of a relationship. She was embarrassed that she was even entertaining such thoughts. He was simply not for her and she would be forgotten the moment she drove away from St. Gabrielle.

She swallowed hard, knowing she would never forget this man.

With the production company in their beds, only a few lights were shining from the motel rooms. They cast a soft light across the parking lot and offered her a mild distraction.

A balmy silence of the night had descended upon the tiny peninsula.

It was so still; she could hear the sounds of water lapping

against the shoreline and feel the light spray of water brought in by a tropical breeze.

Unlike the pristine beaches to the north in Destin or the internationally famous beaches of St. Petersburg, the shoreline around St. Gabrielle and the Sand Point Inn held very little sand, leaving only a crusty waterline of shore that separated it from the dark waters of the Gulf of Mexico.

The moon was full. Its bright outline pronounced in the black sky. A dusky golden haze clung to it edges adding to its glow.

"It'll rain tomorrow," Jon said softly as if as not to disturb the quiet.

At the far end of the parking lot, Sage could clearly see the production trailers and motor homes outlined against the streetlight. A pale blue light was emitting from Jeff Sanders motor home. She guessed it was either a television screen or computer monitor and imagined Jeff even at this late hour going over financials.

She knew McMasters was considering closing down the production and with Jon walking close beside her, she realized she didn't want to leave Florida.

Hillary's motor home, like Connard's, was dark.

Jon said nothing, content to walk beside her.

Retracing their steps back toward the production set, she noted two guards quietly walking about the Inn.

Sage stopped and introduced herself to the guard posted outside the production set. Reading a paperback to kill the quiet hours of the night, he was alert and seemed pleased she had said hello. Like the security guard at the main entrance, he knew Jon.

"All's quiet," Sage said to Jon as they moved away from

the production set. He would be leaving her shortly and she could think of no further reason for him to stay.

As the moon rose higher, it took on a more silvery shade bathing the earth in a soft white light. Out in the Gulf, it hung high over the water casting a silver shaft of light across the restless motion of the black waters.

Pausing at the end of the dock, Jon looked out into the gulf.

"I've been thinking" Jon began softly, "exactly how well do you know Oz and his staff?"

Sage knew where he was going. She needed to correct him right away. "I've known Oz all my life. I met him and his daughter years ago. He's as solid as they come. Are you are thinking he or his staff added the mushrooms?"

"Motive and opportunity."

Sage shook her head but remained remotely open to the possibility. If not Oz, then perhaps one of his employees.

"I don't see how," Sage explained. "Maybe opportunity, but Oz's livelihood is built on his reputation. In Hollywood, one misstep, and you're out of business. New companies are ready to step over your grave without a moment's hesitation."

"What about his staff?"

"He has two guys who have been working for him for years." Sage countered, "You met Manuel. I think the other is Manuel's cousin."

"Would either one of them have a grudge against the studio or maybe Oz?"

Sage tilted her head. "No, I can't believe that. Oz has been around for years and Manuel has been with him since day one."

"Then who..." Jon countered, "Who?"

"The same person who shot Evan Davis," came her soft insistent reply, "I think the better question is why?"

Unwilling to let go of the obvious, Jon held his ground, "Well, since you seem certain it's no one from LA, could it be one of the contestants?"

"Maybe," Sage said taking a step on the dock. "Maybe. I've ordered background information on everyone here. They should be here tomorrow. Maybe I'll find something in their records."

Despite her weariness of the day and late hour, she couldn't resist baiting him just one more time.

"Are you interested in being in the show?" she asked in a teasing voice. "Hillary is always on the lookout for extras."

Jon looked at her in genuine surprise. "Me, no, never! Not interested in being in a movie or TV show."

Casting her eyes down, then out to the gulf, Sage said just under her breath, "Well, you certainly have the looks."

For a moment, Jon stared at her amused, and then burst into a low throaty laugh. His dark velvet eyes were still dancing when he came around to stand in front of her. The corners of his soft mouth were curled slightly, fixed in a grin. He stared at her, his eyes luminous. He bore a look of surprise on his face, as he asked softly, "You think I am good looking?"

Sage kept her gaze steady and clinched her small hands into fists. Her stomach knotted in a dozen places and it was impossible to steady her pulse. There was nothing to do but state the truth. She nervously cleared her throat.

"Yes," she said as her voice broke. She was trying to sound casual and failing miserable at it. "Yes, I think you're very good looking."

In the bright moonlight, Sage watched his eyes twinkle in pleasure. It was impossible not to return his disarming smile.

Looking a bit too smug, Jon folded his arms tight in front of himself.

Sage was both amused and annoyed with herself. She had meant simply to give him a compliment. Why could you not give a man a simple compliment without him thinking a woman was coming onto him?

In a desperate attempt to escape his captivating smile, she moved closer to the edge of the dock.

She had no real purpose in mind other than to change the subject.

Across from her, the moon had sent a long silver shaft across the water. The tropical breeze was light and caressed the dark waters. The effect of wind, wave and moonlight created a magical backdrop for a romantic rendezvous.

The breeze was refreshing and cooled the blush that was warming her cheeks.

Following the call of the warm waters, she took careful steps across the wooden dock. The ancient boards creaked and sagged as she walked to the end of the dock. Jon followed.

Once, in its heyday, the tiny dock had serviced the yachts of millionaires and while the studio had taken care to improve the motel and facilities, the dock remained as the set designers had found it. Stripped of paint and weathered from the tropical sun and one too many hurricanes, the wooden dock was physically sound, and added both charm and a bit of the macabre to the outdoor scenes scheduled to shoot here.

As they reached the end, Sage heard the rhythmic and repetitive thud of a piece of wood hitting one of the pilings.

Jon stopped just behind her.

For a long moment, they both simply stared across the moonlit water absorbing the sultry tranquility of the night.

Jon gently slipped his massive arms around her small shoulders and pulled her body into his.

His touch gentle, in contrast to the hardness his body. His breath was hot and each new kiss sent spirals of pleasure through her. Tired and weary of fighting the day and her raging sensuous emotions, she simply allowed her body to fall back against him, seeking the comfort he offered.

Tomorrow when she was rested, she would find the strength to resist him, tonight she was overwhelmed by her need of him.

"You feel good," he said softly as his tongue grazed her ear.

A delightful shiver of wanting ran through her. Her pulse quickened.

His nearness was intoxicating, deep inside she could feel the delicious flutter of butterfly wings taking her to a place where she should not go. Strange excitement caught her every breath.

Of its own volition, her body was responding to him. Her breasts tingling against the silky fabric of her blouse as a shiver of delight raced through silken thighs and a heat was coursing like a rushing river through her body.

Unexpectedly, his lips moved from her soft thick hair to the nape of her neck, finding their way to her ear before gently, slowly offering shivery kisses along her cheek toward her mouth.

She moaned and reached back. Her hands found his hard thighs. She pulled him into her soft bottom, every soft curve molding into the contour of his lean body.

The fit was too perfect.

"Sage," he muttered in an anguished breath. His hands slid down her blouse to her breasts. His fingertips gently gliding over her hard nipples as the palm of his hand cupped the full swell of her perfectly shaped breasts.

His breath was hard and hot against her neck as he gently began rocking her back and forth.

With each soft sensual kiss, she was growing dizzy with desire.

She was losing control of her body and she didn't care.

She moaned as his left hand slid down to her waist then followed the soft curve to her hips. Her senses were reeling. Her body on fire.

Turning around to face him, her arms flew about his neck, and her lips found his. He moaned in surrender to her. She realized she owned this moment. She owned this man.

"Jon," she cried as his tongue caressed her lips before parting them to sensually explore the recesses of her mouth. He pulled away, his lips raining kisses on her cheeks before once again covering her mouth.

His breath was ragged. His body hard and tense as he pulled away.

"Honey," he whispered in an anguished cry.

"I know," she said in the same moment. The world was spinning too fast.

His voice was dark and husky as he pinned her to him, "I want you to know that you are in danger of being ravaged right here, right now!"

Drowning in the seduction of surrender, she knew it was wrong to want him so. Yet, it wasn't the time. Not yet. Not yet.

"Take this as fair warning: this will be very the last time I'm a gentleman with you, Sage," he said bringing his mouth down on her. A moan of ecstasy slipped through his lips and she knew his fiber was being tested.

She couldn't resist a giggle. He pulled away from her clearly annoyed she didn't appreciate the magnitude of his restraint.

Softly she reached up to touch his handsome face. As she cupped his cheek in her hand, the pain in his eyes softened. His need of her was undeniable.

"I suppose you are used to men with better manners," Jon apologized, with dark passion in his eyes.

"You just surprise me Jon," she answered softly. Her voice carried her gratitude. They needed to hold their passions in check just a bit longer.

His voice was husky as he replied, "Yeah, well, at, the moment I'm kinda surprising myself."

With both their hearts pounding, he brought her into his arms once again, this time only to hold her dearly.

She felt her breasts crush against the hardness of his chest as he clasped her body tightly into his. His touch was unbearable in its tenderness.

Sage closed her eyes in wonder. Instead of becoming more familiar, Jon was becoming more enigmatic. With his ragged breath on her cheek, she could hear his name echoing in the black stillness of her soul as she slowly returned to her senses.

Drawing away from him, she knew, as did he, whatever awaited them would have to wait until the threat to the lives around them was over.

As he read the understanding in her eyes, he relaxed, guilt leaving him as a passing shadow.

Whatever regret they shared was gently blending into the moonlight. Their sense of responsibility and duty to others bound them closer than any stolen kiss ever could.

Below her, the earth was once again firm. Sage moved out of his arms and once again heard the annoying sound of knocking against the dock.

Standing beside her, Jon stood thunderstruck, wondering what in the hell was a matter with him? He was hypnotized by her touch, the sweet taste of her mouth, her silky, soft skin, and the dark passion that radiated in her blue eyes. She was liquid fire in his arms and he was flying through space and time with fragmented desire and need of her.

In his arms was the most ravishing woman he had ever known and he knew she wanted him as badly as he had needed her. In her arms, he was more than he ever hoped he would be. He was drowning in his need to protect this woman whose inner strength and courage matched his own.

His senses were filled with a heady surge of conquest. She was his to claim. What in hell was keeping him from taking her? He didn't understand.

Then he knew. He understood.

He didn't want her just for the night.

He took in the soft flowery scent of her hair, and tried to cool the aching hurt that was growing inside of him. He was the last person he would have suspected of chivalry and he was uncomfortable with the role when all he wanted to do was ravish her.

Her breath was now steady and his senses drugged by its sweetness. He wrapped his arms around her; this was all he would ask for this night, lest he become lost in her forever.

Irritated by the constant slapping of wood in ear's shot, Sage reluctantly pulled away from him, annoyed anything should spoil this perfect moment.

Standing at the edge of the dock, she looked into the dark water.

Turning back to him, she asked. "Do you hear that sound?"

"What sound?" Jon asked following her over to the

edge. In the darkness he could see nothing but he trusted her instinct.

Then he heard it, a soft grating sound of wood against the dock.

Driftwood, he thought recognizing the pitch of wood hitting wood under the dock, no doubt brought in with the waves.

"It's beautiful here," she said allowing her mind to lazily drift in and out of the magical moments of the night, "Have you ever been out to LA, Jon?"

She couldn't see him but knew he was frowning. "Once. All I remember was the traffic."

Sage smiled. "Yes, that does take some time to get used to."

Drawing a deep breath, he stared down at the dark water. "Sage, you know you might like living in a small town."

Sage shook her head. She knew what he was asking. In terrible sadness, she said softly, "My dad is depending on me taking over his business and it's something I have wanted since I was a little girl. Like it nor not, I belong in California."

An unwelcome tension settled between them. The magic that seemed real enough to touch was gone, leaving in its wake a well of loneliness.

Jon shrugged, his jaw tightened.

Sage swallowed hard. She knew he had let her go.

A fear, stark and vivid raced through her and she regretted her words. Still, they had been the truth and now spoken she could not take them back.

Telling him she wished things were different would solve nothing.

Her heart was aching. How could she be so close to him

and know soon enough she would return to the opposite corner of the world, never to see or touch him again?

She couldn't think or imagine a world without him. How could she deny her heart, she asked herself, knowing she simply had no choice.

With nothing else to focus on, she turned her attention back to the irritating sound of the wood scraping under the dock.

Looking down into the dark waters, she saw the source of the constant rattle. A small, narrow piece of fiberglass had returned from the gulf.

Taking a closer look, its shape took form. Her sharp intake of breath drew Jon's attention.

"Oh my God," she cried pointing to the arched bow, its single strand of white nylon trapped on jagged splinter wood on the piling. "Is that what I think it is?"

"I think it is," he agreed.

"We'd better retrieve it before it drifts out," Sage said bending down but she couldn't reach the bow.

"Allow me," Jon said pulling a pair of plastic gloves from his pocket.

Without hesitation, Jon slipped out of his shoes and socks, and jumped feet first vanishing into the dark water. Less than a second later, he bobbed up and with a single stroke swam to the piling.

Taking care not to lose the bow in slippery fingers, he lifted it from the broken timber and with a long reach of his arm brought it onto the dry dock.

With a swift and powerful strength of his forearms, he pulled himself back onto the dock.

Grinning at his prize and dripping wet, he reached for his shoes and socks.

"You found the bow," Sage cheered ignoring her part in the discovery.

"You found it," Jon corrected her; "I merely retrieved it."

Sage let her eyes fall. "So, whoever shot Evan Davis threw the bow off the dock, only it didn't quite make it out into the gulf. Or, if it did, it came back in with the tide."

"Good work," Sage said hoping to mend the strain between them.

"Yeah," Jon laughed deprecatingly, "but trust me, when we walked out here, I had my mind on anything but work."

Still dripping with water, his clothes soaked and clinging sensually to his hard body, he gave Sage an awkward grin. "Got a towel?"

Sage grinned. "I'll round one up. Do you think we will be able to pull any fingerprints from this?"

Jon shrugged. "I doubt it but at least we'll have it checked. The State Crime Lab might find something. I'll get it to them in the morning."

"You folks all right," the security guard called out walking down the dock.

Sage assumed Jon's splash into the water had caught his attention.

"Yeah, we found something." Jon answered for them as the security guard joined them at the end of the dock.

"Stay here," Sage said to the both of them, "I'll go see if I can find something to wrap that in."

Without giving Jon a chance to protest, Sage hurried across the parking lot toward the kitchen. She was confident she would find something to wrap their find in.

As she hurried though the shadows, she wondered if indeed they might find fingerprints. If they did, then this game would be soon over, and the filming would go on as scheduled.

The sooner the better, she thought, for all concerned, for all the right reasons.

The kitchen was in back of the motel behind the small dining room they had used for storage.

Too late she remembered there was no outside light on this side of the Inn. Still, there was enough moonlight to help her find her way.

Reaching for her keys to unlock the back door, her fingers touched the doorknob.

It slid from her, opening of its own accord into the dark kitchen.

Sage stopped.

The room was pitch black. Instinctively, she sensed something was wrong and debated whether she should return for Jon or the Security Guard. Though both would willingly accompany her back to the kitchen, she felt foolish to ask either.

She shook her head. Her mind was working overtime, there was nothing to find except for a stack of dirty dishes and cooking utensils and something to wrap the bow in for safekeeping.

Still, the door was open. With shallow and uneven breaths, she reminded herself that someone on Oz's staff or hers had not taken the time to lock the door. In light of the food poisoning or perhaps because of it, attention to detail must be a priority. This sort of negligence was stupid and dangerous, in more ways than one. She would have to speak to everyone in the morning.

A warning whispered in her head. She ignored it.

Stepping into the dark kitchen, she realized she didn't remember where the light switches were. Using the palm of her hand, she felt along the wall near the door where she presumed the light switch should be.

A slight movement to her right caused her to stop.

With no time to react, she met a dark massive figure moving quickly toward her. He slammed her against the wall.

She grabbed at the dark mass, clawing her way down a fleshy arm.

"Bitch!" he hissed before giving her a sharp left hook to her jaw.

Sage fell to the floor. She screamed and pushed herself away from him but not far enough to escape a hard metallic pot that hit her forehead.

With pain ripping her head in to two pieces, Sage rose. Her assailant tried to swing at her again but this time she was prepared. Dizzy from the assault, she offered him a sharp jab with her left fist, a right cross, and a powerful roundhouse kick to his head.

She screamed in Japanese. Years of martial arts training pooled with a powerful surge of adrenaline, she moved as she was trained, without thought, without fear toward her attacker.

Instead of holding for her attack, he turned and ran out the door.

Sage was too weak to follow. She stood, poised in a full karate stance, conscious of the warm sticky blood sliding down the side of her face. He was gone. She was too weak to follow.

She dropped her arms and moved slowly back to the doorway. Her fingers found the light switch. She flipped it on.

Light flooded the room. She stood looking out into the darkness, not sure she was out of danger.

"Sage!" Jon screamed entering the kitchen. His expression

shifted to rage as he saw her. He quickly gathered her into his arms.

"I'm okay." Her voice was barely audible. She brought her hand to her forehead and pulled it back in horror. Her palm was red with her own blood.

"Get a medic in here!" Jon shouted to the guard who had followed him into the room.

"No!" Sage cried in anger.

"Hell no," Jon screamed at her bringing her face up for him to study.

She saw a glazed look of panic, rage, and guilt. His arms held her steady. His broad shoulders were heaving as he breathed. Gone was the cool professional.

"GET THE DAMN PARAMEDIC!" Jon shouted to the guard who was standing helplessly in the doorway. His eyes were sick with fury. The guard turned and ran from the kitchen.

"Jon, no," she pleaded softly, tugging his shirtsleeve. "You must listen to me. I got a bump on my head, I'm all right."

Jon was now visibly shaking. He wasn't listening to her. She tried again, "Think, Jon, think."

His breath was jagged as he looked beyond her into the darkness. Drawing her close, he said in a guttural threat, "I'll kill the bastard!"

"He could have killed you!" he screamed in rage.

"But he didn't, I'm all right," Sage countered him, trying to sound more calm than she felt. "He must have heard me. Things are confusing at the moment."

"Who was it?" he demanded. "Did you get a look at him?"

"No."

"Sage, we need to get you to the emergency room."

She looked at him, tears threatening to spill. "Jon, the last thing we need is another emergency here. I need to sit down."

Lifting her with ease, he carried her to a straight back chair by the dishes.

"All right, start at the beginning." Jon said, sounding more like a law enforcement officer.

Flashes of anger shadowed his handsome face, but at least, Sage thought with relief, he was willing to listen.

"It was dark," she began, "the door was ajar. I tried to find the light. I couldn't hear a sound from..." She stopped in her narration and turned to the far corner half expecting to find someone standing there.

She continued softly, "I heard a sound and the next thing I knew I was on the floor. I tried to fight back but he just turned and ran. I should have followed."

"Did you recognize the assailant? Was anything familiar?"

"No," Sage answered but the slight movement of her jaw sent a sharp pain to the top of her head.

Seeing her flinch, Jon lifted her chin and cursed again. His dark eyes went black in fury.

"I want the paramedic to take a look at you. If you won't let one come here, then I'll get you to the hospital myself."

He was angry. She wanted to cry "don't leave me," but she bit her tongue.

"Why the hell did I let you come in here by yourself?" he said. She heard the guilt rising in his voice.

"It was my fault, I should have known better," Sage apologized with regret, "Its okay. I've had worse accidents on a surfboard. I just want to have a shower and go to bed."

"What can I do? I feel so damn helpless," Jon said pulling her to him.

"It's all right; I am a little shaky but ..."

"I will be the judge of that," the blonde haired paramedic said coming into the room. "The guard said you were injured. Let me take a look at you? Were you attacked?"

"No," Sage lied, "I fell."

The paramedic frowned. Despite his size, he tenderly parted her hair. "Small cut," he said, pulling out a pencil flashlight from his pocket. After checking both eyes, he tilted her head left and right, up and down before slipping the light back into his pocket.

"You fell, huh?" He said stepping back from her. "What? Were you standing on one of the tables?"

Sage said nothing.

"Well, young lady, it looks like you fell," he continued as he lifted her chin, "into someone's left hook, though outside of some swelling I don't see any serious damage. A good night's rest wouldn't hurt either of you. Unless you have anything to add or are experiencing more symptoms than you are telling me," the paramedic said soberly, "The last of the people with food poisoning have finally gone to bed. I'm going home myself."

"Go home," Jon interjected. "The rest is police business. I'll take care of it."

"Suit yourself," he replied shaking his head.

Jon looked at the guard, "Make sure he gets to his car."

"Wait," Sage called out to guard, "call your supervisor, and double the security staff as soon as possible."

"One more thing." She cautioned the guard as he was leaving, "Keep what happened here between us, at least for the time being. In the morning I want you to contact my assistant security chief, Ken Kendrick, Double K. Let him know what happened, he'll know what to do."

After the guard and paramedic left, Jon turned to her. In a soft voice filled with quiet determination, he said slowly, "I'm staying with you tonight."

Sage tried to grin but her jaw twisted in pain. "I appreciate that but I don't really think I am up for..."

Jon frowned. "I'll sleep outside your door if I have to."

She knew it was pointless to argue and in truth, she didn't want him to go.

Leaning against the table beside her, she stood. Jon slipped his arm around her.

"The bow?" Sage stammered remembering the reason she had come to the kitchen in the first place.

"I found some plastic in my vehicle." Jon replied quickly, "I doubt if we will find any fingerprints on it anyway. If he or she took the time to throw it off the dock, it's probably wiped free of fingerprints. Come on," Jon said starting to lift her, "we need to get you to bed."

Sage was too tired to argue and her whole body was beginning to throb.

With his arms snug about her, Jon allowed her to show him the way to her room.

Giving him her keys, he unlocked her door and easily found the light switch.

Exhausted, Sage almost fell on the bed. She had no strength left. As her eyes filled with frustration, she clamped her lips shut to imprison a sob. For the first time in a long time, she felt helpless, defeated and in her weariness blamed herself for everything.

"Come on, honey," Jon said in a voice so tender it startled her, "I'm going to help you shower. Let me take care of you."

Of its own volition, her hand reached up to touch his hand, but he clasped it and brought her to her feet and into his arms. With his lips upon her head, she felt his breath warm and sweet.

"Wait here," he said softly. She stood there, using the last of her strength to do so.

From the bathroom, she heard a torrent of water as he turned on the water. Instantly the bathroom filled with hot, inviting steam, its warm spray mist curling into the bedroom.

Jon returned to her and tenderly led her into the bathroom.

Standing in front of the mirror, she watched as his fingers began to fumble at her blouse. He slid her blouse off her shoulders and the silky fabric fell slowly to the floor.

She heard him suck in his breath as he released the lacy bra. She looked up to find his eyes gazing at her peach-colored, full breasts.

Unabashed, he wordlessly continued, unfastening her belt and pulling her shorts and panties to her ankles. Kneeling behind her, he unlaced each shoe and discarded her clothes and her lightweight hiking boots under the sink.

He gently eased her naked body into the shower and watched as the beads of water danced atop her silky skin.

Whatever thoughts she had were lost in the hot stream of water. Sage closed her eyes allowing the hot droplets of water soothe her aching muscles and the painful memories of the day. Taking a small step closer to the showerhead, she welcomed the sweeping warmth of pulsating water as it freely cascaded down her face, wetting her unbound hair and her tense, tired body.

Less than a second later, Jon joined her. His soapy hands began to gently massage her shoulders and wash her breasts. He paused to kiss her, taking care to wash each part of her body with a tenderness that was almost unbearable. His gentle massage sent currents of desire though her. His hands moved slowly down the length of her back kneading each tight muscle before sliding across her silken belly.

Aroused she moved sensuously closer to him allowing him to explore the soft lines of her waist and her hips. His soapy hands toyed with her hardening nipples.

Their bodies were moist, he poured creamy shampoo into her hair, it slid down her perfectly shaped body to disappear in the warm water pooling at her feet.

Pushing her closer to the showerhead, he began to gently wash her hands, her fingertips then moved up her forearms to her small shoulders. When his fingers began making slow sensual circles in her hair, she was weakened by the pleasure.

Allowing the water to kiss her lips and fondle her breasts, she wondered when she had ever been held with such tenderness. He took his sweet time washing her stomach, her legs, and her aching calves, each muscle relaxing with his touch.

Abruptly, the water stopped and she felt a soft dry towel wrapped around her.

Effortlessly, he swept her into his arms and took her to the bed. Pushing back the covers, he laid her atop the cool sheets.

"I'll sleep outside in the Explorer," he said in a whisper as his lips feathered hers.

"No," she protested softly, "I need you here."

Barely conscious, she felt the warm lay of covers atop her and in the distance she heard the snap of light switch.

Though her eyes were closed, the room seemed darker, safer because he was near.

He slid under the covers beside her and gathered her into his arms. She felt her body and her soul melt into his.

"I'll never let anyone hurt you again," she heard him say as she drifted off into a deep sleep.

Out in the darkness, he stood watching the light go off in her room.

Damn Sage McCall. Two more minutes in the kitchen and he could have finished what he'd started earlier that day.

He smiled at the thought.

Somehow they had found the bow that should have drifted off to into the gulf. He had seen it covered in plastic lying in the back of the police vehicle. That must have been why she had come into the kitchen. Who knows? Who cares?

For a moment, he had debated breaking into the police vehicle but why bother? He knew full well it had been wiped clean. He'd made sure of it.

Sage was becoming a bother. He would have liked to go in there right now and finish her but he didn't want to tangle with the Police Chief.

At least not tonight.

Though he hated to admit it, he was a bit shaken. She'd fought back with a strength that had surprised him.

He saw two security guards who were now making their way toward his location. They didn't see him. He would remain hidden until they passed by.

This was just too easy; he thought with a smile and tomorrow was another day.

CHAPTER SEVEN

For the second time in two days, Sage woke to pounding on the door. She rose slightly. As she rose, a sharp pain ran from her chin across her jaw line. She flinched, as a second spasm bit at the top of her head. Moaning softly, she touched her swollen scalp.

Jon lay next to her, his long legs covering her silky thighs and calves. His massive arm casually, possessively, lay across her small waist. Warm body heat was emanating from his every limb, burning her with desire.

Still asleep, his body's dark tan seemed bronze in the dark room and it magnified the inky blackness of his short hair. The shadow of stubble on his face accented his rugged masculinity.

She had slept naked with him and regretted there was no memory of the night.

With the pounding on the door, he rolled slightly. At once, his dark eyes flew open, in one fluid moment; his hand went to the nightstand beside him. Before she could speak, Jon sprang from the bed, instantly alert, his police revolver pointed at the door.

"Don't shoot," Sage pleaded softly, her entire body was throbbing. "It's probably Double K."

"Oh yeah?" Jon said laying his revolver on the lacquered wood bureau. Shaking sleep from himself, he raked his fingers through his hair. His bare chest glistened in a slither of sunlight that was seeping into the room. A pair of short blue boxers covered his firm, hard posterior and touched the tips of his upper thighs.

Despite the pounding her head was taking, she took in the sleek line his body made in the dimly lit room.

"Just a damn minute," he yelled at the door, jerking his pants off the chair. Slipping them on, he crossed the room. Pausing for a moment, he looked back to her. She could see the tenderness in his eyes. "How do you feel?"

"Like I've been run over by a truck, a big truck," she replied and added though the knocking had stopped at the sound of Jon's deep voice, "Answer the door."

Jon stood for a moment, "I'll get you some ibuprofen. Let me see who this knucklehead is."

Holding her head, Sage sat up and brought the sheets up over her breasts as she watched Jon fumble at the door lock before opening the door wide.

With his arms folded over his massive chest, a black frown deepening the lines on his face, he looked first to Sage then Jon.

"She's untouched," Jon said with a wave of his hand, motioning for him to come into the room.

"How are you feeling?" Sage asked Double K as she rose higher, keeping the folds of the sheet tight around her body.

"My stomach is still upset," Double K said coming into the room, "but I feel a whole lot better than you look. What happened? You got hit last night, why didn't you come get me? I'd have taken care of you."

His last sentence pronounced with a hard glance toward the Police Chief.

Jon faced Double K without explanation or apology.

"I'm okay," she muttered wrapping the sheet around her.

Annoyed at their behavior, she mused the testosterone level in the room was on overload. Both men watched her rise from the bed, she took two steps away from it before collapsing into a nearby chair. Holding her head with her right hand and the sheet about her naked body with her left was proving more a challenge than she anticipated.

Before she could speak, Jon related the previous night's events, culminating with bringing her to the room. He omitted giving her a shower.

Sage felt her face burn slightly at the end of his tale.

Double K looked at her and grinned.

"You say a paramedic took care of her last night?"

Sage shifted in the chair. They were talking like she wasn't in the room. "Yes, Double K, a paramedic looked at me last night."

Double K relaxed. Looking at Jon, he said, "Thanks for watching out for her last night."

Before Jon could respond, Double K added roughly, "You should've come and woke me up. Oz woke me up this morning yelling something about a guard wouldn't let him go into the kitchen."

"Yes, that's right," Jon said walking back into the room. He sat on the edge of the bed. "Every criminal leaves something at the scene. Every criminal takes something from the scene. Fingerprint, footprints, hair, fiber. I want to find this guy before he raises the bar."

"Yeah," Double K agreed, "get in line."

"Oh God," Sage said at once glancing toward her radio clock. "What time is it? We have eighty plus people to feed this morning and we can't go into the kitchen!"

"Got ya covered," Double K said. "Oz found a hotel

restaurant and they are catering breakfast. Food, plates, juice, coffee, everything should be here in about twenty minutes."

Relieved, Sage hated to ask but knew she must, "What about Hillary?"

Double K shrugged, "Haven't seen her yet, but no news is always good news."

"All right, we'll be out shortly. Double K, I want this kept between us. Between finding Evan with an arrow in his chest, the food poisoning, I don't want to hear my attack leaking out. Now, we need to get dressed and I need a truck load of ibuprofen."

"Double K," Sage called out as Double K turned to leave. "The Chief went in the water last night. His clothes are wet; could you bring him a shirt and pair of pants?"

"Sure," Double K said. Looking dispassionately at Jon, he asked, "You look a thirty-two waist? Shirt, large?"

"That'll work," Jon said with an appreciative nod.

Double K turned and left the room.

Alone, Sage and Jon looked at each other, each feeling a bit awkward.

"Thank you for taking care of me last night. I slept like a baby."

Jon grinned. "You didn't look like a baby."

A blush warmed Sage from head to toe. "You looked?"

"Hell yes," Jon admitted to her. Seeing her frown, his grin became broader, "did you look at me?"

Sage laughed. "Don't make me laugh; my jaw hurts."

It seemed like only minutes before Double K returned. He knocked only once, entered and tossed a McCall uniform to the Police Chief.

Jon grabbed the outfit and without a word disappeared into the bathroom to change.

With a grin, Double K asked, "And you are going to tell me nothing happened between you two last night?"

Sage shook her head. "Nothing happened, no joke."

Double K grunted. "Maybe he's gay?"

"He's not gay," Sage shot back. "He was going to sleep in his car...just to stay close, to protect me."

Double K grunted with approval. He didn't try to hide the smile that played at the corners of his mouth or the twinkle in his eyes.

Sage pretended not to notice.

"Well, I need to go. Get dressed," Double K said, as he was about to leave, "we need to figure out who hurt you. And put some makeup over that black bruise under your chin."

With a quick nod, he turned and left the room, keeping whatever else he was feeling to himself.

Sage sat, feeling too tired to rise. She closed her eyes and waited for Jon Maddux to emerge from the bathroom.

Examining his face, Jon rubbed his beard. There was nothing he could do about the dark shadow that covered his chin and he sure as hell wasn't about to use her little pink electric shaver on his rough beard.

A wire jeweled basket on the back of the toilet held a neat array of feminine grooming products. None of which could help him.

Picking up one bottle of skin lotion, he shook his head, like she needed anything to make her skin softer!

No shaving cream, no razor, he'd have to swing by his house on the way to work later.

With a shrug, he grabbed a thick washcloth to wash his face, it would have do. He had no hesitation in using her toothpaste and brush.

All through the night, he had held her, listening to

her jagged breath. Twice she had moaned softly and he was instantly awake but it was only bits and pieces of a nightmare that had disturbed her.

He had brought her small body closer to his each time, holding her tight, willing the demons of her sleep away.

Nothing in his life had prepared him for the rage he had felt when he found her lying on the kitchen floor. Nothing!

At that moment, every bit of training and discipline went right out the window as he could have easily taken a bat to the person who had harmed her.

He had almost turned his anger on her when she refused further medical treatment but her reasoning was infallible. She had taken a hard hit but she would survive. She didn't panic. She didn't cry. She kept a cool head reasoning with him until she convinced him she was right.

Taking a breath, he tried to think of a man or woman he admired more than this wisp of a girl who had challenged him at every turn.

He remembered too easily, the long smooth silky line of her back to her small round bottom. How soft and supple it felt in his large hands.

His body ached deep inside him as he'd gently kneaded her full, perfectly shaped breasts in rich, soapy lather. His fingertips had stroked the pink aureoles, flickering the tips of each causing them to rise under his touch. Her full breasts had begged to be sucked, kissed, stroked and yet, he had only massaged them, dumbfounded as to where he found such self-constraint.

The curve of her waist was smooth and he'd allowed his hands to roam freely in heavy lather down it. Her tummy was flat and creamy as his hands had made their way downward, over her silky thighs to her soapy calves and small delicate feet.

Supporting her full weight with his body, she had been limp in his arms. He hadn't dared to turn her around, knowing the temptation he was only touching would have been more than he could have handled.

Even now, he remembered her blue eyes seductively innocent and filled with trust in his tender care.

It took all he had to keep from ravishing her. Even now in the room next to him, she sat with no makeup, an ugly bruise under her chin with only a soft sheet around her. She was the most beautiful woman he had ever known.

With a hard breath, he slid into the black shorts and jerked the black polo shirt over his head.

Taking a moment to admire his own physique, he found himself wondering how he measured up to the handsome men in her life.

For now, he could only request God grant him two prayers. The first was simple; he prayed when he caught the SOB who had hurt her, he wouldn't kill him on the spot. The second was more private. He prayed that God would give him strength to live without her.

Sage smiled when he reentered the room, well pleased to find him in a black short sleeve polo shirt with McCall Security printed just over the pocket. The powerful outline of his shoulders strained against the fabric. Sage was acutely conscious of his tall, athletic body. Her eyes strayed too long on the pair of black shorts; they fit him a little too snug.

Frowning at his reflection, his voice clipped out, "I look a school crossing guard."

"You look fine," Sage said trying not to giggle.

Wearing a frown, he turned to her, his eyes taking in

every curve of her body. Though the sheet covered her body, she felt naked and exposed.

His eyes darkened dangerously and his lips parted in wanting.

She sat transfixed under his heated appraisal. Even a child would have felt the want in his eyes.

His voice was strained as he forced himself to look away. "Maybe, we should go for coffee."

With her heart pounding, she cast her eyes down. This was no man to tease or trifle with. Sitting there with only soft flowing sheets gathered around her, she was straining his moral fiber to its limit. She had visible proof of it.

Moving with catlike ease, he came to her. Lifting her up into his arms, his eyes drank in her lips, her nose, and each smooth delicate line of her skin.

His gaze was intoxicating and her body was tingling with hungry desire. All she had to do was to drop the sheet. The thought of what would naturally follow left her senses reeling.

Of their own volition, her full lips parted slightly.

Watching her, he sucked in a breath. "You need to get dressed!"

"Damn," he said shaking his head. "Why do you have to be so beautiful, so rich, and so Californian?"

Her eyes flew open wide.

"You make that sound like a bad thing," she cried. Moving past him to her bureau, she pulled out a soft lacy white bra, white silk French cut panties, as well as a neatly folded pair of tan shorts and a black McCall Security polo shirt.

"My Dad's well off, Jon," Sage reminded him in a low silvery tone, "not me."

Jon was silent.

She swallowed hard. The sudden silence between them

was leaving her with an inexplicable feeling of emptiness and she ached in pain.

There was nothing more to say. The momentary happiness of just minutes earlier had vanished in harsh reality. Why should his words stab at her heart like a knife?

She went into the bathroom, closed the door, and dressed as quickly as she could. She took care to apply her make-up and hide her bruises.

Looking in the mirror, she stared long and hard at the pretty blonde girl staring back at her. How much longer was she going to deny her attraction toward him? The thought both astonished her and filled her with sudden clarity. He was right. She belonged in LA. He belonged here in this place. It felt all wrong.

"Ready?" Jon asked when she emerged minutes later.

Sage nodded. Attaching her cell phone and radio to her belt, she quickly decided she couldn't think about this now. She didn't have time to think about this now; she'd have to think about this tomorrow.

Jon opened the door for her and let her pass.

Drawing a fresh breath of cool morning air, she realized she wanted him more than any man she had known. There was no help for it, she thought miserably.

The activity of people moving to the event tent had a sobering effect on her. She fell to earth. This was real, she thought, surrounded by the unreality of a television production set. This was her world. Jon was right to remind her of it.

By the time she reached the tent opening, they found the round tables were back in place. The cast and crew were already seated, eating, and passing each other jellies, butter, and toasts. There was no sign that the day before this had been a make-shift triage. Sage sent a thank you to the production assistants who always seemed to move like magic off and on the set throughout any film assignment.

"Good grief," Jon said his eyes wide with surprise, "how do you people do it so quickly?"

"Hollywood magic," Sage replied realizing she was ravenous. "Let's eat."

A couple of female makeup artists were sitting by the buffet table. They watched Jon as he crossed in front of them. Though both women were strikingly beautiful, even by Hollywood standards, Jon didn't notice either one as he filled two plates.

Returning to their table, he served Sage the smaller of the two.

"You've got to eat," he said placing it in front of her. Without waiting for her thanks he picked up a knife and fork and unceremoniously began attacking his own breakfast.

Double K joined them with a cup of coffee and a small stack of powered donuts.

"Second breakfast," he said taking a bite of pastry. He glared at Jon and their eyes locked.

Sage nibbled on a biscuit as she watched the two men. Though no words were spoken, an understanding and general acceptance of the other seemed to pass between them.

Interesting. Looking to Double K, she asked, "No one has been in or out of the kitchen since last night?"

Double K gave her a quick nod.

Talking around a bite of ham, "I'll call my officers out here to gather prints but so many having unlimited access to the kitchen area, I doubt if we come out of there with only a single suspect."

"What about the eighty plus people we have to feed?"

Sage asked taking a sip of coffee, "We have a logistical problem here."

"I understand that but everything, and I mean every food item brought in here, has to be secured. The fool behind this may have something more on his mind than a few mushrooms."

"I'll see it gets done right," Double K volunteered.

"Good," Sage said taking her last bite of bacon.

"What about the attack on Sage?" Double K asked with his voice once again taking on a gruff and protective tone.

"That depends on Sage," Jon said sipping his coffee, "and how much she remembers."

Oz came over with a cup of coffee and sat down.

Sage looked at him.

"You're amazing," she said, "How did you get this spread together so quickly."

Oz chucked. Looking across at the lavish morning buffet, he said, "I let my fingers do the walking and got lucky with a local caterer at the last minute."

"So," Oz said, "how's your jaw?"

"Sore," Sage answered touching the bottom of her chin. Did everyone in the entire company know?

"I'm sorry," Jon said to Oz, "but your kitchen will be out of service until we get some fresh supplies in there."

Oz nodded. "Understood. I have already ordered lunch. Presumably, I will be starting fresh with everything since someone was in the kitchen last night. By the way, think we will get to work anytime soon?"

Sage shook her head. "Half of the crew is still going to be feeling under the weather from yesterday's bout of food poisoning. I don't think anyone will be complaining too much as we are all being paid."

"You think McMasters will close down the production?" Oz asked under his breath.

Sage looked at him and shrugged. Besides a paycheck, so many here had a lot riding on this production. She felt her body tense and looked back to find Jon's dark eyes upon her.

Placing his cup of coffee on the table, his mouth grew tight and his jaw line rose. "I will do what I can and see if there is a way to speed this up. Maybe we can get a set of prints off the bow."

Sage smiled. This wasn't the same man who had tried to obstruct their every move since arriving here.

Keenly aware of his wide-shouldered, powerful body and long muscular legs, Sage gave Jon a smile. She knew he wanted to solve these crimes not only for the greater good, but he wanted to solve them for her.

She let her eyes soften as they touched his face. In a voice barely above a whisper, she said, "I know Hillary will appreciate that."

A look of understanding passed between them. Without ever meaning to, she felt her mind, her body melting into the ever present and invisible warmth he wrapped about her. It was too easy to get lost in him. How long could she keep her aching heart at bay?

"Back to the big question." Double K said too loudly. The deep resonant sound of his voice temporarily broke the spell Jon was weaving around her. "Who's behind this?"

"If we figure the why, Double K, " Sage said noting Oz twist in his seat, "we can figure out the who."

Sage noted the way Oz twisted in his seat. All this police business was no doubt boring him.

With fresh resolve, she had to clear her head of the

handsome Police Chief and get back to the business of solving this case.

"Well," Oz interjected, "I have a bunch to do, least of which is a major clean up, if I have your all clear, Chief?"

"Sure," Jon said glancing at Sage for her approval. She concurred.

"Wait," Jon said to Oz as he was about to leave the table, "can you tell me about Manuel."

Oz looked surprised and his face colored brightly. "Manuel has been with me for years, I trust him with my life."

"Anyone else hanging around the kitchen?" Jon asked, his eyes expressionless.

Oz blew out a long breath. "One of the contestants, a chef from New Orleans. No, you can't possibly think René Devereaux could be mixed up in this. No, No, I don't believe it."

"Take it easy," Sage said smoothly, "we are just trying to get some answers at this point."

Sage accidentally rubbed her chin, which sent it throbbing. The ibuprofen had yet to start working. She tried to separate René Devereaux from the rest of the contestants but for the moment was at a loss. She couldn't recall his face. "By the way, how tall is he?"

Oz shook his head, "About my height, five foot ten inches, but he is..."

"Under suspicion," Jon answered for him. Looking at Sage, he turned to Oz, "I've got to be going. We found the bow and maybe we'll get lucky and find a fingerprint as well. Miss McCall, thank you for your hospitality."

Seated next to her, Double K snorted. Sage ignored him. Nothing happened! Why didn't he believe her?

Turning to Jon, she gave him an easy smile. He was leaving

and she didn't want him to go. As if to read her thoughts he said, "I'll be back as soon as I can."

Sage rose as if to walk Jon out to his vehicle but he shook his head. "Finish your coffee and try to get some more rest."

Sage nodded. She missed him and he hadn't even left the room.

His eyes lingered on her a moment longer than they should have. With a slight nod, he left without another word.

Sage turned to Double K; she had no intention of resting or sitting idle. "We're going to restart our own investigation. We have to find out who is behind this."

Double K gave her a terse nod. "Do you think McMasters is going to pull the plug?"

"I don't know," Sage said slowly. "I do know Nick well enough that he's not going to risk anyone's getting hurt and I know he's catching a lot of negative publicity right now. My Dad will probably give us a heads up about this soon enough. In the meantime, we have a job to do."

Double K seemed pleased with her fresh determination.

"I need to go check on the coffee," Oz said with a nervous glance toward the beverage table. He hurried over to the buffet and in minutes was absorbed in seeing dirty cups and dishes got removed from the dining area.

"So what's your plan?" Double K asked wiping the powdered donuts from his mouth. "That is, of course, after you call your Dad and tell him about your attack?"

Sage frowned. She didn't want to alarm her father anymore than he probably was.

Taking a long breath, she finished the last of her coffee and said, "It's back to basics. We're going to interview everyone again. I especially want to talk to this René Devereaux and find out where he was last night."

Placing her cup into the saucer, she looked to Double K. "The guy who hit me was about five-foot ten, heavy set. It was too dark to distinguish any features and he moved fast. I don't think I'll be able to forget that voice."

She paused then added, "I'm tired of waiting to see what this character will do next. It's time we get on the offensive. I want you and Cowboy Bob to touch base with everyone. Ask probing questions, see what they think or feel about the show. Find out who has a grudge against McMasters. I just feel if we find out why, we can find out who."

Double K was clearly pleased and his grin spoke volumes.

"While you are doing that, I'm going to go through everyone's employment records as well as the background information on the contestants. They are supposed to arrive today. Someone has had to have seen something. Someone knows something."

"You want us to question men and women?"

"Everyone," Sage replied firmly. "I believe the person who hit me last night was a man, but I want the women questioned too."

Double K leaned slightly closer to her. "And who gets to interview Hillary?"

"I will," Sage replied, "and I will speak to Jeff Sanders and Connard."

"Good idea."

Cowboy Bob walked in and strolled over to the table where Sage and Double K were sitting.

"This just arrived," Cowboy Bob said handing her an oversized UPS package address to her. The sender's inscription read McCall Security.

Sage reached out for the package and laid it beside her.

"Thanks," she said. "This must be the background information on the contestants and employment history I've been waiting for. Maybe we can find some answers in this."

Double K gave Cowboy Bob a list of directives.

"When do you want me to start?" Cowboy Bob asked with an eye toward the breakfast buffet.

"Right after you have something to eat." Sage interjected, "I'm gong to go over everyone's background before I join you. I want additional security posted in and around the trailers and motor homes today. I want to double the guards on patrol at all times."

"You got it," Double k grunted with approval.

"One more thing," Sage said readying herself to leave, "we need to take a look at a copy of the script."

Cowboy Bob chuckled, "Script? What script? I thought everything was real."

Sage laughed as she rose, "Cowboy, it's too real. I'll catch up with you two later."

Leaving Cowboy Bob and Double K, Sage hurried toward her motel room. She hoped that inside the package she would find something that would lead them to her attacker. She could not let him harm another person in her charge. Somewhere in the package there had to be a trail for her to follow. Time was running out.

Opening the door to her room, she stopped, unprepared to find the bed unmade and every inch of the room filled with the memories of the night before. Though Jon Maddux was by now in St. Gabrielle, his presence filled every inch of the room.

Sage remembered feeling the warmth of his breath, the light feathery touch of his fingers racing up her arm and his virile scent that was becoming familiar to her. She remembered the flutter of her heart as his lips traced the soft contours of her mouth before they sensuously covered each inch of soft skin.

Her breath quickened as her eyes fell on the towel he had casually thrown on the bed. She remembered too clearly the sheer beauty of his naked muscular body.

Last night in the darkness, her body had been surrounded, sheltered, and protected by the warmth of his powerful arms and the heavy line of his long muscular legs. With her eyes wide in wonder, she recalled the hardness of his manhood against her soft bottom, still struggling to understand why he had not taken advantage of her. She would have let him.

Standing there, mixed feelings mingled with a haze of swirling desires. Where was the self-assured woman she had been just yesterday? Who was this awkward girl who was hungry for this man and what his body and heart offered? How could she feel so lost without him?

Deep inside, her heart ached with excitement.

Closing her eyes, she tried to regain her balance.

As the reality of the moment came back to her, she forced the memory of Jon Maddux to a safe distance.

When she reopened her eyes, she felt deceptively calm.

With a firm grip on the package, she entered the room intent on giving the paperwork her full attention.

Tossing the covers over the bed, she quickly opened the package, allowing the contents to spill across them. Setting aside the employment records of the production crew aside, she was most interested in the contestant information.

Leaning back against the headboard, she paused before reading the first record.

Who was behind these crimes? She had to know. So far he or she had shot an already deceased Evan Davis, poisoned the crew, and assaulted her. Was this the work of a single man, she wondered, or were more involved?

Was there a possibility the incidences were unrelated? Had her assailant meant to inflict harm or had this person meant to kill?

Looking down at the files, she came back to the same question that most troubled her: why? Sage opened the first file folder labeled private and confidential, and she began to read and scan the pictures for possible clues and directions.

David Garrett, age twenty-seven, six-feet tall. As she read and thought, oh yeah, he is the good-looking fireman from New Jersey. Tall, distinctively handsome, she remembered. Though he had a muscular build, he was too tall to be the man who'd hit her the night before. Still, she read his background expecting to find the unexpected.

Only minutes into his paperwork, she smiled. David Garrett was as he seemed, a Sunday school teacher with a stable career and the all American family. This guy was a Boy Scout. She flipped through his medical information and his releases. Nothing stood out about him and she moved on to the next file.

Todd Morris, a student from UCLA. From sunny California, Todd was five foot eleven inches, the right height range but was trim and athletic. The man who attacked her was heavy-set. Still, she dutifully read Todd's information. In his reason for being on the show, he had written 'I love reading mysteries and hope one day to be a scriptwriter. I think my experience in *Murder in Florida* will help me achieve my goals and give me good experience.' He concluded his note with "I have good instincts in solving crimes. I usually know the ending of a good mystery long before the final scene."

Sage chuckled softly and wondered if she should invite him into their investigation.

The next three were women, a waitress from North Carolina, a real estate broker from Colorado, and a stock analyst from New York.

René Devereaux followed. She held her breath and she took care to read every word.

René, Sage read, had listed himself as a professional chef from New Orleans. However, his resume revealed he was little more than a short order cook. His career was strictly hands-on experience with no formal culinary training.

McMasters Studios, for whatever reason, had decided to portray him as a bona fide Chef, probably the work of the publicity department. A chef would certainly garner more attention than a short order cook.

Devereaux employment had never been steady. He was divorced, and his hobbies included hunting, fishing, and being outdoors. She glanced at his photo.

He was stocky, with thinning brown hair and had small dark eyes. As a man, he was indistinguishable and could blend unnoticed in any crowd.

This man was the right height and the right weight. He was familiar with the kitchen. Sage took a closer look at his application.

Like most of the contestants, he had in his application his love of mysteries and listed *Law and Order* and *CSI* as his favorite TV shows.

Sage leaned back against the headboard and took a breath.

As an avid outdoors man and southern cook, he would certainly know the difference between edible mushrooms and poisonous. Though it did not state whether he hunted with a bow or rifle, she surmised his experience as a hunter would give him working knowledge of a bow and arrow.

But, Sage, thought, how much experience would shooting an arrow at close range take? Even Hillary or Connard could have hit that mark, she thought with a shake of her head.

This was too easy. Something didn't feel right. René was the right height and build. Hanging out with Oz, he would have known his way about the kitchen. She laid his profile aside and had to consider him as suspect.

Were there others?

She tried to recall the raspy whisper of her attacker but the attack had happened so fast. She had been caught off guard. A mistake she vowed would never happen again.

She quickly scanned the remaining contestants: a librarian from Kansas City, a commercial fisherman from Washington State, and a used car salesman from Duluth. The entire lot of them, all self-confessed crime/drama buffs. No one who stood out, except for René Devereaux. She would interview him first.

As she laid the folder beside her, the phone rang. She heard the exhilaration in his velvet-edged voice as she said hello. She listened to his quick intake of breath. Of its own volition, a warm glow flowed through her and her heart sang with delight.

"How are you, Sweetie?" Jon asked from town.

"A little better, now that I have rested a bit," she replied. Her heart hammered against her ribs. She waited until her quickened pulse subsided before she asked, "How about you?"

"Trying to focus on what I have to do to keep you and everyone else safe, but my mind keeps drifting back to last night."

Sage colored fiercely. Too quickly the night returned, a

night filled with the memory of bruising kisses. Her body tingled remembering the touch of his fingers. She recalled the smoldering passion that thrilled her and the scent of his body. His face haunted her. His voice left her defenseless.

"I want to see you," he said, his voice sounding strained.

Despite herself, Sage laughed. "I am sure you do!"

She heard Jon choke.

"I didn't mean that way," he apologized then laughed, "Maybe I did."

"Do you have any information for me, Officer?" Sage asked trying to sound more serious than she felt. She was helpless to stop the light laugh that broke free from her soul and danced across her heart.

She heard him smile, before he replied, "The lab boys are saying the mushrooms in the sauce are a common variety of nightshade found growing wild throughout the south."

"Any possibility they were originated from *The Pizza Guy?*"

"No. We tested his sample but found no trace of mushrooms in the spaghetti sample we received from *The Pizza Guy.* The mushrooms on the pizza were organically grown so obviously the added mushrooms came from person or persons unknown. This type of mushroom is relatively mild but turns toxic when added to a tomato sauce. Trust me; I have learned more about mushrooms in the last hour than I knew existed."

Quickly, Sage told Jon about René Devereaux.

"Sounds like a good suspect. Wait until I get there to question him," he said with cool authority.

"All right," she said with no intention of waiting for his return. "What time do you think you might make it back here?"

"Probably late afternoon, unless you need me before then," Jon said, his voice trailing off softly.

"Jon about last night," Sage began softly, "I just want you to know..."

"That you don't go to bed with every Police Chief you meet after you have been mugged," he finished for her.

She laughed. "That sounds so provincial; you are probably thinking I never set foot out of Beverly Hills."

The sharp knock prevented her from saying more.

"Hold on," she said laying the receiver on the nightstand.

She opened the door to find Double K, Cowboy Bob and Reece standing sheepishly before her.

"What's wrong?" she asked looking at Double K.

"It's René Devereaux," Double K said, out of breath.

"What about him?" Sage asked sharply fearing his answer.

Double K took a long breath, "He is gone!"

CHAPTER EIGHT

Sage stared at Double K. His every word struck her like hammer blows. "What do you mean he's gone?"

"We went to his room, knocked on the door, no answer," Double K replied. His deep voice was strangled. A look of dread, sharpened in his brown eyes. His voice was labored, tight, as he continued: "His clothes are there but his bed hasn't been slept in. We even checked with the maid. We've searched everywhere. He's gone."

Sage listened quietly. Grisly images began to build in her mind and an icy fear tightened around her heart.

Double K coughed and shifted slightly. "No one has been in or out of the Sand Point Inn except for law enforcement or medical personnel. Sage, René Devereaux is nowhere to be found."

Sage leaned back and closed her eyes. Knowing Jon was on the phone a few feet away she could only assume he'd had heard their conversation. She opened her eyes, the knot in her stomach tightening, "Does anyone remember if he had food poisoning?"

"No," Double K answered quickly, "but now that you mention it, seems like I do remember him helping out. I saw him last night but not this morning."

Sage took a long breath and returned to the phone. She could feel the muscles of her forearm harden as she brought the receiver to her mouth. "Double K is at the door. One of the contestants is missing."

"The chef?" Came Jon's sharp response.

"His bed wasn't slept in last night. Double K says no one except medical or law enforcement has been in or out. Jon, trust me on this, if he'd made his way through the media encampment, he would have been on the news by now."

There was a short pause before Jon said simply "I'm on my way out to you."

Holding her emotions in check, Sage looked across the room to where Double K stood. "We're going to conduct a search to see if we can locate him. If he turns up, you'll be the first to know."

Returning the phone to its cradle, Sage glanced at her watch. She would have all of one hour to find René before she had to make the call to LA.

With her every nerve tensing and time slipping away moment by moment, she knew she had to inform Hillary and Jeff Sanders as soon as possible.

Grabbing her two way radio, she slid it in her belt and hurried to join her security team.

"I know you have checked everywhere," she said softly to the trio, "but I want us to check again. Maybe, this time, he'll turn up."

First to Reese and Cowboy Bob she said, "Find Oz. Ask him if René has been seeing anyone here. Maybe he's in a woman's room. Try to find out when he was seen last. Double K and I'll notify Hillary before we check the production trailers. Keep your walkie-talkies on and your eyes open."

Reese and Cowboy Bob spun on their heels and hurried away.

Sage and Double K immediately began their jaunt toward Hillary's motor home.

"Have you heard or talked to Jamie Wolf this morning?" She asked almost at the motor home.

"Yeah, he's doing much better," Double K replied as if grateful to have a change of subject, "but he doesn't remember anything about the attack."

Stopping two short steps away from Hillary's motor home, Sage gave the door several sharp knocks. An immediate barrage of little barks answered her knock as Pepe announced her arrival.

Hillary swung the door open. Finding Sage, Hillary sent her a brutal stare.

"What now?" Hillary snapped, and her voice was curt. She made no attempt to hide her irritation. "I'm trying to get some rest!"

Behind her was Connard dressed in a light blue *Ralph Lauren* polo shirt with beige, front flap chino pants, and buff European loafers. Pepe was breathless in his arms.

From his vantage point at the motor home's door, he stood several feet over her and Double K. He took full use of his two-foot zenith to give Sage and Double K a condescending stare.

Sage drew a long breath, knowing what she was about to say wasn't going to get a sympathetic response.

"One of the contestants is missing. We're conducting a search now."

"Oh my God!" Hillary wailed. "Who? Not anyone important I hope! If anyone else dies, Nick McMasters will have a fit!"

Connard paled slightly and tightened his grip on poor Pepe.

Double K gave Sage a sidelong glance but remained silent.

"It's René Devereaux, the chef from New Orleans. At the

moment, we don't believe he's dead. He may be wandering around but we do need to find him. We checked his room. All of his things are still there and the bed didn't look slept in."

"Don't you need a warrant for that sort of thing?" Hillary asked not bothering to hide her disapproval.

"No, Hillary," she explained, "the police need warrants. We're private citizens, we were merely trespassing."

Connard raised an arched eyebrow.

"Have you contacted Nick or your father?" Hillary asked her voice dripping with resentment. It turned cold and emotionless as she spat, "You know Nick knows about all of us getting sick."

Hillary's pretty face drained of all color. Panic was reflective and frightening in her blue eyes, and she continued breathlessly, "They are having a meeting at the studios today. I think Nick might close down the production. If that happens, I don't know what I'll do! Sage! You have to do something!"

Sage frowned.

Shamelessly, Hillary continued her voice raising a shrill octave with each phrase from her trembling lips, "I know Nick will listen to you, I know he will. You have to tell him it's all right."

"I'll do what I can," Sage promised Hillary. "Now I have to inform Jeff Sanders."

"No, I'll do that," Hillary sniffed, "you go find that what's his name, René, whoever he is and you can tell him I'm not pleased with this little disappearance act of his!"

Hillary almost fell into Connard, signaling the end of the conversation or at least her interest in it. "It's all too horrible!"

"Connard," she wailed turning to her assistant, "I can't bear all this stress, its simply horrible. Find me something to take. Hurry!"

With a final accusatory stare at Sage, Hillary slammed the door shut. From behind it, Sage heard Hillary shriek in wonder about why this was happening to her.

Double K looked at Sage and snickered. "I thought she took that well."

Sage half smiled. "Yes, considering the alternatives, she did. As long as we're here, let's walk around the production trailers."

The trailers stood at the far end of the parking lot. One held electrical equipment, the second trailer props and third additional sound equipment and cameras.

Sage guessed this area was once intended for overflow guests but looked ill-used even in the Sand Point Inn's heyday.

Nearest her, the asphalt was broken with tall grasses popping through the broken pavement.

Beyond the black pavement, lay tall wheaten grasses that lead to green leafy vines, rising from the forest floor and wrapped their way up the tall scrawny pines and small discarded branches. Long strands of Spanish moss cascaded from low hanging limbs and draped their way through a stand of live oaks.

The entire scene reeked of flies, mosquitoes, and small crawling things. The air was alive with the hum of beetles and the sounds of locusts.

Mid-morning, a slight steam seemed to be rising from the moist earth warning Sage of hidden dangers and unseen risks.

The exotic calls of unfamiliar birds voiced a warning as they approached.

Just over her head, Sage heard the flutter of wings but saw nothing through the canopy of dark green foliage.

There was no trail leading into the cypress swamp, only a tiny hollow in the tall grasses perhaps made by rabbits to scurry through after a quick taste of new grass growing though the pavement.

Sage drew a soft breath, this too was Jon's world, a world that was primordial and both untamed and seductive. It reminded her of him but then everything did. There was no escaping his presence even when she was alone.

"Sage!" Double K called startling her.

Instantly, she was brought back to the moment.

Leaving the Cypress Swamp to the wild things living there, she followed Double K's voice to the back of one of the trailers. As she joined him, she followed his line of vision to the metal roll door and the dark smear against the side. It looked like...blood!

Though smudged, Sage could make out a clearly identifiable palm print on the trailer. It was as if its owner had but for a moment braced his hand against the door before vanishing.

Whose? A member of the crew who had inadvertently injured himself or the blood trail of René Devereaux?

Double K cursed under his breath. "Now what?"

Sage didn't reply, intent on following the downward angle of the smear to the ground.

It took her only a moment to find a second splattering just a few feet away. A third lay just before a small hidden path that led into the swamp.

Sage stood motionless for a moment debating if she should follow.

In following the trail they would and could damage any evidence or scent that René Devereaux or whoever may have left behind. Yet, she knew whoever had passed this way had been injured. She had no choice.

"Let's follow the tracks," she said drawing an uneasy

breath punctuated with uneven gasps, "but try to stay off of the blood trail."

Together they took either side of the path and evenly paced themselves along both sides of the narrow path.

As the tall grasses gave way to the clusters of thick palmettos, tall thin pines, and cypress, the trail of blood stopped amid the damp wetland of covered in wet leaves and cypress knees that jettisoned out of the ground.

She heard a sound and turned just in time to see a raccoon vanish into the bush.

Ahead of them lay the murky dark waters of a creek and the erratic hum of flying insects and locusts hidden in grassy marshland.

Searching the ground nearest them again she realized they had lost the trail. She looked up to Double K who could do little more than shake his head.

"We need to get some dogs out here if we are going to find anyone." Double K said taking a few more steps into the swampy forest.

Sage nodded. "I'm going to keep moving forward and see if I can find anything. I want you to..."

"I'm not leaving you, Sage" Double K interrupted with his jaw clenched and his dark brown eyes were fastened on her in challenge. She could tell by his tights jaw line and the wrinkles that shadowed his brow, he was not going to do her bidding this time.

She gave him a nod knowing there was no point to argue. "All right, I'm going to call Jon Maddux; we need a search and rescue team out here as soon as possible."

Still along the tree line, she punched in his number on her cell.

"Do you have access to any search dogs?" she asked when he answered.

Jon was silent for a moment. "Yeah, we have a local K-9 search team group here. Their dogs are used throughout Florida and went to New York after 9/11. Why?"

"We found a blood trail that leads from the back of the prop trailer into the cypress swamp. We've followed it as far as we can."

"I'm turning into the Sand Point Inn now. Where are you?" Jon asked, his voice sounded strained. He was worried about her. She heard it in his voice, felt it in her heart.

"Drive toward the motor homes," she answered, signaling Double K to head back to the parking lot. "We're behind the production trailers."

As she moved through the tall grasses, she heard the sound of his Explorer roll onto the broken pavement just before he came into view. She turned off the cell phone and stuck it in her pocket.

Seeing him, she felt a soft smile upon her lips.

Across from her, Jon got out of the Explorer. When his eyes found her she watched the smile on his mouth curl into an ardent grin that brightened his dark brown eyes.

As she hurried toward him, she felt a warm glow flow through her entire body. Her mood was suddenly buoyant.

Jon could feel his face brighten at the sight of her. His smile broadened and he knew the spring in his step was visible.

They could barely reach each other fast enough.

God she was beautiful, Jon thought, feeling his heart pounding in hard beats at the sight of her. He had driven too fast to reach the Sand Point Inn but it wasn't the investigation that pushed him, it was being close to her.

Watching her, he was spellbound. She moved like a

dancer, her shapely legs easily moving with ease through the tall grass. Memories of the night before sent ripples of desire through him.

The McCall Security uniform she wore did little to cover the exquisite body he knew that lay beneath the layers of cloth.

In the bright sunlight, her long golden hair was shining like spun glass. A few tiny wisps had escaped her ponytail and clustered into short curls around her heart shaped face

He remembered the melting softness of her perfectly formed body, the moist satin feel of her breasts, and the honeyed taste of her sweet lips. Her blue eyes were shining in welcome. This both startled him and took him by complete surprise.

This was a woman beyond his reach. Yet, she seemed elated to see him. On so many levels he was free falling, helpless to stop his descent into a place of sensory pleasure that he couldn't name. Every inch of his body quivered with life. And there was no use denying it. He felt himself being tightly wrapped around this little wisp of femininity, who'd proved adept at handling herself and every situation that confronted her. She would never need him, he realized with a mixture of pride and dejection. He needed her to.

His gaze traveled over her face and he had to fight the overwhelming urge to take her into his arms.

Someday soon she would have to return to California. He knew when she did he'd crawl every inch of the way to find her there.

"Show me the blood trail," he said, reaching them.

Though his words were uncompromising, his tone was soothing in its warmth.

Sage smiled, the air around her seemed electrified by his presence.

"The blood is bright, looks fresh," Double K said turning to retrace his steps. He doubled back along the trail expecting Sage and Jon follow him. They did.

He stopped where he and Sage had found the last droplets of blood.

"They stop here," Double K said coming to a halt, "just beyond that tree."

"Let's go," Jon said headed toward the water's edge.

Sage and Double K followed, both on the watch for water moccasins, coral snakes, as well as poison ivy and sumac.

Less than a quarter mile from the Sand Point Inn and the comforts of twenty-first century technology, Sage felt she had traveled a time warp to an era when man struggled for life and nature won each game of life and death.

Sage could see no visible movement to the slow flowing stream except for a small brown leaf floating along the brackish water. At some point, the creek would join with other streams and would eventually find its way to the gulf.

Sage had thought all the water on this coast was crystal clear but this water was dark and looked deadly.

Across from her a graceful blue heron stared but showed no intention of relinquishing his favorite fishing spot to a group of intruders.

High overhead was a small flock of roseate spoonbills, their pink and white feathers stunning against the pale blue sky.

Looking again at the heavy marsh, Sage began to see the brilliant colors; vibrant reds, lavenders of flowers as well as bright red and black berries. Though primeval, incredible beauty untouched by human hand lay all around her.

Jon stood quietly. Sage came up behind him.

"There," Jon said softly pointing his finger toward the opposite bank.

Sage looked but could see nothing on the bank, then midway across the creek she gasped as she saw a pair of black eyes staring back at her. Behind the lifeless eyes, barely visible above the water's surface a craggy dark gray ridge barely tipped the murky water. Had she not seen the eyes, she would have easily mistaken the dull silvery hide for a piece of driftwood.

Her short gasp caught Double K's attention.

"Gator!" She cried, her voice cutting the silence. "He's staring right at us! I didn't even see him!"

"That's the idea," Jon said slowly folding his arms across his chest.

Double K moved in for a closer look. "How big is he?"

"He's about nine to ten foot head to toe," Jon said with a measured sigh, "looks like an old bull."

Sage inched closer to Jon.

Jon chuckled. "Nothing to worry about; he is just protecting his territory. They got their name from the Spaniards; they called them El Lagarto, the lizard."

"What do they eat?" Double K asked inching his way to the water's edge to get a better look.

"They can kill almost any animal they can find and that includes birds, turtles, snakes, fish, and sometimes humans."

Double K shifted nervously. Double K was out of his element. Sage had little doubt given the choice of confrontation, Double K would be happier facing an LA street gang than a ten foot bull alligator. Sage stood transfixed by this ancient creature.

The gator made a swish of his tail but it didn't appear to be threatening; at least, not yet.

"There are three more gators over there on the bank," Jon

said pointing out three small ones lying in a small patch of sunlight that had slipped into the swamp.

As Sage looked across the creek, several young alligators rose and angled their webbed feet toward the water before smoothly gliding into the stream.

Double K grunted. "You say they can attack people?"

"They can," came Jon's cool reply. "Most gator attacks occur when people swim during feeding times, sunset or sunrise. Gators have been known to come in and try to drag a person who is standing too close to the water's edge. If they are successful, they will try to drown their victim by going into a death roll. By the way, in case you were thinking about it, it's best not to swim in gator infested waters."

Double K stepped away from the bank. "Wasn't planning to."

A worried thought crossed Sage's brow. "Do you think who ever left the blood trail could have been...?"

"Eaten?" Jon finished for her. "I sure hope not. I'd hate to make divers go down in this gator infested pool."

Sage physically shook.

"Let's go back, and leave this old man alone." Jon said in a soft voice. "Hopefully your guy has turned up by now."

Sage was relieved and ready to go.

When she turned back to give the big gator a final look, he was gone.

Making sure she stayed up with Jon and Double K, she asked, "If we've been living a quarter of a mile from the alligators all this time, why haven't we seen any?"

"They have pretty much everything they need right here. Besides, if they see you first, gators will usually mosey away. If you are in their water, you are in their territory. Remember the most dangerous are the ones who don't leave when they see a human. They are the ones who have lost all fear of man. Their habitats are being destroyed by developments, pollution, and loss of their food sources. That's why they go looking for food. Every now and then gators will have to be removed from lawns, garages, golf courses, and swimming pools."

As they walked on, Jon continued, "They have moved off the endangered list and I'm afraid even with licensed wildlife officials relocating nuisance gators and licensed hunts they are going to continue to be a problem for Floridians. Not that I am entirely unsympathetic but when man and nature collide, nature never wins. Let me just say, I hope whoever it is didn't try to cross the swamp last night. Gators are only part of the danger."

Reaching the production trailers Jon asked, "Have you checked inside the trailers?"

Sage shook her head.

"The trailer doors are locked," Double K said but moved past them toward the farthest trailer. "I'll double check."

"I'm going to call in for the search team," Jon said moving toward his car. "If René tried to make it through that swamp last night, there won't be much to find."

Half listening to Jon on his police radio, Sage and Double K checked the trailers, careful to make a wide berth of the blood smear by the door.

"Nothing," Double K reported when Jon rejoined them.

"While we are waiting for the SAR team," Jon said in a troubled tone, "I'd like to see his room."

Sage nodded and turned to Double K. "Do me a favor and check in with Cowboy Bob and Reese. See if they've turned up anything."

"Will do," Double K agreed hurrying off to find his partners.

Saying little, Sage took Jon to René's room and opened the door.

Jon walked about the room checking the closets, opening a few drawers finding René's wardrobe intact. His shaving cream and razor sat undisturbed on the bathroom countertop. His bed looked as though it had not been slept in.

"I don't get it," Jon said "nothing has been touched, his clothes are here and there is no sign of abduction. He didn't have a private vehicle here, did he?"

Sage shook her head and quickly related his background information. Jon's ruggedly handsome face tensed.

"As a hunter, he's someone who could have a working knowledge of a bow and arrow, though at that range it wouldn't take much skill."

"I came to the same conclusion myself," Sage agreed.

"And if he is familiar with the outdoors and a cook or chef, he probably knows which mushrooms are unsafe to eat." Jon paused before he asked, "and I seem to recall you saying he's about the right height and weight of the man who attacked you?"

Sage nodded still feeling the bruise on her chin.

"Well, he's somewhere," Jon said, "We need to find him."

Leaving the room untouched, Sage and Jon were approached by a small group of stunt men and crewmembers. Their faces were dark, their strides were angry, and they stopped abruptly before Sage.

"What is going on?" One of the stuntman demanded a bit too loud.

Sage recognized him as Stuart Dunbar the stunt coordinator. He was brawny with rock hard abs, wrestler's arms, and, in Sage's opinion, more muscle than brains. He liked using his beefy size to intimidate but Sage knew with her third degree black belt she could easily take him down if she had to. His temper was always in fifth gear, too bad; she thought if he worked on his personality as much as he did his muscles, he could attract more ladies with his amazing dark blue eyes and dark brown hair.

Without apology Sage looked at him and there was no need to beat around the proverbial bush.

"René Devereaux is missing," Sage answered. There was no use in keeping this from them and if they had seen René, it could help. Looking straight at Stuart, she asked, "Have you seen him?"

Stuart threw up his hands in disgust, "Is that all? That little weasel, he probably went home. He was talking about it."

Sage noted the sneer and look of contempt on the stunt man's face and read it easily. Anyone who wasn't willing to jump from a twenty-foot high building, dive off a cliff, or career around in a speeding vehicle was a lesser man in his eyes.

Still, she heard a ring of truth in his words and she was able to put a finger on what had been bothering her all morning. René Devereaux was on the soft side. He didn't seem the type to attack her or anyone. While he may have been a fisherman and hunter, he was no athlete. But why did he leave? Where had he gone?

"You said he was talking about going home?" Sage asked hoping he knew more.

Stuart's eyes narrowed and he answered too quickly, "Yeah sure, he was, half the production crew is."

"Have any of you seen him?" Sage repeated hoping someone had seen or knew more.

The stunt men shrugged.

Someone asked, "Have you heard any more about McMasters closing down production?"

"You'll have to take that up with either Hillary or Jeff," Sage answered candidly, "I don't know. Look, I know you are all getting restless and are eager to get to work but you will have to take that up with Hillary."

"Do you know why we got sick?" Mike Murphy asked. In his mid-thirties, Mike was a carpenter who worked with set design. More educated than his Neanderthal companions, Sage always thought he was an odd addition to this tight knit group of friends.

"Mushrooms," Jon interjected. Until that moment, he had deferred to Sage. Now was the right time to step into this conversation. Back in his police uniform, he pushed his thumbs into his belt and rested his hands on his gun belt. The gesture did not go unnoticed. They had pushed as far as they were going to.

Jon's icy stare drilled into the self-proclaimed leader of the group. He tried to cool his temper and his words as he explained, "We just got word a short while ago. It was a type of wild mushroom. Not lethal but toxic when added to tomatoes."

"Did it come from the caterer?" Mike asked looking a bit relieved.

Jon shook his head. "The caterer's food was thoroughly screened. Whoever put mushrooms in the sauce did it here at the Sand Point Inn."

Stuart Dunbar's face darkened. "If I find that little weasel Devereaux before you, I'll ..."

"You'll what?" Double K asked gruffly coming up behind them.

Stuart turned and stared at Double K. Double K towered

above the stunt coordinator and dared Stuart Dunbar to finish his boast.

"You'll do nothing but bring him to us," Sage warned him. "Look Stuart, this is important, if René Devereaux is involved in anyway, he'll be thoroughly questioned by the local authorities. Last thing this production needs is to lose one of its key stuntmen because he can't keep a cool head."

Two of his companions said something low into Stuart's ear. Apparently Sage's words hit a small note. Stuart shifted restlessly. With a dark scowl on his face, he seemed to settle down a bit and gave her a reluctant nod. With that, he left taking his companions with him.

Speaking to the stunt men hadn't been a complete waste of time. She had learned that René Devereaux had been talking about leaving. Had he simply been frightened enough to go home, without telling anyone? This didn't make sense but again she didn't know why. She was about to mention this to Jon when Double K's cell phone rang.

Double K answered the phone and a smile crossed his lips.

"That's real good news."" he said to the caller, "I'll be there to pick you up shortly."

"That was Jamie," he explained putting the cell phone back into his pants pocket, "they're releasing him from the hospital. Okay, if I go pick him up?"

"Yes," Sage said relieved to hear this news, "but hurry back. I know I am going to need you here. And make sure the media stays away from the both of you."

Cowboy Bob and Reese walked up that moment to join them, and Double K quickly shared the news about Jamie.

"No sign of René Devereaux, I take it?" Jon said to them when Double K was finished.

Cowboy Bob shook his head. "We checked everywhere. No one has seen him."

"Did anyone check the kitchen?" Sage asked on a hunch.

Reese looked at Cowboy Bob then back to her. "No, at least we didn't. Some one put up crime scene tape around it, so we didn't go in."

Sage and Jon looked at each other. "Let's check it anyway, to be sure."

With quick steps, they hurried to the kitchen. Cowboy Bob and Reese hurried in their wake, a sheepish expression on both their faces.

"Think he would have gone to the kitchen?" Sage asked, trying to keep up with Jon's impatient stride.

Sage was desperately hoping this wasn't going to turn into another wild goose chase.

Reaching the kitchen, they all stopped short. The door was ajar. Jon knew it had been secured the night before.

With his every sense taunt, he slowly lifted his gun from the holster and raised it with both hands to his chest.

Looking down at Sage, he said in a low growl, "I'll go in first."

Using his foot, he slowly pushed the door open.

Stepping into the kitchen, Jon kept his gun in his line of vision. Scanning the room, he found only stainless steel tables, an empty sink, and loose utensils lying in the drain.

Turning back to Sage, he motioned for her to enter the room.

She did, inching along the back wall.

Jon took slow deliberate strides toward the large double door refrigerators.

Sage froze. She heard something.

She caught Jon's full attention and with a single snap of her fingers pointing toward the pantry door.

Working as a team, she maneuvered her way to the wooden door and placed her small hands on the handle.

Jon slowly eased to the front of it. With his gun brandished directly into the center of the pantry, he gave Sage a nod.

She brought back the door with a jerk. Jon stepped in front of the large pantry; he was ready to fire.

"Don't shoot, don't shoot," came the frightened cry.

Sage looked to find René Devereaux in a near fetal position against a dark corner.

Shivering, his eyes filled with terror, he showed no signs of resistance.

Jon held his gun in check. "Stand up. Put your hands on top of your head!"

Slowly and meekly, René rose.

He was physically shaking, his eyes focused on the tip of Jon's gun.

"Don't shoot me," René whimpered, tears streaming down his face. "It wasn't me, I swear it wasn't me!"

"Keep your hands in the air and step out of the pantry," Jon said taking a few steps away from the door. His eyes narrowed as René passed Sage. The gun held steady in his hands.

"Why are you hiding?" Jon demanded.

René was shaking so hard he was having difficulty keeping his hands in the air. He voice cracked as he whimpered, "Because he said he was going to kill me."

CHAPTER NINE

Who's going to kill you René?" Sage demanded.

René's eyes were welling in pools of terror and tears. His lips were quivering, and his sagging overweight body was shaking in fear.

Standing next to him, Sage was doubtful that René was her attacker.

The attack had been quick and gave her little time to defend herself. She remembered the rapid charge. This overweight man didn't look capable of moving that fast. Her attacker had been leaner, but it was all such a blur, she just couldn't be sure.

Jon lowered the gun.

Before he had returned it to his holster, René had dropped his fleshy hands over his face, his knees buckled and he fell to a kneeling position on the floor.

"I'm Jon Maddux, Chief of Police," Jon said sounding exasperated. "No one is going to hurt you."

Unconvinced, René sat, cowering before him.

"René," Sage said kneeling beside him. She placed a gentle hand on his shoulder and he flinched from her light touch. "No one is going to harm you. You have nothing to fear."

Something in her voice or her manner had gotten past his fear, for René slowly slid his fingers down his face.

Trembling, unable to fully remove his hands from his face, René looked at her. Sage offered him a friendly smile but René was too paralyzed to move.

Jon was growing impatient. "Can you stand up?"

René nodded and with Sage's help rose to his feet.

Cowboy Bob and Reese were now in the room. Cowboy Bob offered René a rickety wooden kitchen chair to sit down in. René slumped in the chair.

"René," she began as if scolding an errant child, "You have to tell us what's going on. Who's going to kill you?"

"I don't know," he sobbed, "he left a note in my room, it said if I told anyone what I saw he would kill me."

"Who?" Sage demanded, "Where is the note now?"

"I threw it away and ran out of my room. I went over to the trailers. I was trying to find someplace to hide; that's when I cut my hand. Look, I didn't see anything, I don't know what the note was about, I don't know anything!" René cried. His eyes were saucer wide and his voice straining in terror.

As René buried his face in his hands, Sage looked at Jon and shook her head. He was too terrified to say more. They were going to have to remove him from Sand Point Inn and get him calm before he would be able to tell them more.

Jon leaned over René and put his hand on his shoulder. "I'm going to put you into protective custody. Until I'm satisfied that you are telling the truth, you can plan on being the guest of the St. Gabrielle Police Department."

"Am I under arrest?" René sobbed looking up at Jon. "I want to go home. I don't care about being on television. I want to leave as soon as possible. I honestly didn't see anything!"

"Someone thinks you did," Sage said keeping her voice soft and her gaze steady. "Chief Maddux is right; you'll be safer in town."

Without giving René a chance to respond, Sage turned to Cowboy Bob and Reese. "Would you escort him to Chief Maddux's SUV?"

Cowboy Bob and Reese took either side of René and lifted him from the chair. He offered no resistance, leaning slightly against the men for support.

As they passed the kitchen door, Jon looked at Sage. "Do you believe him?"

Sage leaned into him, and tilting her face toward his giving him the only answer she could. "I believe he is truly frightened of something or someone."

"Who?" Jon asked and his question hung in the room like an ax waiting to fall.

In the quiet of the room, Sage could feel his heart beat and sense his thoughts. He knew he was close to having the answers. She saw the thunder in his dark eyes; his expression was taunt and watchful.

Looking down at her, he said quickly, "Well, I need to call off the search team. If you don't mind, why don't you come with me to the station? When Mr. Devereaux calms down, we may be able to figure out who and what he's afraid of."

Sage gave him a quick nod.

"Let's get him out of here as quickly as we can," Jon said touching the small curve of her back.

The warmth of his hand on her sent spirals of pleasure though her. His touch was possessive, protective, and she relished in the heady sensation it gave her.

Too quickly, they were at the Explorer.

After Jon unlocked the back door, Cowboy Bob and Reese helped slide René into back seat. Jon opened the front passenger door for Sage.

In a matter of minutes, Jon, Sage, and René were on their way to St. Gabrielle.

Reaching the highway, Jon called his dispatcher advising him he was en route with a suspect.

Somehow Jon's vehicle had made its way up the entire drive unnoticed. Seeing them near the gate, the guard on duty opened the gate at the last minute. Jon wasted no time in speeding through the media encampment toward St. Gabrielle. The reporters and news vans paid no attention to Jon's Explorer. They hadn't seen the slumped passenger in the back seat.

Sage glanced back at René but he seemed wrapped in a cocoon of his own terror and oblivious to his surroundings. She was beginning to suspect they would learn little from him this day.

Jon reached across the seat and found her small hand. He squeezed it, and brought it to rest on his thigh.

His hand was wonderfully magnificent in his strength and utter maleness. His long fingers seemed on fire with warmth and the simple contact sent delicious pleasure through her. Her heart was racing with desire.

How safe and protective she felt when he was near. Would she ever know such sweetness and care again? Trying not to think on this, she turned her attention to the road, mindful of each stroke of his powerful fingers. How could she ever bear to leave him? New thoughts, implausible thoughts were beginning to form. She was breathless as they reached the small town of St. Gabrielle.

St. Gabrielle's main thoroughfare was lined with ladies boutiques, a pharmacy, a hardware store, and a couple of restaurants. At the end of Main Street lay the town's picturesque waterfront park. Young mothers with strollers were leisurely chatting with friends along a waterfront walking path. Old men were laughing and playing chess under swaying palms. An old-fashioned gazebo was the park's centerpiece. Empty this late afternoon, during the summer months Sage could almost hear the music of small philharmonic bands and long political speeches made every Fourth of July.

To the west of the commons was a small fishing pier that jutted into the Gulf of Mexico. Fishermen lined either side of the railing and appeared to be doing more socializing than concerning themselves over the catch of the day.

Sage watched a windsurfer dance across the sparkling water passing too close to a small fishing boat. The entire scene was framed with enormous clouds that hung layer upon layer against a pale blue sky. All that was missing was a musical score from a vintage TV show to create Hollywood's version of small town Americana.

Sage could understand why Jon had not wanted America's attention brought to this peaceful place filled with gentle people.

The police station, like the town, was quaint, and housed in a red brick building with an arched doorway. City Hall was next door and directional signs pointed to town manager's office and various community services and departments.

Jon pulled into the parking space designated for the Chief of Police.

Inside, the small police department was filled with high tech computer equipment atop old oak desks.

A female dispatcher brightened at the sight of them and waved as she took another call. Passing her, Sage heard something about a cat and the fire department. She smiled realizing all the more how very far she was from LA and big city problems.

Jon led the way through the modest police station past his own office to a multi-use room with a battered wood conference table in its center.

René sat down at the first available chair and laid his head on the table.

"Coffee?" Jon asked them both.

René was noncommittal. Sage nodded.

Jon muttered their request to the officer who had followed them back and came back into the room moments later with three cups of coffee.

René ignored the coffee, Sage and Jon. His face facial muscles twitched in erratic spasms. His and his eyes darted around the room picking out objects but seemed unable to focus on any.

Jon sat opposite René and Sage took the head of the table next to him.

"Mr. Devereaux," Jon began, "who are you hiding from?"

René looked to Sage. His lower lip was quivering as he said softly, "I want to leave. I want to go home."

Sage nodded. In soothing low tones, she said quietly, "I understand, but first, we need you to answer a few questions."

René's face turned into a mask of terror, his voice constricted as he whimpered, "I want to lie down."

With a pitiful look of appeal, tears once again welling in his eyes, René collapsed again on the table.

Jon drew a jagged breath and turned to Sage. He slowly shook his head.

Rising, Jon said to René, "Mr. Devereaux, I'm going to put you into one of our holding cells and let you rest for a while. You are not under arrest but I am putting you into protective custody. The jailer will see that you have something to eat, and drink. I want you to calm down and we will talk later. Is that all right with you?"

"You will be safe there, René," Sage said in a whisper. René gave Sage and Jon a nod.

Sage managed a smile at him and held his hand as Jon left the room. A moment later, Jon returned bringing with him the officer who had served them coffee earlier.

Murmuring instructions to the officer, he helped René rise. After a bit of a shuffle of feet, René stood. In less than a second, they were gone, leaving Jon and Sage to stare at each other.

"That was going nowhere fast. Let's give him a couple of hours," Jon said drawing a hard breath. Shooting Sage a disarming smile, he added, "Come on, I'll buy you lunch. There's somewhere special I want to show you."

His smile had sent her pulse racing she knew she could deny him nothing. Leading her back to his SUV, this time he took great pains to gallantly open the door.

Though he seemed reluctant to leave her side, nevertheless, leave her he did to take his place behind the wheel.

Placing the key into the ignition, his eyes were compelling, magnetic as they slid down her face to focus entirely on her lips.

"Better get going," he said too quickly, "before I get arrested in front of my own damn station."

Sage laughed as Jon backed the Explorer out onto the street. Intent on their destination, he drove across town back to an obscure restaurant and bar with a neon sign that read, 'Paradise Bay. Home of the World's Best Cheeseburger.'

"Be right back," he said with a grin and was gone. Less than five minutes later, he returned with an oversized sack that filled the Explorer with the heady aroma of grilled burgers and homemade Texas fries. The smells were intoxicating.

"That smells good," Sage said with a backward glance at the bag. "But I take it you are going to make me wait for lunch."

Busy shifting gears, Jon got back on the highway and headed back toward the Sand Point Inn.

Halfway there, Jon pulled down a side road and took a single lane drive into an orange grove.

Where was he taking her? Sage wondered with a smile, and guessed he wanted to share a special picnic place on the water.

"I'm taking you to my house," he said answering her private thoughts.

Sage was pleased and found herself curious as to what type of house Jon would call home.

When the Explorer cleared the orange trees, Sage discovered a modest Spanish style home.

The home was small, constructed of pink coquina with a flat Spanish style roof. It was settled just off center on an acre of land. The view of the gulf was spectacular.

It was easy to see Jon living here, Sage thought looking about. It suited him.

The grounds were neatly kept with ferns relishing the shadows of shady oaks. Easy to keep tropical plants and shrubs grew around the house itself. The landscape had been well-planned and required little maintenance. A seventeen-foot center console fishing boat was moored to a small dock at land's end.

Jon brought the SUV to a complete stop. With a measure of pride, he said, "This is my place."

"It's lovely," Sage replied. He seemed pleased at her reaction.

"Actually," he explained a bit sheepishly, "I'm just renting. The house actually belongs to a retired couple from up north. Nice folks, but the wife's mother has gone into a nursing home and they won't be able to enjoy this home as much as they would like. So, I rent this place for a song and I think they like knowing the house is being occupied by the Chief of Police. It's quiet, peaceful and for me, for now, its home."

Sage heard just a trace of loneliness in his voice. Her every emotion longed to cover it. In her mind's eye, she saw LA with its eight million people. How lonely it was going to be without him there.

"Come on in," Jon said in welcome. He grabbed the bag from the back seat. "I'll show you around."

Without waiting for him to open the door, Sage stepped out of the Explorer and walked toward the back entrance.

A beautifully carved stone walkway led a few feet to the back of the house.

Jon unceremoniously opened the door to the kitchen and allowed her to pass.

The kitchen was small and boasted wide burgundy colored tile and fine oak cabinets. A single discarded coffee cup lay in the dish drain and outside of morning coffee, Sage guessed the kitchen enjoyed little use.

The kitchen opened to a small dining area with a light colored pine table with beige tile on the top of it. A large bowl decorated with chili peppers sat atop the table. It was filled with bright red apples and a cluster of green grapes.

The single room housed a Spanish style fireplace in one corner, and a large, comfortable floral sofa with matching high back chairs.

The television was small and the main focal point of the room was a double set of French doors with a breathtaking view of the Gulf of Mexico.

"Here," Jon said opening the doors, "let's get some fresh air in here."

With that a light breeze filled the house.

The invitation was irresistible and Sage walked out onto the red tiled porch. Oversized patio chairs were scattered about the broad porch and a porch swing swayed in the growing gulf breeze.

Sage glanced heavenward and saw thunderheads thickening. The bottoms of the heavy cumulous clouds were growing flat and darker by the minute.

A thunderstorm was less than an hour away. She could think of nowhere she would rather be than with Jon in the warm shelter of his home.

The waves were growing choppy. White caps swirled atop the waves. Looking across the gulf, she brought her attention to a boathouse near the house.

"The boat is mine," he said with self-satisfaction. "It may interest you to know that I am actually closer to you by boat than in driving distance."

Sage couldn't keep the laugh inside her. "That is good to know."

"Well, I did promise you lunch," Jon said turning back toward the kitchen.

"Perfect," Sage said with a smile. "Mind if I look around?"

"Help yourself," came Jon's easy reply.

The small house had only two bedrooms. The back bedroom was a guest room though it looked like it had been years since it was last occupied. The front room was Jon's.

The bath was neat and a bit Spartan with only Jon's after shave and electric shaver adorning the counter top.

Taking a second look at Jon's bedroom, Sage noted the McCall Security uniform across a wicker chair. She liked seeing it there.

The bedroom boasted an oak dresser with an exquisitely

carved mirror. The four-poster bed was unmade. It looked inviting, too inviting.

So, this was where Jon slept, she thought with a sharp intake of breath. Her mouth curved into an unconscious smile.

Two French doors in his bedroom opened onto the porch. She guessed Jon spent many a night enjoying the cool breeze that drifted in from the gulf. She knew she would.

"Let's eat out here," Jon called to her and she joined him on the open verandah.

He had taken the time to carefully place four cheeseburgers on a plate and a pile of fries in the bowl.

"This is perfect," Sage said her heart singing with joy. Without waiting for him to ask, she reached across the table and put one of the cheeseburgers on the plate and Jon offered her a hearty serving of golden steak fries that looked too perfect for ketchup. With her mouth watering with pleasure she brought the cheeseburger up to her lips. "Jon, these look great. Everything does."

"You look great," Jon said watching her. He had wanted to add, you look great here. Instead he popped open a beer and offered it to Sage.

"Sorry," he said sheepishly, "I'm out of diet sodas."

Looking at his own beer, he wondered when, if ever, he'd had diet sodas in this house? This is stupid. He should have served her something special but for the life of him couldn't think of what would ever be special enough for the beautiful Sage McCall.

Sitting across from him, cheeseburger in hand, her legs gathered under her Indian-style, she looked like a teenager.

Watching her take big bites of the cheeseburger, he felt his heart surge then grow tight, constricted with emotion. He could hardly believe his good fortune. Watching her, he knew this extraordinary beauty, who had eaten at some of the finest restaurants in the world, was sitting here with him, eating cheeseburgers.

"This is absolutely fabulous," she said her eyes shining.

Jon grinned, realizing he had pleased her. He wanted to please her!

Together, they watched as the dark clouds grew thicker.

The internationally famous cheeseburgers of Paradise Bay were lost on him this day. He was lost in beautiful heart-shaped lips, the rhythmic soft sound of her voice, and the luminous blue of her eyes.

Sage could only manage one cheeseburger though Jon ate two. He told Sage about a family of raccoons who traveled the length of his yard each night. He tossed the remaining cheeseburger and fries out onto a palmetto patch where the treats, surely, would be discovered later that night by the family.

"I suppose we should head back to town," Sage said realizing their meal was at an end.

Dark gray clouds had blackened the sky and the water was now choppy and rolled over the grassy bank of the yard. Jon's boat, though secured, bobbed like a toy. Even from this distance, Sage could hear the hollow sound of the boat scraping at its moorings.

"Let's let this storm pass before we leave," Jon said as the first heavy drops of rain splattered on the porch.

Though covered, it was only a matter of moments before the wind brought the rain under the canopy and across the porch. It stung at Sage's arms and legs in bites that left cold water droplets on exposed skin.

Knowing she should retreat to the safety inside the house,

she lingered just a few moments longer, watching the storm clouds churn and swirl in the black sky.

What had started in heavy drops had turned to a deluge of hard pounding rain.

With her every sense alive, she stood still, unable to take her eyes away from the torrential downpour. Her heart was pounding as she watched lightning flash across the sky. Its thunder ripped the heavens and rippled through her body, her ears ringing with its violent vibration.

"Let's get inside, young lady," Jon said gently touching her arm. His hand meant to guide, meant to protect, and touched her deep within her soul. He felt it too as she turned to him, lightning flashed a second time, this time unleashing a dark look of wanton desire in his eyes.

Her body ached for his touch.

"Jon," she said in a whisper as he brought her into his arms. It was all he needed to hear, her soft voice melting any doubts of resisting her.

He had stayed his every emotion too long. His need of her was physical and all-consuming.

Pushing back her head, he stared into her stormy blue eyes. He had to be sure. He had to be sure she wanted him not for this moment but for all time. He could settle for no less.

In his arms, her heartbeats were hammering in an erratic rhythm though his were far louder than her own.

Gazing into his dark eyes, Sage saw his need of her.

A smile crossed her lips and her small hand found its way to his cheek.

With the wind threatening to rip them apart, they stood motionless, gazing steady into each other's eyes. Not one single breath lay between them.

In his powerful arms, so far from the Hollywood Hills, she knew she had at last found home.

His arms tightened around her. His mouth came down heavy on her lips.

Her pulse quickened and his lips turned soft, sensual, and caressing. A hot ache grew within her. Blood surged from her fingertips to her toes warming that inside her which most belonged to him. Only and forever him.

Her arms found his broad shoulders as he easily lifted her.

Without bothering to close the French doors behind him, he carried her to his bed and laid her gently in its center.

In an instant, he was beside her, his mouth covering hers, his massive hands cupping her breasts, fondling them, groping them, and tearing at her shirt.

Her calm was shattered with each supple caress of his mouth. Her body strained to meet his in desire as his tongue gently began exploring the soft recess of her mouth.

Her nipples were swollen as her body strained upward into his and the thrill of his hardness had her own blood pounding in her brain.

The ecstasy was unbearable as his soft, passionate kisses explored the satin skin of her face, traveled slowly, sensually down her cheeks to the hollow of her neck, lingering there before moving across her creamy shoulders.

His fingers nimbly unbuttoned the top button of her shirt. His lips hungrily following in their trail, kissing, tasting the soft skin of her upper-breast all the while easing the lacy cup of her bra aside.

As his tongue began to caress each swollen nipple, her senses reeled with pleasure. She fought to pull his shirt from his waistband. At least she had her hand under the fabric of his shirt. He groaned with the pleasure of her touch as she kneaded and stroked the rippling hard muscles on his back.

He rose. His velvet eyes dark with passion as he pulled at his shirt and quickly stripped off his pants and shorts. His eyes never once left hers and she slid out of her tan shirt. The lacy bra fell aside exposing two perfectly shaped breasts.

Impatiently, he found the back of her shorts and slipped them down the silky lines of her outer thighs, taking her panties with them. His body moved to cover hers. His hands slid upward to her soft round bottom, kneading each cheek as she writhed overloaded in carnal sensations.

Her hands explored the hard lines of his back, his waist, and slid down to his hips, and rock hard ass.

A scream of pleasure ripped through her as she felt her skin become heated where his touched her.

His mouth once again claimed her, bruising her lips.

Her body burned with desire.

His muscular foreleg found its way between her silky thighs and, with ease, he parted her legs.

She could bear it no more as she welcomed him into her body.

"Sage," he cried entering in her.

Locked together, they began to move in rhythmic sensuality like the waves upon the gulf waters, rising in rhapsody before falling in divine desire.

His breath came in searing cries that electrified the scorching sweetness that raced uncontrolled through her senses. Gusts of uncontrollable pleasure exploded over and over until she was lost to everything but the movement of his body within her.

As if unable to hold himself in check any longer, she felt his body rise, strain, and heard his cry of surrender.

His body spent, he rolled off of her but took care to bring her into his side.

It was over. She was his.

On the verge of drifting into dreamy sleep, she savored the smoldering embers of their fire. She was so completely comfortable to lie with him, wrapped in the warmth of his powerful arms.

The room was filled with his heavy breathing, and Sage knew he had fallen asleep. She desperately wanted to remember this moment, but the combination of the heat his body offered, the even rise and fall of his chest, and the steady pounding of rain against the roof and windows were lulling her into a deep and dreamless sleep.

Even in sleep, he reached out to her to hold her, treasure her. He pulled her closer still and she heard the soft sound of her name on his breath.

Oh God, she though blinking away her tears, she realized she was falling in love with Jon Maddux. The thought sent a wakeful ache though her as all the old reasons argued with her heart.

"Sage," she heard him whisper from heavy sleep. "I don't want you to go anywhere...without me."

"How can I, Jon," she replied in a whisper. Her heart fluttered wildly. Oh sweet impossible dream, her soul cried longingly, perhaps, perhaps they would find a way.

Weightless in his arms, she fell into a deep sleep where all dreams came true.

CHAPTER TEN

Outside the house, the fast moving thunderstorm with a band of heavy rain had moved inland. Though, some distance away, Sage could still hear the distant rumble of thunder, the spray of wind sheers and lightening heralding its path across the dry land.

Left in its stead was the last of a light, soft, steady rain that filled the air with a clean, fresh fragrance of renewal. The only loud sound was the drainpipe, just outside the bedroom water still rushing down its pipe sending the overflow into the already saturated ground.

Sometime during her sleep, she must have gathered the bed sheets around her. They felt cool and silky to her skin.

Most of all, she felt Jon.

His legs brown and firm, were wrapped over her smaller limbs, his arms around her shoulders and his long fingers holding her still. She was keenly aware of his hard muscular chest and his trim waist that curved to the muscular thighs. His body felt and was magnificent.

Pressing her face into his chest, she caught the arresting scent of his after-shave. Content to make this moment last through eternity, she lay in his arms listening to the still quiet of the house.

From somewhere in the living room or kitchen, she heard the soft clicking of a clock marking time. She should fully wake; instead, she nestled down into the feathery softness of the bed.

Lying on her right side, she snuggled closer into Jon hard body. She felt sated and luxuriant in a euphonic sensuality that tantalized her skin and body in physical pleasure.

Even before she ever opened her eyes, she felt his eyes, warm and intent upon her. Slowly, she opened her eyes to find his face only inches from hers.

Drops of moisture clung to his damp forehead and his skin glistened in a light sheen that gave his tan an illustrious glow.

Jon was breathtakingly handsome with his warm brown eyes that were almost startling in secret expression. His face melted into a smile that touched her heart and she saw a new contentment on his handsome face that hadn't been there before. Jon Maddux had found in her, peace.

"Hi," he said leaning closer to her to give her a soft kiss. The sensual feel of his lips sent her reeling with desire.

"Hi," she replied in a whisper when his sweet kiss was complete. Too content with the moment to move, she lay close to him. Regretting she had to, she asked, "What time is it?"

"Not sure," he said, his voice deep in drowsy sleep. "The world stopped a couple of hours ago for me and I'm not anxious to ever restart it again."

Sage smiled and snuggled closer still, the rain outside turning into a soft drizzle. She wanted this moment to last.

The shrill pitch of a cell phone broke the spell. Both Sage and Jon rose from the bed each looking for the direction of the ring. It was Jon's cell. Sage fell back against the pillow.

Jon reached for his phone and answered.

"Yeah, what's up," he said to the caller. After a pause, his face changed. Gone were the soft lines, replaced with a dark profile that was sharp and alert. His lips tightened into a grim smile as he said after a short pause, "All right, thanks for calling."

"What is it?" Sage asked gathering sheets around her breasts.

Jon deposited the phone to the nightstand. With a frown, he pulled her into his arms one last time and said softly, "Honey, we need to go."

Sage lingered only a moment. She knew their time had run out.

Pulling away from him, she rose, tossing back the light covers and grabbing her discarded shorts, shirt, and underwear.

"Do I have time for a quick shower," she asked as she hurried into the bathroom. She had decided she was going to take one whether they had time or not.

"Yeah, "Jon said, "I guess we both do but not together."

Sage blushed.

"There's been a break in the case. They found bite marks on the bow."

Sage stopped dead in her tracks and looked back to Jon, "Human?"

Jon shook his head, "No, dog bites. Little ones."

Dog bites, Sage repeated in silence. Incredibly, then she knew...Pepe!

"We need to get back to the Sand Point Inn," she said as she hurried into the bathroom. Breathless with rage, she yanked the shower curtain back, stepped into the shower and pulled it back in place harder than necessary. She twisted the knob and relished the instant flow of hot water that did little to cool her fury. Enraged, she scrubbed her body too hard, too fast, and too angry with herself to put it into words!

"How could I have not seen this?" she shrieked slamming the faucet shut. "Hillary!"

Why, she asked herself, and then answered: of course, publicity for the show. Why else? Quickly she scrubbed her body with a washcloth and shampooed her hair. Less than five minutes later, she stepped out of the shower. Toweling herself, she dressed quickly.

She drew a cool breath. Who else had access to the only dog on the set besides Hillary? Only one other person: Connard.

She replayed the night of her attack. Connard was the right height, the right weight. Only the image had seemed heavier, more powerful and evil.

Why had she not considered Connard? Did his over-the-top effeminate manners throw her deductive thought process to the wind?

"Do you mind?" Jon said stepping into the shower.

"How could I have been so stupid?" Sage said slipping out of the shower. She grabbed a towel and took note of the hot sudsy water was already rushing over Jon's hard body. Sage tried to ignore the long powerful lines of his shoulders, his nice hard butt and the way the soap slid down his distinctively muscular thighs and calves.

"Don't be too hard on yourself," Jon cautioned her, "the bite marks could have occurred prior to the incident. We need to talk to Hillary and that fellow she works with...what's his name?"

"Connard." Sage spat over the blow dryer she was using.

Two minutes later, Jon pulled back his shower curtain, and smiled at her.

"Throw me that towel," Jon said. A wicked glint flickered as his dark eyes met hers. With a fresh blush, Sage smiled at him and handed him a fresh towel from the rack behind her.

As good as he looked with clothes, he looked better without them.

Jon was out of the shower and dressed by the time she finished drying her hair.

"You're beautiful," he said with a smile. With a single stride, he crossed to her and placed his hands on her small shoulders.

His lips parted hers in a light and tender kiss. She quivered at the sweetness, her entire body pressing into his powerful arms and her mind reliving each sensual moment of their passion. She wanted more.

Keeping her in his arms, he held her dearly before gently pushing her away so that he was able to look down at her face. His dark brown eyes studying her eyes, her lips, her neck, her face as though he wanted to place this moment in his memory for a lifetime.

"I suppose we should go," he said, a roguish grin curling his lips with delicious mischief.

Sage laughed. There were other things to do besides taking the handsome Chief of Police back to his bed, but for the moment she couldn't think of a single one.

"All right," she agreed trying to recall a time when she felt as happy.

"Woman!" He groaned gently pushing her out of his arms, "One more come hither stare and we'll be back in bed. Come on, you nymph, let's get out of here. You are just too damn tempting."

With light, easy banter dancing between them, her hand in his, he gently pulled her though the house, her easy laughter leaving a trail in their wake.

Outside, he opened the door to the Explorer and gave her one sweet kiss before he rounded the vehicle to the driver's seat.

"Thanks for lunch," Sage giggled as Jon backed the Explorer out of the parking space.

She watched as his playful mood shifted to quiet reserve.

"The dog could put Hillary at the crime scene," Jon said driving through the orange grove to the main highway. As he turned onto the road, he added, "It wouldn't take that much physical strength to fire the arrow into Evan or injure Jamie Wolf?"

"She's familiar with the set," Sage agreed. Was Hillary capable of such physical violence? In her mind's eye, she replayed the moment she was hit; was it Hillary who had attacked her?

"Hillary doesn't strike me as an outdoor kind of girl who would know about wild mushrooms," Jon said, a thin smile on his lips. He brushed his fingers through his short hair and kept his eyes on the road ahead of them. "She was sick as a dog when we found her."

"She wouldn't have poisoned the crew with the mushrooms then left half a plate in her motor home for us to discover. Would she?"

Trying to put all the pieces together, she took in a long breath. "This brings us to another point. Is she working with an accomplice? Maybe the two incidents are not related."

Easing the Explorer over to the center line, he gave a small armadillo on the side of the road a wide berth. Righting the vehicle in the lane, he glanced at Sage and said. "You said yourself she enjoys publicity? Do you think she wanted it that bad?"

Sage laughed, "You can never be too thin, too rich, or have too much exposure in Hollywood, good or bad."

"Would René Devereaux be frightened of Hillary Kenyon?"

She was silent.

As they passed an open pasture, she watched several white cattle egrets walk gracefully in the trail of a small herd of Black Angus. Off in the distance an osprey soared toward a huge nest atop a utility pole then it vanished into an oversized pile of wood.

"Sage, are you still sure it was a man who attacked you in the kitchen?"

"Yes, yes, I am sure. The person who hit me was taller than Hillary, and had more bulk. The voice was hoarse, raspy, and low. It was a man's voice."

"What about Connard?"

"I have thought of that. Connard is very slim. The man who hit me had more bulk."

"And you've had so much experience in being hit by a man?"

Sage laughed. "I can assure you, I'm a third degree black belt; I've been hit many times. I've been thinking since you got the call about the bow but I'm sure that the hit I received came from a man, not a woman."

"Third degree black belt?" Jon said with a sudden grin, "I'm impressed...again."

Sage snuggled up to him, "Your father doesn't own a security firm in Los Angeles. And I've been taking those classes since I was a child."

"You're the woman of my dreams."

"But I live in LA, " Sage reminded him softly, "and I'm going to have to go back there."

"We're going to talk about that," Jon said firmly reaching out for her hand.

"Well, without completely ruling Hillary out of the picture, we know that whoever our suspect is, he or she is well-organized, has outdoor skills and some working knowledge of poisonous mushrooms. And technically, he hasn't killed anyone."

"Yet," Jon added as they approached a minivan bearing Michigan tags, "and there was the attempt on Jamie's life and yours."

Jon easily overtook the vehicle and passed the family of four.

A woman in her early forties was studying a Florida road map, two teens in the back were asleep and the man looked relaxed and oblivious to the passing police vehicle. With luggage piled high atop the minivan, they grew small in Sage's side mirror as Jon distanced his SUV from the out-of-state visitors.

"The kitchen was dark and the set was dark when Jamie came upon it, so whoever hit Jamie and attacked me knows both places well."

Sage's cell rang, it was her father.

"Hi, honey," he said, "I thought you should know that between the negative publicity and pressure from the network, the studio is canceling *Murder in Florida*. Nick is on the phone right now with Jeff Sanders. They are going to send everyone home."

"But we need more time to find out who…"

Her father didn't let her finish. "Nick says he's not willing to risk anyone else's life and is pretty adamant about this."

"What about the crew?"

"Not to worry, Nick is bringing the same group back for a new TV movie he is planning to film in Arizona. By the way, your sister Fallon is going to star in it. Nick's going to direct this one."

"Good for Fallon, Dad, but we are hardly close to finding out who did these crimes."

"Honey, I have to go. I'm swamped with work here in LA," her Father concluded. He sounded tired. "Frankly, Sage, I need you and our guys back here for several high priority assignments. I'll let you know when I learn more. Take care, Sweetie, I'll call later. You're doing a great job."

Sage sat stunned. While she wasn't surprised, this was too soon and too sudden. She dropped her lashes to hide the unexpected hurt.

"What's wrong?" Jon asked.

Trying to swallow the hard lump her throat, she said softly, "The network has cancelled the show. Nick is closing the production and is going to send everyone home."

"When?" Jon said angrily. "I won't have time to close this investigation and it's going to be next to impossible if everyone leaves. When is this going to happen?"

Sage shook her head. "The studio will probably send the contestants and members of the crew within the week. The rest will close up shop and leave shortly thereafter."

Jon gripped the steering wheel a little tighter, his brows set in a straight line and his eyes narrowed in displeasure. "You may have the okay from McMasters Studio but you'll need one from me. I have no intention of sweeping this under the rug because some studio head in Hollywood wants everyone back in California."

Sage could think of nothing to say. She knew as well as he did, without clear evidence or a single suspect, there was nothing he could do to keep the company in Florida.

The distance between them grew unbearable. Already the ache of loneliness was choking her breath. She watched as a dark shadow passed over his handsome features. She wanted to touch him, assure him, but didn't know what to say.

His warm brown eyes raked her face, her lips, before melting deep within her eyes touching her soul. Turning his attention to the road, he cleared his throat. In a soft voice that deepened in sensuality, he said, "Sage, I don't want you to go."

She stared at his well-defined profile unable to speak, unable to say she didn't want to leave him, either.

In a husky whisper his voice broke. "You could stay."

Sage looked outside to the window. Her vision transfixed on a billboard that offered tourists a free breakfast for a hotel night's stay.

She shook her head. "You could come to California."

A tortuous flash blazed deep in his dark eyes and thrust a cut deep inside her chest.

"Yeah," she said looking down at her hands that suddenly had nothing to do. "I know"

"Even if I came to California, Sage," he said surprising her, "what would I do?"

Her heart jumped with the possibility. "'I'm sure that my Dad…"

"Sage," he interrupted with words as hard as stone, "I can't go to work for your father, Sage. I have to be my own man."

Though his words had sounded hard, his eyes smoldered with longing.

"Look," he said with more tenderness than she could bear, "we don't have to worry about this now. We can figure something out. Right now, we need to question Hillary. All we have at the moment is more questions than answers."

He was right, Sage thought trying to stay the ache in her heart. She offered him a sweet smile and saw it returned.

"I don't know what's going to happen, Sage," he said. She

could hear the strain in his voice, "But I'm not ready to lose you to California."

Sage gave him a short nod and took what felt like her first breath since ending the call to her father.

Arrival at the Sand Point Inn turn-off took away any words, thoughts, or longings. Focusing on breathing, she stared at the edge of the road assured that somehow, they would make this work.

At the moment, right or wrong, she had to concentrate on finding who shot Evan and was frightening René Devereaux. Was it the same person who had poisoned the crew and assaulted her?

With her growing feelings toward Jon safely tucked in her heart, the future would simply have to wait.

She had to find out who had harmed so many. Sage was beginning to believe while Hillary Kenyon was no longer her primary suspect, she was part of the puzzle.

Pepe's bites on the bow placed Hillary at the scene but had she shot Evan? She would know in a matter of moments.

A small contingency of reporters and news vans were still parked outside on the grassy entrance of the barred gate. The Explorer's return drew little attention and no frantic rush toward the police vehicle. Good, Sage thought, they hadn't gotten wind of René Devereaux's involvement.

A security guard Sage didn't recognize waved them through the gate. Sage gave him a short wave as they passed him.

Jon drove through the main parking lot to the motor homes.

Hillary was outside with her car keys in hand, her designer handbag flung over her shoulder and Pepe carefully tucked in her arm.

Dressed in an *Armani* black silk top and matching slacks, her hair was impeccably twisted into a neat French twist. She looked dazzling as she jerked her *Gianni Versace* sunglasses away from her eyes. She glared at Sage and Jon as the SUV pulled next to her.

Her makeup flawless, her mouth twisted in an aggravated curl.

"Hillary," Sage called out as she got out of the Explorer. "We need to ask you a few questions."

Impatiently, Hillary shifted her slight weight to one foot, digging her designer shoes into the pavement.

"Now what?" She snapped, her silky voice thick in defiance. Raising a fine arched eyebrow, she turned slightly and inserted the key into her silver Porsche.

"Look, whatever issue the two of you are having, you will have to solve for yourself," she explained in a huff, "but I've just found a suitable dog groomer for Pepe and I'm on my way into town right now."

Jon's eyes narrowed and grew hard. "Your dog is going to have to wait."

"That's quite impossible," Hillary snapped with a wave of her hand at him.

"We can talk here," Jon said in a cool tone, "or we can talk at the station. Your choice."

Glancing at her Rolex, Hillary had to brush away her diamond tennis bracelet to read the dial. "Okay, you have exactly three minutes."

Jon looked at Sage as though not quite believing Hillary would question his authority. The woman was either mad, insane, or had no respect for the law.

"Answer his questions, Hillary," Sage warned her.

For a breathless moment she refused to even soften her

impatience, but taking heed of Sage's word of warning and the dark look across the face of the police chief, Hillary finally shrugged her perfectly shaped shoulders.

Jon did not wait for her compliance. "As you are aware, Ms. Kenyon, we found the bow which we believed was used to shoot Evan Davis. We have discovered it had small dog bites on the weapon. We believe that the bites came from your dog."

Hillary squirmed and shifted Pepe from her right arm to her left.

Pepe who had been watching the exchange was suddenly alert to the mention of his name. Ignoring Sage, he gave Jon his full attention, his small eyes black and riddled with apprehension. His diminutive lips curled slightly to reveal tiny white teeth. Though his small white legs dangled freely under Hillary's hold, and his every white curl was in place, Pepe had obviously decided he wasn't going anywhere without a fight.

Hillary tucked Pepe closer to her.

"We can take a mold of your poodle's teeth to confirm a match, Ms. Kenyon," Jon said his eyes blazing in warning.

"You can't prove anything." Hillary snapped, "It's my word against yours!"

"We can prove everything, Hillary," Sage said pushing out her words. "And mark this; I'll make sure Nick McMasters will be aware of your cooperation in this investigation or lack of it."

"You little witch," Hillary spat, "you wouldn't dare!"

Jon remained quiet. Hillary had just been threatened with exposure to the Studio, the Hollywood community, and the possibility of arrest and still she kept her silence. She held her poise one moment longer before she slumped, and gave Sage and Jon a forced smile.

"All right, All right," Hillary hissed, "I was there the

night you found Evan's body. I came in the back door as you entered. It was dark, you didn't see me."

Sage swallowed hard. She was numb with rage. She felt Jon touch her shoulder. It did little to soothe her anger.

"You came in the back way," Jon repeated as though to prompt Hillary to say more.

"Yes," Hillary replied. Now that she had begun, she seemed almost eager to explain her participation. "I couldn't sleep that night. Pepe had wanted to go out. I saw lights on the set and went over to find out what was going on. I heard you say poor Evan was dead. I was about to leave when I almost stumbled over your security guard, what's his name."

Hillary ignored Sage's sharp intake of breath.

"He opened his eyes," Hillary said miserably, "and just looked at me."

"My God," Sage said taking a step toward Hillary, "why didn't you say something? Jamie Wolfe nearly bled to death."

"Well, he didn't look that bad," Hillary whimpered.

Sage was too furious to speak.

Hillary glanced down at her polished nails and yawned. "Like I said, he didn't look so bad; besides, he's not my responsibility."

"Every damn thing on this set is your responsibility, Hillary." Sage reminded her. For one incredible moment, Sage thought she saw Hillary flinch.

With guilt in her eyes, Hillary bit her lip and looked away. When she turned back, she had regained her composure.

"Where did you find the bow?" Jon asked keeping his emotions in check.

"It was already on the dock," Hillary stammered. "Pepe found it. I took it away from him and threw it into the water. At that time, I didn't know Evan had been shot with the stupid thing. I just didn't want Sage or Double K to know I was on the set. You have to realize, as a director, I have enough day to day problems of my own to deal with."

"Didn't it occur to you that it was an odd place to find a bow? Evan Davis was dead; it could have been part of the crime scene investigation?" Jon asked unwilling to believe anyone was so stupid. In a low growl he continued, "Had Jaime Wolfe died, I could have charged you as an accessory to murder."

Hillary gave Jon a hostile glare but said nothing.

"Did you see anything or anyone else?" Jon asked sharply.

Hillary shook her head. "No, I saw nothing more. Now your three minutes are up! Can I leave? I just can't be any later than I already am."

With that, she turned and gently deposited Pepe on the passenger seat. Pepe sat and waited for Hillary to join him.

"Where do you think you are going?" Jon demanded.

"I do have an appointment as I mentioned earlier with Pepe's groomer. I've told you all I know. I'm sorry about that security man of yours but I can't tell you anything more. Now, if I'm not under arrest, I need to leave."

Jon folded his arms in front of him. His eyes were black and dazzling with fury.

"I don't want you leaving the county or the state, Ms. Kenyon," he warned her ignoring Hillary's sneer. "Is that clear?"

Hillary laughed and slid into the driver's seat. "Perfectly," she snapped as she turned the Porsche's powerful engine on. Over the motor's whine, she cried, "You forget I'm not going anywhere. I'm the director!"

With a slight wave of her beautifully shaped hand, Hillary

circled her car around them in a hairpin turn and headed down the main road.

"She actually is a good director," Sage said watching the Porsche speed away. "But she's a poor actress. I actually think she's telling us the truth, even though I could strangle her for not alerting us about Jamie. The kid could have bled to death."

Jon stared down at her then burst out into a hearty laugh. "The kid, as you put it, is only two or three years younger than you."

Sage grinned and turned her head away.

Jon rose to his full height and said just under his breath, "I have a laundry list of charges I could bring against her. At least we found, Jamie's angel. It wasn't you after all. It was Hillary."

"Yes," Sage agreed. Hillary was his angel in white as she remembered seeing Hillary dressed in her white flowing nightgown that night. With a toss of her long blond hair, she laughed. "Imagine anyone thinking Hillary is an angel."

Across the parking lot, Sage could see groups of cast and crew headed toward the event tent.

"Look, it's almost dinner time," Sage said with a glance at her watch, "Why don't you stay?"

Jon smiled. "I will for a quick bite but just to be with you. Then, my angel, I'll have to head to town and see if René Devereaux is ready to give us more information."

On the way back to the tent, Sage and Jon looked toward the dock and found a bright shiny twenty-five foot sport fisherman moored to the end of it. The boat looked empty.

"Where did that come from?" Sage asked, her first thought being a reporter had found his way to the Sand Point Inn by water.

Halfway down the dock, she was relieved to see Oz pop up from the cabin. With a big grin toward Jon and Sage, he motioned them to come aboard.

"Yours?" Jon called out admiring the boat with its walk-around cabin with a custom built hard top. The sleek white lines and silver railing around the bow glistened in the late afternoon sky.

"All mine," came his proud reply. "I bought her a week ago from a dealer in Crystal River."

"She's beautiful," Sage agreed, genuinely thrilled with Oz's new acquisition.

"Permission to come aboard, Captain?" Jon said already taking the step onto the boat.

Oz laughed and stepped out of Jon's way. Onboard, Jon turned and offered Sage his hand.

"Welcome to the Carol Ann," Oz said swinging his arms proudly to show off the fishing boat.

Trying not to let the sadness steal her smile, she looked about, realizing Oz had named the boat after his late daughter.

"What's she got?' Jon asked looking at the massive 225 outboard motor.

Leaving Jon and Oz to discuss the powerful engine and complement electronics, Sage went below to the cabin. It was small but offered a bed and a small galley.

Looking about the neatly trimmed cabin, she saw two gas cans in the galley. They should be secured, she thought, but was sure Oz would take care of this detail before he ever left the marina.

"How are you going to get her back to LA?" Sage asked returning to the deck.

"I'll trailer her out to California," Oz said pointing out the boat's trailer at the far side of the parking lot, "but not before I spend some time fishing with my brother in east Texas."

"Look," Oz said sounding very excited, "It's about time for the caterer to set up but I'd like to give you two a quick inaugural spin right after dinner?"

"Not me," Jon replied with a note of regret. "I'm afraid I have to head back to town for some unfinished business."

Oz looked disappointed.

"How about you, Sage?" He asked. His face brightened with anticipation of her reply.

"I'd love to, Oz," Sage replied with regret, "but unfortunately I have a lot of paperwork. How about tomorrow?"

Oz grinned. "Tomorrow it is!"

"By the way, what's for dinner?" Sage asked as she climbed out of the boat to the dock.

"Buddy's Bodacious Barbeque, your recommendation."

"Congratulations on the boat," Sage called to Oz. "She's a real beauty."

Jon easily stepped from the boat to the dock and they walked away from Oz and the Navigator.

"Hungry?" Sage asked Jon as they reached the parking lot.

"I'm hungry for a lot of things, but right now, I will settle for dinner." Jon said under his breath.

Even before they reached the tent, the succulent smell of rich barbeque filled the air.

Sage wasn't surprised to find Double K, Cowboy Bob, Reese, and Jamie Wolfe eating at the far end of the tent. Her security team was almost finished when Sage and Jon joined them with their plates.

They sat down with her men and began eating.

"Look guys," Sage began in low tones, "keep this under

wraps but it looks like Nick McMasters is going to close down the production."

No one looked surprised.

"Too much bad publicity," she continued. "My dad says it's all over the news. The network has backed away from the series."

Double K pushed himself away from the table. "So when is Jeff Saunders going to tell everyone?"

"My guess is there will be a major announcement tomorrow some time," Sage replied.

Cowboy Bob whistled in anticipation of the uproar the news would create.

"Shouldn't be too much of a blow to anyone," Sage added, "Nick is going to use most of the crew on a feature film which is scheduled to start in four weeks. Fallon's going to star in it."

Jamie Wolfe stopped eating and grinned. "That's great," he said with a sparkle in his eye. "Any chance I could get assigned to that project?'

Sage returned his smile; she knew he had a crush on her beautiful sister.

"What about Hillary?" Double K asked with a frown.

Sage shook her head. "She's Nick's problem; but sorry guys, no vacations for any of you. The firm is overloaded with assignments right now. Dad needs everyone back."

The men nodded in unison. Each in their own way looked relieved and happy to leave Florida for the bright lights and excitement of Hollywood.

"Keep this between us," Sage reminded them and was immediately greeted with mummers of compliance. Sage nodded her head in silence.

"Well, we've got a bit of work to do," Double K said rising from the table.

Cowboy Bob, Reese and Jamie were immediately to their feet. With nods toward Jon and Sage they left, Jamie grabbing another slice of pie as they passed the dessert table.

Jon ate a few more bites then dropped his fork onto his plate. He was no longer interested in eating.

"I have to get back to the station and see if René has calmed down enough to talk," he said looking around the tent. With a wicked grin, he added, "The only bright side to all of this is the Mayor and his group of cronies are getting the short end of the stick. They had banked on scoring big when the show came out."

"I'll walk you out," Sage said as she rose to follow him.

Silently they walked to the Ford Explorer.

"I thought you wanted us to leave," Sage teased trying to cheer him as they reached the vehicle.

"Yeah," Jon said his dark eyebrows slanted in a frown. "I did. But that was before I fell in love with you."

CHAPTER ELEVEN

Sage felt her heart jump as she raised her eyes to study his handsome face.

Jon did not turn away; he held his gaze steady. His velvet brown eyes were smoldering with the raw honesty of his words. His lips curled tenderly and he gently placed both strong hands on her shoulders and pulled her to him.

Watching her reaction, his dark eyes filled with shifting stars.

Sage stood astonished. The flesh beneath his fingers was on fire. With his words ringing in her ears, waves of euphoria washed over her. Unexpected, his words had caught her off-guard and took her by complete surprise.

He had said he was falling in love with her and she knew it was true. Tears threatened to spill down her heart-shaped face.

Before she could reply, he brought a single finger to her lips. His eyes were full of sparkle, his smile sweet as he silenced her. His gaze was soft as a caress. His eyes were dancing with light.

"Don't say a word, honey," he said in a whisper. "Now is not the time and this is not the place. We'll talk later."

She stared at him in silence.

His handsome features relaxed a bit. He took in a long breath as if to will himself back to earth. "I've got to get back to town, and question René Devereaux. He's had plenty of time to settle down. I want you to rest. I have a hunch I can do more with him by myself. I'll call you when I'm finished."

"All right," Sage agreed.

She sounded so reasonable to her own ears, so mature and sophisticated when all she wanted do was stop the world from spinning. He was right this was not the time and this was not the place to say more about their feelings. He was right about René, too. Without any of the television show staff present, he might feel safe, safe enough to tell Jon what he knew.

She looked down at the ground then back to Jon.

"If I'm not present, René might talk. It's worth a shot." Sage said allowing the gentle off shore breeze to finish her sentence. She looked across the water to the setting sun and shyly bowed her head, hiding a secret smile.

The sunset was dazzling. Long streams of rose-colored pink twisted with shafts of violet and intertwined with orange rays of light creating a startling panorama of color that stretched endlessly across the horizon.

The gulf waters were darkening to a deep azure blue and moved in lazy motion carried along by a fresh breeze.

Sage slowly turned back to Jon, and found his eyes fixed on her face. The look of respect and adoration was undeniable. She could only offer him a warm smile and a nod of her head.

Hurry back to me, she wanted to whisper but instead said, "I'll look forward to talking to you later."

He gave her a curt nod and pivoted but turned back again to kiss her forehead.

"Come, walk with me," he said in a husky whisper, "before I forget what I should be doing instead of standing here like a teenager looking at you."

Sage laughed and resisted the urge to curl her arm about him. Too many eyes would be watching them in so open a space. For now, she wanted to keep this special feeling private between them.

They crossed the parking lot in silence. Hillary's Porsche was sitting beside Jon's Explorer and there was no sign of her.

"I'll call you," Jon promised opening the door. Pulling her close he brought her face to his before his hand possessively slid down to her soft round bottom. Giving it an ever so soft squeeze, he grinned wickedly and his eyes warmed in a gentle smile.

"Gotta go," he said his voice now strained with desire.

Sage nodded and stepped away from the vehicle.

"Bye for now," she said in a soft whisper not sure she wanted him to go.

Jon winked at her and a second later he was gone, driving too fast away from the Sand Point Inn and her. The sooner he left, she thought with a smile, the sooner he would return.

Like a child she watched his SUV barrel down the long drive.

Walking back to her room, she tried to focus on the spectacular sunset, which was caressing the gulf waters. The sun's bottom tip was dipping into the gulf setting the water on fire with color.

So absorbed in a quiet moment of euphoria, she barely noticed Double K walking up to her.

"What's up?" he said softly. "Did René Devereaux fess up?"

Sage shook her head. "Not a word. He's too upset to talk. Jon has gone back into town to speak to him."

Double K grunted and ground his fist into his palm. "I should be the one interrogating him. I'm not constrained by all that legal mumbo jumbo."

"Like the Miranda Rights?" Sage said with a laugh. Double K grinned.

Sage didn't bother to hide her snicker. "He's not under arrest, though Jon is holding him as a material witness to a crime."

"Well," Double K growled, "He did have access to the kitchen."

Sage grew thoughtful. "I did and I have gone through that moment a hundred times in my mind. My attacker was stronger and leaner."

"But," Double K said in low tones, "it was dark, and you know as well as I do shadows, movement, types of clothing could distort an image."

A sudden chill ran through Sage and she took in a sharp intake of breath. Sounding more confident than she felt, she said, "Well, he's in custody now. Jon has gone to question him. We'll get our chance to question him."

"What about now?" Double K snapped not willing to let this go.

"Now, there isn't a lot we can do but if it will make you happier I promise we'll talk to him tomorrow, one way or the other."

Double K grunted and Sage could tell he didn't want to wait until tomorrow to grill the man who may have hurt her.

"Well, me and the boys got some rest today and we're planning on staying on top of everything tonight. You look tired. Tomorrow isn't going to be any easier. Why don't you take off and hit the sack. I'll keep an eye on everything here. Come on, I'll walk you back to your room."

Silently they walked back to her room. Sage had dismissed the possibility of René Devereaux. Why? Because he had shown fragility? He was the right height though he did seem a bit too heavy. Double K could be right. In the darkness, shadows could have distorted his figure.

Criminals from petty thieves to the serial killers were known for their skill of deceptions. Was René the cowering victim or a deadly predator? How better to deflect and redirect his crimes than to feign terror toward an unnamed suspect? He had played his part well. Looking at him with new eyes, she now wondered if perhaps they'd caught the culprit after all.

By the time they reached the door, she began to doubt herself all the more. This was an easy out but she didn't want to make another misstep in this investigation. She wanted to talk to Jon before he talked to René.

"Try to rest a bit," Double K said giving her a short squeeze, "Me and the guys will keep an eye on things."

Sage had barely closed the door when the motel phone rang.

It was the Mayor of St. Gabrielle.

"Good evening, Miss McCall," he began a bit too cheerful for her current mood. "I wanted to call you and assure you that you had the support of our town and my personal offer of assistance. We want to do everything in our power to make your television show a success."

"Thank you," Sage heard herself respond. She wasn't about to tell the Mayor that the Studio was already making plans to close down the production. News of that would travel soon enough. "Jeff Sanders is really the person you need to be talking to Mayor Frederick. I'm only the Security Chief for the location."

"Well, just the same," the Mayor drawled in a whiny southern accent, "I just wanted to you to know we're standing by you and the Studio."

"I appreciate your taking the time to call," she said ending their call. "Have a wonderful evening."

"You as well," he replied slowly.

He sounded as though he wanted to say more but allowed her to end the conversation on her goodbye.

Returning the phone to the cradle, Sage couldn't understand why the Mayor was contacting her but her short and to the point response toned the nature of the call.

She could only guess that in calling her he was hoping to glean some inside information. She was sure the media was hinting the production might close. This wouldn't be a big surprise to anyone, including the Mayor.

Grabbing up the employment histories and background information from the dresser, she wanted to call Jon and she wanted to go over the information again. She turned on the television but ignored the rerun of her favorite sitcom.

Glancing at her alarm clock, she saw it was now almost seven thirty. She put in a call to Jon but his cell was turned off. She left a message only asking him to return her call.

Sitting Indian style on the bed, she began to read but an hour and a-half later could find no new clues in the employment records or backgrounds of the contestants.

Her cell rang breaking the silence of the room.

"Hi," Jon's voice said over the line. He sounded tired. "How are you?"

"Tired," came her weary reply, and an instant smile crossed her face. "How's Mr. Devereaux?"

"He's seems to have settled down a bit but is still refusing to talk. Maybe he doesn't know anything as he claims or maybe he just hasn't put the pieces together yet. Either way, he says he wants to stay in the holding cell at the jail." Jon stated matter-a-factly. "I spoke to him for quite a while and he seems to be getting more comfortable with me. If he's comfortable, he'll talk."

"Double K seems to think that René might be the man who attacked me. I'm not sure, my attacker was about that height but I had the impression he was leaner."

"Yeah, that thought crossed my mind. He doesn't seem bright enough but then he could be smarter than the both of us. Anyway, he had his day to settle down; tomorrow, we're going to get down to business."

"The mayor called," Sage informed him.

"That pompous ass. What the hell did he want?" Jon growled into the phone.

"To let me know that he and the town are supporting the production."

"I told you before the Mayor is an opportunist. He and his group of buddies' bought the Sand Point Inn. When the show airs, he'll make a neat little profit. If the show closes now, he'll lose his investment. He was in with me earlier and angry, of course, at me for not resolving this problem. Wait until he gets the official news tomorrow. I'm sure all hell is going to break loose."

"This isn't the first time you have had a run in with the Mayor."

"Hardly," Jon said sarcastically. "That guy's had it in for me ever since I gave him a DUI for drunk driving. And I don't mean a few drinks. After a local football game, he nearly ran over a group of kids. There were plenty of witnesses and he did this right in front of me! I locked him up."

"What happened?"

"What usually happens when the drunk driver is a politician? His Judge buddy let him off with a slap to the wrist and he's been after me every since. When he hears the Studio is closing the shoot, I'm sure I'll be to blame about that as well."

"What about your job?" Sage asked softly.

"At this point, I don't know and I'm not sure that I care anymore. It's an uphill battle to give my guys raises. Hell, they wanted to lay off two of my men last year. I got into this to be a good cop and do my job, not for the politics."

"You've done all you can," Sage reminded him softly.

"I'm not so sure," Jon argued. He sounded anxious. "There're so many questions left unanswered. Look, it's after nine thirty, why don't you get some rest. I think I'll head back over to the station and give René Devereaux one more chance to talk to me tonight. If I learn anything I'll call you right away."

"Jon," Sage said hearing the fear in her voice. She stopped, not knowing what to say. It seemed childish to simply keep him on the line. "Good night. Call me if you learn anything more."

"I will, Sweetie, and I miss you too," he said in a raw husky voice that was weighted in sensuality. His voice cracked with longing as he continued, "I want to be with you. And Sage, I meant what I said to you earlier. We'll talk as soon as I get this René Devereaux thing over. Tomorrow, we'll have all the answers we need to know."

"Call me if you hear anything," Sage said reluctantly letting him go.

There was nothing more she could say. She needed to think...about everything.

Across town, Jon slammed paperwork on his desk. Patience was not his forte and he was about at the end of it. He was sure René held the answers he needed.

He didn't like Sage being alone without him but she had

four big guys there to stand guard over her. The best thing he could do to protect her was to get some answers out of that fat Louisiana short order cook.

He leaned back in the chair, and, in his mind, he saw her lying naked in his arms, her perfect body molding into his.

She was the most beautiful woman in the world and she deserved someone better than a dirt water Police Chief. But, he argued with a smile, he had seen himself in her eyes today and realized he was now something more. She had made him so. She wanted him and he felt it in each hungry kiss.

Just thinking of her it he grew hard and shifted in his seat.

Remembering the melodious sound of the rain, the sweet taste of her mouth, the velvet silkiness of her soft skin was a pleasure too sweet for words. He made a vow to cherish this beautiful woman who had given him a gift, an unexpected chance at life.

Glancing at his watch, he took an uneasy breath. He would not keep Mr. Devereaux waiting a moment more. The one thing he could do this night was to keep her safe.

Sage leaned back against the headboard of her bed and smiled. She couldn't wait to be in his arms again and she was glad he had called.

Glancing at the mound of employment records and background information on the contestants beside her, she dutifully brought them into her lap and began reading one after the other.

A little over an hour later, she took the stack of paperwork to the dresser, took a shower and changed into an oversized tee shirt from her college days. Glancing at herself in the mirror, she laughed wondering what Jon would think of her well-worn nightgown.

Her eye caught the stack of papers but her eyes were tired and strained, and she could simply read no more. She turned off the lamp and settled back in bed.

Realizing the news broadcast was on; she reached for the remote and turned up the volume.

Murder in Florida was the second story into the news. The story was filled with more speculation and innuendoes than fact.

The reporter rehashed the death on the set, hypothesis on the autopsy, and the mysterious food poisoning, somehow tying it into a local Indian curse.

Sage half-smiled wishing this could be attributed to a ridiculous legend.

With the entrance of the Sand Point Inn in view, her hired security man in the background, the reporter concluded the story with several questions, the last with speculation that the Studio might be considering closing down.

Shifting her pillows under her head, she laid back, grateful he ended the segment without mention of René Devereaux. So, Sage thought with a satisfied smile, they would have René and his secrets one more day.

Before she could click off the television set, the broadcast went into the next story, sharks in record number off the Gulf Coast.

A perky blond, with short curly hair and collagen lips, began the next story before Sage could turn off the television.

"Sharks are not new to Florida," she said flashing a brilliant smile to the home audience, "but a strange phenomenon is occurring for the second straight year in a row. Great schools of Black Tip sharks are gathering off the west coast of Florida."

The screen changed to the same reporter wearing

headphones seated in what appeared to be the cockpit of a helicopter.

"Scientists are baffled as to why the sharks have returned," she shouted.

The television picture shifted, showing the beautiful clear waters of the Gulf of Mexico. With the reporter's voice filling the background, the camera captured the helicopter's fast flight over the water. The scene was mesmerizing.

"Black Tip sharks are not the largest of sharks, but they are fast and aggressive and are generally found in the warm waters of the Atlantic and Pacific. Black Tip sharks can grow up to six feet in length and are easily recognized by the clear black marking on their dorsal and pectoral fins."

The picture held on an astounding shot of sharks, swarming endlessly in the blue water.

The perky blond reporter continued, "Sharks such as the Black Tips are best suited to a long distance cruising. They are, however, capable of high speeds of up to close to twenty miles per hour. They detect their prey by smell, motion detection, and eyesight and by sensing electrical currents created by the nervous systems of their prey."

The scene changed back to the studio where the two attractive news anchors were feigning interest. With a staged frown, the dark haired male anchor asked, "Do environmentalists know why this is happening?"

On cue, the flaxen blond, now dressed in a different outfit from her taped report, glanced over her shoulders into the live shot of the Gulf of Mexico.

Sage recognized the scene as the St. Gabrielle Fishing Pier. Behind her an excited group of teens, who should have been in bed, waved at the camera.

Unflustered by the activity, the reporter answered the

anchorman, "No, Scott, the scientists are as baffled as we are by the activity."

"Thanks, Shelly," the anchor replied with a shuffle of papers.

The perky blond nodded and the anchorman informed the audience weather was next.

"That right, Scott," the weather man said standing in front of a map of Florida's west coast, "Tomorrow promises to be another picture perfect day in paradise."

Sage switched off the television and plunged the room into darkness.

She settled in the bed. It was too easy to remember Jon's arms around her.

With her eyelids heavy, she reached across the bed to touch the pillow where he had laid beside her.

The red digital number of her clock radio flipped from eleven twenty-three to eleven twenty-four. She was asleep before it registered eleven twenty-five.

She woke the next morning at quarter to seven and turned off the radio. Brushing her hair from her face, she looked at the telephone. The night must have been peaceful.

She showered, changed into a fresh McCall Security uniform, and headed toward the event tent. The rich smell of coffee touched her as she entered.

Pouring herself a cup of coffee, she joined a sleepy Double K sitting alone at one of the tables. Members of the production crew and a few contestants were slowly coming into the tent walking straight for the lavishly prepared buffet table.

"Anything new?" she asked taking a sip of hot coffee.

Double K shook his head and shoved his breakfast plate away. "Jeff left word he wanted everyone here at eleven a.m. for an announcement. Half the crew thinks the Studio is going to shut down the production. The other half thinks we may be resuming the shooting schedule. I don't think closing the production will be unexpected at this point. Not for the veterans anyway."

Oz walked in the tent, taking a moment to examine the steaming trays of eggs, bacon, ham, potatoes, pancakes, and fruit. He gave Manuel, his assistant, a wave and came over and sat down with Double K and Sage.

"Seems like I remember you promised to go for a ride on my boat today," Oz said beaming at her. His mood was buoyant. His eyes were bright in anticipation.

Sage couldn't help but smile.

In the same instant, she also realized with sadness how desperately Oz wanted someone to share his new boat with. He had friends in LA who would gladly join him, but here, he only had a handful and those were too busy to spend an hour or so with him on the boat. She gave him a nod.

"Absolutely," she said taking a sip of coffee. "I understand we're having a major announcement at eleven but a short trip would be nice. Double K, I'm sure there is room for you if you want to join us?"

Before Oz could readily agree, Double K shook his head. "No, I can't. I get seasick if I look at the ocean too long."

Oz and Sage both laughed.

"Well, Manuel has everything pretty much under control." Oz said with a backward glance at his assistant. He looked down at his Timex and grinned. "It's going on eight now. How 'bout you meet me at the boat in forty-five minutes. We'll shove off and be back by ten."

"I'll see you then," Sage promised.

Oz brightened. "Great!"

Sage grinned; a couple of hours on the water was just what

she needed. It would give her the fresh perspective on a lot of things.

"What do I need to bring?" she asked deciding she would eat a light breakfast after all.

"Just yourself, Sweetie," Oz said sounding very, very pleased.

Oz hurried over to Manuel and after a few words, Sage watched him hurry away to ready the boat.

Poor Oz, she thought privately, he seemed so excited just to have someone share an hour or two on the boat with him.

"Well," Sage said turning back to Double K, "if I'm going to go out on the water. I need to eat something."

Double K rose when she did and followed her over to the breakfast buffet.

Grabbing a plate, Sage looked at him, and he grinned as he began filling the plate.

"I'm a growing boy," he explained with a sheepish grin. Sage could only laugh.

They were almost finished breakfast when her cell phone rang. It was Jon.

His voice was rich, warm, and filled with longing.

"I missed you last night. When I finished with René I even thought about coming out but figured you were already asleep. Did you get any rest?"

His voice wrapped around her, filling her every sense. Sage smiled into the phone.

"Yes, thank you," came her happy reply. It was good to hear his voice.

"Well, the mayor wants my head on a platter and he has gotten everyone up in arms. I checked in on René Devereaux. He's having some coffee now. He looks like he's rested. I'm going to take in his breakfast, which should be here any minute. He looks ready to talk. I'll call you if I learn anything and should be out today between eleven and twelve."

"That would be a good thing," Sage replied already eager to see him. "Jeff is going to make 'the' announcement' then. A little moral support would be appreciated."

"OK, honey, see you then."

She glanced at her watch. She was fervently alive just knowing she would be with him in a matter of hours.

Leaving Double K alone to finish his pancakes, she returned to her room to wash her hands and was on the dock at eight forty-five.

The engine of the boat was purring.

"Ahoy?" Sage called out. "Permission to come aboard."

"Welcome aboard," Oz said coming from the open cabin.

"What can I do to help?" Sage called to him.

"Well, you can help me cast off," Oz said pointing to the mooring lines.

They worked in unison and in a matter of minutes; Oz had the boat headed out into the gulf.

Less than a mile off shore, he stopped and disappeared into the cabin. Returning on deck, he held two tall glasses of what looked like orange juice.

"I almost forgot," he called out to her over the outboard, "I made some mimosas for us. I know it's early but thought it would be fun to inaugurate the Carol Ann properly."

It was a bit too early to drink, but Sage accepted the mimosa. How could she refuse?

"To the Carol Ann," Sage said raising her glass.

There seemed to be an edge of impatience creeping into his strained voice as Oz lifted his glass to hers. "Yes, to the Carol Ann."

At the soft clink of dime store glass, Oz pulled away

slowly. For just a moment, Sage watched Oz's face tense. His blue eyes turned cool and icy. A spasm crossed his face, and then he smiled, vanquishing his dark thoughts.

Perhaps, Sage thought sadly, his murdered daughter crossed his mind. She felt sorry for him and tried to smile.

He licked his lips, pleased she had toasted with him. Returning to the helm, he pushed the throttle forward.

Sage leaned against the boat's hand rail and looked across the expanse of blue water. It was going to be a beautiful day.

"Have you seen the reports on the Black Tip Sharks?" Oz called out to her.

"Yes," Sage shouted back over the rush of wind and rumble of the motor as the boat hit the breakwater. "I saw a report on the news last night."

Though the waves were minimal, the speed of the boat across the water was jarring. Sage wished Oz would slow the boat's speed.

She looked across the horizon. Light white puffy clouds were filling the sky. The sun was behind them but she could still feel its warmth on her back and arms.

At last slowing the boat, Sage leaned back and took another drink of her mimosa. The orange juice tasted sweet. She could feel the euphoric effect of the alcohol as her muscles began to relax. She realized for the first time in days how tense she had been.

The light spay of water was exhilarating and felt refreshing to her face and arms. She was decidedly enjoying the moment, allowing her thoughts to drift toward the handsome Chief of Police.

She turned to look at Oz. His eyes were fixed on her and his lips were curling into an ugly grin.

Sage regarded him, not quite capturing his full expression. She called out, "Everything okay?"

Her voice sounded distant. She was drifting in a sea of tranquility and realized, without any sense of alarm, that she didn't care whether he answered or not.

"Couldn't be better," he shouted turning his back to her again. "This is working out better than I planned."

Sage looked back out to the gulf. The waters were sparkling with shards of light.

Somewhere deep inside her a warning thought began to form. She looked around, the day couldn't be more perfect and she had known Oz for years.

She leaned back and closed her eyes. She felt weightless, floating in a perfect harmony of spirit. When was the last time she had been so peaceful? It had been years!

Then, she thought of him.

Jon.

There was nothing to fear.

"Look!" Sage called out as a school of dolphins leap from the water.

The moment seemed magical.

Oz slowed the boat to a full stop and vanished into the cutty cabin.

Sage rose to follow him, but he emerged moments later with two large five gallon drums. He seemed to be walking in slow motion.

She wanted to ask him what he was doing, but couldn't form the words or even manage to phrase so simple a question.

In a growing daze, she watched him open the containers and slide red chum into the water.

As he made a second trip into the cabin, Sage looked back

to the shoreline. If anyone was looking for her, the small boat wouldn't even be a speck on the horizon.

Opening up the second five-gallon bucket, he glanced at her and smiled. The chum was leaving a long bloody red streak atop the blue water.

It smelled of death.

"What are you doing?" Sage finally managed to ask feeling her breath quicken.

Nauseating spurts of adrenaline rushed through her body fighting the drowsy sensation that was threatening to overwhelm her.

"Chumming the waters," Oz replied casually in a voice that lacked emotion. "Just wanted to see the sharks. This should draw them. No need to be alarmed, Sage."

Sage shook her head. She was dizzy and wished she hadn't drunk the mimosa.

Nothing was making sense. She began to struggle to fight her way back to consciousness.

She began to rally her thoughts and tried to rise but fell back against the seat as the long sleek body of a five-foot shark glided across the bow of the boat. Her body felt heavy.

"They smell the blood," Oz said pointing out a second shark.

Watching for the two sharks at the bow of the boat, she glanced to her left just in time to see a third shark, its black dorsal fin cutting the water as it swam down the side of the boat.

The sharks began to swirl and dart, their ashy gray bodies just feet away from the boat. As one of the sharks turned, Sage saw its white underbelly with a dusty band of darker gray color extending backward along each side. Its pectoral fins were black-tipped. Their eyes were black and lifeless as they swam through the water too close to the boat.

Try as she could, it was a struggle to focus.

Setting the Mimosa down beside her, she realized she was disoriented.

She had been drugged.

Grabbing the back of the seat, she rose and staggered toward the cutty cabin.

Before she reached it, Oz was at her side.

"Where do you think you are going?" he asked his lips pursed with suppressed fury.

"I don't feel well," Sage heard herself reply.

"Come sit down," Oz said softly, "I'll get you a glass of water."

She turned from the cabin door, allowing him to guide her back to her seat, but not before noticing a commercial video camera on the table inside. On the floor, two large red gas containers sat on the floor.

Why would Oz have a video camera in the cabin, she wondered, finding it strange and out of place?

She was trying desperately to shake off the queasiness as he gently settled her back in her seat.

Watching Oz idly she noticed for the first time a long streak of a scratch along the back of his arm. "How did that happen?"

"You did it."

"I did it?" Sage heard herself laugh. "When could I have possibly scratched you, Oz?"

The sharks were now circling the boat. More than she could count. Their speed was increasing; the water was boiling with their movement.

She looked up at Oz, her stomached knotting. When had she been close enough to scratch Oz?

Then she remembered.

She remembered what she had forgotten the night of the attack.

She suddenly knew when, she knew where.

With her heart pounding, her breath ragged, she watched as Oz's face contorted grotesquely changing into to someone she did not know.

In numbed horror, her face grew pensive. She stiffened at his touch, loathing his hand upon her. Fear was welling inside as she tried to wake her dulled senses.

She glanced at the Mimosa struggling to fight off the effects of whatever drug he had hidden in the sweet orange mixture.

"You know, Sage," he began softly, "I always liked you, even when you were a little girl. You kinda reminded me of Carol Ann when she was your age."

Sage sat quietly. Carol was, she remembered, his murdered daughter.

"You don't really remember her do you? You were just eight when you met her. She was almost twenty."

"I remember her," Sage lied reaching for her cell phone at her side.

Oz easily gripped the phone and easily pried it from her fingers. In a single movement, he tossed it overboard.

The small splash instantly drew the closest sharks to the spot where it hit the water.

"I remember the day I first saw you, Sage. We were filming some movie, I forget which, but you came in with your Dad. I talked to your father and you spoke to Carol Ann. She was going to follow in my footsteps just like you are doing with your father."

Sage offered a smile to Oz, trying to access a distant memory but couldn't. She could feel the small hairs on the back of her neck stirring. A knot was constricting her throat.

"You know they never found the person who killed my wife and my little girl." Oz said evenly. A crazed look deepened in his smoldering eyes. In an almost wistful tone, he added, "Just another unsolved murder in Los Angeles. Carol Ann and her mother weren't movie stars. They weren't important enough to anyone but me."

"Oz," Sage stammered, her eyes darting maniacally about the boat for something to defend herself with. "I'm so sorry."

Oz gave her a monstrous glare then his face sharpened in disgust. His eyes took on a haunted expression and she realized what she should have seen, what someone should have seen long ago.

Oz was totally insane.

"You're a sweet girl, Sage. That's why I am going to hate doing this."

"Do what?" Sage asked with a forced smile.

The veins in his neck tightened in a stubborn line and his smile was malicious. His eyes regarded her in bitter triumph.

"Why, Sage," he said his voice dripping with spite, "I thought you might have guessed by now. I'm going to kill you."

CHAPTER TWELVE

From outside reality, Sage fought through the cobwebs of a drugged-filled haze. Her limbs were heavy. It was hard to stay awake.

The drugs were whirling through every fiber, every cell of her body. Their unspoken pleas, like a siren's call, were willing her to just let go and sleep.

Sage blinked hard struggling to throw off the effects of the narcotics but they were overpowering her.

Through a blurry vision, she saw Oz standing across from her. With his fat arms crossed over his chest, he looked deceptively calm and relaxed. His voice was shrill, his eyes as lifeless as the sharks schooling around the small boat.

Sage struggled to focus. Her mouth was dry and her limbs weighted.

All she had to do was sleep.

Sleep.

His words had struck her like hammer blows and she knew, he was only waiting for the effects of the drugs to subdue her.

From behind a wall of a drunken stupor, she willed herself to live. Her mind struggled though a shadowy haze of tangled thoughts and emotions. She saw images of her Father, her family, and Jon.

More real than life itself, she knew in her heart, she was in love with Jon. She knew he was in love with her.

Her head was reeling, her heart driving her forward, she willed herself to live. She willed herself to stay alive.

She glanced overboard just in time to see the large dorsal fin of a Black Tip Shark part the water. The shark was followed by another, and then another, each slithering through the water faster than the one before. Their search was becoming reckless, their turns murderous and quick.

Death was in the air and they could smell it.

Her cell phone lay at the bottom of the Gulf of Mexico. Her gun safely stored in her motel room.

She glanced about looking for something, anything that would help her live just a few more moments.

"Why do you want to kill me, Oz?" She asked. It was becoming impossible to speak, to keep her tone even and her words clear.

He rolled his eyes at her and his face twisted into a hideous sneer.

"Same reason, I shot Evan with an arrow," he said as if he were talking to a child, "same reason I put the mushrooms in the sauce."

"You attacked me in the kitchen," she stated, her mouth was fuzzy, her words slurred.

Oz chuckled. "No one suspected me."

"Did you write that threatening note to René?"

Oz gave her a casual nod. He appeared in no hurry. "I did. He saw me add the mushrooms to the sauce and didn't say a word. Of course, he didn't know they were poisonous at the time. He even ate some of the spaghetti. Got sick like the others. I guess it will be a matter of time before he puts two and two together."

"I thought you liked him?" Sage heard her voice say. It sounded weak, soft, and distant.

Fighting the blackness that threatened her, she looked at Oz, unable to turn away. "I thought you liked me?"

"I do, I do," he spoke in an odd, yet gentle tone, "but when you took René to jail, I knew he'd talk sooner rather than later. As you can see, I have no choice but to act now."

He took two steps from her and looked passively at the thick gray swarm of sharks swimming faster. Their speed was increasing as they churned the water in search of the kill. He seemed pleased. He turned back to her.

"If it will make you feel better, Sage, I even thought of killing René but he's a nobody. No one would really care about René. Hillary, Connard, even Jeff might get a short mention but Sage McCall. Your father will insure your death will be noted. The publicity from this will be alive for months. That's why I had to pick you, Sage, you understand, don't you?"

Sage didn't understand. She wasn't meant to.

"So," she said formulating her thoughts into words, "you did this hoping to gain publicity for yourself?"

"Me?" Oz asked as though genuinely surprised at her question. "No, not me. I'm just the messenger, the sacrificial lamb, so to speak. And I know I will have to endure public ridicule from people who don't understand. I understand, all too well, that I'll have to go through the trial, the endless interviews, psychological profiles, the media, and the made for TV movie. I really don't want the publicity but I have no choice."

He stopped and his fleshy face brightened. "Say, I hadn't thought of it until right now, but they could get your sister to play you. Nick McMasters could produce it. He has the inside track, after all. Hillary could direct, I always thought I'd like to have George Leggett to play me. He's such a wonderful actor, what do you think?"

Oz's eyes were glazing over and Sage was fighting her way back to consciousness. She felt drained and hollow, and fatigue was ever-threatening to envelop her into darkness.

"I think you're insane," Sage said, her words lingering on her tongue.

Oz slapped his thigh and howled, "That's what my lawyer is going to say!"

An icy chill ran down her back and her small hands balled into fists. She dug her nails into the palms of her hands. She was in a macabre dance with a mad man and there was no way out. A sudden stab of regret hit her chest, why hadn't she seen this before.

She watched him; he was beginning to move like a caged animal, close to the kill.

"I still don't understand why, Oz," she apologized struggling to understand.

He seemed in no hurry. It was as if he had all day.

He did.

"Because of the publicity," Oz said not bothering to cover his yawn. He took in a long breath and articulated each word carefully so she would understand. "Sage, my dear, as you are aware, Americans can't get enough of murder. They watch it every night, every day, it's on the news, hell, and we even have channels devoted to crime and punishment. Hollywood glamorizes murder and it's getting worse every day. People are desensitized to death. So I intend to put it in their faces. They need to see a real live murder. Yours."

"This is nothing personal Sage," he added in a voice that was as cold as death. "But someone has to do this. I knew you would understand."

Incredibly, Sage realized the boat was his confessional. He was asking her for absolution.

"My death won't stop Hollywood, Oz." She argued but her reasoning went unnoticed. He was lost in his insanity and from his madness there was, for him, no chance of return.

"Maybe not," he said, "but it's important to try."

He shifted about keeping his eyes on her. "You know when I found Evan, he was already dead. I thought just shooting him would do the trick and the close down the show. It didn't of course. I even heard Nick is going to start shooting again this week. Jeff is supposed to do the big announcement today."

Sage shook her head in a defiant struggle to throw off the effects of the drugs. There was no use telling him Nick intended to do just the opposite. Oz had come too far to ever come back. Her fate was sealed.

Deep inside her adrenaline was pushing her back to sanity.

She had to know the truth, all of it. Each question, each reply was buying her precious moments while she struggled to keep her voice edged with control.

"Where did you get the bow and arrow?" her voice cutting through the quiet calm of the morning. "The prop trailer is always locked."

"It wasn't earlier that day. I helped the Production Assistants bring some things over to the set. No one noticed I had picked up the bow and arrow."

Sage shuttered. Had Oz intended on using the archery set on a live target? She thanked Evan Davis for his life and for his natural death.

Looking into the twisted face of evil, Sage cried in a burst of fierceness, "What about Jamie Wolf?"

"Oh Jamie, nice kid," came Oz's velvet reply. "He came in through the back. I hid in the shadows and hit him before he even knew I was there. You never suspected it was me, did you, Sage?"

Sage looked at him and slowly shook her head. Double K had been right. The darkness and the swiftness of the attack had been made by a heavier man.

"Your boyfriend suspected me," Oz said with a frown. "He asked me questions and came back and asked more. But he trusted you and you trusted me."

"And you think by killing me, you are going to stop the film industry from making movies about murder?"

"I think the American public will tell Hollywood they've had enough."

There was nowhere to run in this small boat.

"Is that why you brought the camera?"

"Oh you saw it?" Oz asked genuinely surprised. "Yes, I'm going to film your death for the home audience. Everyone will see it Sage. Your Father, your Mother, your beautiful sister Fallon, Nick McMasters, your boyfriend, and millions of Americans, over and over and over again."

Oz laughed as only one insane could. "And the icing on the cake is your boyfriend will be there to oversee everything. I'm sure I can taunt him enough and he'll snap. I doubt he'll be able to keep his cool for very long, especially about you. I could tell that the night when I attacked you."

"It's all worked out then," Sage said her voice sounding groggy to her own ears.

No, Sage thought, she had to rally; she wasn't going to die like this.

"You will never get away with this." Sage warned him.

Oz only laughed. "Oh, I have no intention of getting away with this. I might get off scot-free. I could wind up on all the talk shows, go on college lectures, people will send money to a foundation with my daughter's name on it."

Sage felt sick to her stomach. Although her arms felt heavy, and her feet felt like they had weights in them, powerful forces were welling inside her. She had no intention of dying.

There was a faint glint of humor in his dull eyes as he said wearily, "You don't have any choice. I gave you enough muscle relaxer to knock out a horse. I can't believe you haven't passed out by now. Maybe you should drink some more."

"Its time, Sage," Oz said quietly, his voice took on an ominous quality that was unmistakable. He was deranged; streaks of madness were visible in his light blue eyes.

"You're not going to kill me, Oz!" Sage warned him, her voice dark and insolent.

"Sage, I'm sorry honey, we've just been out here too long. Someone will come looking for you and I can't let that happen. Here, let me help you take another drink."

Oz casually reached across her for her mimosa as a small wave knocked the Navigator jarring the boat.

Sage realized if she were to have one chance to live, she would have to take it now. She had to move. She had to move now!

As Oz leaned over, in one fluid movement Sage brought her legs up to her waist and kicked, knocking Oz to the deck.

Pushing herself to rise, she propelled herself forward; she had to make it to the cabin.

About to slide down into the cabin, Oz was miraculously upon her and grabbed a thick hank of her golden hair, yanking her backwards.

"I didn't expect that," he hissed trying to pull her to the back of the boat. In her drugged state, it was easy.

Fighting the pain, she jabbed her elbow into his chest

and he fell into her. She turned and in one fluid movement slammed his face with her backhand.

He screamed in pain and tried to grab her but she whirled, slamming her foot into his abdomen, and again, a second kick into his stomach.

Oz fell.

Sage ran to the console, her senses were too dull to put up much more of a fight to her assailant. Madness was on his side. She had to find something to fight with.

"Sage, it doesn't have to be like this," he said, incredibly rising to his feet.

Without waiting for him to come to her, she grabbed the boat's radio.

"Mayday, Mayday," she screamed into the hand held mic, "This is Sage McCall."

Damn, she didn't know where she was!

"I'm in the Gulf of Mexico, approximately forty-five minutes somewhere west of the Sand Point Inn. Oswald Anderson is trying to kill me!"

Behind her she saw Oz and heard his laugh. "I don't care who you tell, Sage. Don't you get it; no one can get to you in time. Now are you going to come with me, be a good little girl? The sharks are waiting."

"No," Sage protested, with the last ounce of strength in her possession and turned toward him sideways in a defensive horse stance, her legs bent, her arms raised for striking.

Oz bunched his fleshy hands into fists. A burning hatred blazed in his crazed eyes. His nostrils were flaring and he hurled his huge body toward her.

Sage's kick was high and it cut his brow.

He took a step back.

"You bitch," his hissed in the same tone he had used the night of her attack.

Her adrenaline was spent. Beads of perspiration were dripping from her forehead as the drugs began dulling her senses once again. Her arms fell slightly.

Oz noticed the slight movement and sneered at her. They both knew at that moment this was one battle she would not win.

As he began to move slowly forward, she caught a glimpse of the boat's emergency first aid box beside the captain's chair and a flare gun beside it.

She pressed her weight into her forward leg and with as much force as she could muster she heel kicked the emergency case. The lid fell open exposing a first aid kit and a flare gun.

She stepped back, ripped the flare gun from the casings, and pointed it at Oz.

He stopped cold.

"I can blow a hole through you, Oz, and I will. "She said evenly. "I want you to go back and sit down. Now!"

Oz stood motionless.

Sage brought the gun to his forehead. Her fingers were cold on the trigger.

"Move," she said her voice groggy from the narcotics.

With his attention on the wide barrel of the flare gun, he began to step backward.

Sage moved slowly forward, keeping pace with him. She had no plan except to bind him with the mooring rope before she totally lost consciousness.

"Sit," she ordered him.

Seeing her weave, Oz darted around her quickly and was now at the front of the boat. He lunged at her and she fired at him. The flare streaking passed him into the cutty cabin.

With a sudden pop, the cutty cabin exploded into flames. The shot had hit the extra fuel Oz had brought onboard.

Oz turned back to her. His eyes were glassy with fear. He knew, as she did, the boat was going to explode.

The yellow flames hurled from the cabin rose five feet across the deck.

Oz stumbled toward the back of the boat and stared at the circling sharks.

There was nowhere to run, for either of them. She could count her life in minutes.

Sage lunged for the radio.

"Mayday, mayday," She screamed into the mic, "This is the Carol Ann. There's been an explosion on board. We are surrounded by sharks, if anyone can hear me…."

It was over. All was lost. She still wasn't prepared to die.

"What is your location, Carol Ann?" came a loud reply over the speaker. "This is Coast Guard Skipper Lt. Jake Murray, and we got your earlier transmission. We're on our way. Repeat—What's your location?"

"I don't know, " Sage cried. "There is no time, the boat is going to explode."

"Our helicopters see your fire, Carol Ann, stay calm."

"Stay calm my ass," Oz said turning toward Sage.

Below them the she heard a pop, pop of exploding canisters. Then a large deafening boom. It rocked the boat. Sage grabbed for the back of the captain's chair. Oz fell onto the deck.

"That was the propane tank, you bitch," Oz said rising again. "In about two seconds this boat is going to explode. You have ruined my plans, Sage; my only compensation is you are going to die with me. We're going to be blown to bits then eaten by the sharks."

Black smoke was billowing all around them.

"I'm not going to die!" Sage screamed at Oz.

His laugh was diabolical and it cackled over the roar of the cabin's fire.

"I'm going to stay with the Carol Ann," he screamed, "like I should have stayed with my daughter the night she was murdered! I figure we have about thirty seconds before she explodes. So like I said, you will be eaten alive or you will be eaten dead."

Black smoke was darkening the boat.

Sage knew she did not have a chance to survive the explosion.

The coast guard was on their way. However slim, she had one choice. She had to take it.

Climbing to the rail, she could barely see the water under the thick layer of smoke.

"You could have been famous," she heard Oz scream at her, "Here, wait, let me watch you die!"

Sage didn't wait. With the drugs still trying to take full effect, she dove headlong into the cool water. She dove at a hard angle hoping to distance herself from the boat.

Diving as far as she could, she turned upward toward the surface, pushing herself further away from the boat.

As she surfaced, black billowing smoke was curling about the boat, Oz's dark silhouette poised against the bow, facing in her direction.

She heard him laugh again and with a gulp of surface air, she dove once again.

Twelve feet underwater, she felt the hard brush of a shark against her leg. She stopped her dive and pushed herself away from the predator.

Muffling a scream, she felt a second shark tug at her leg. She kicked and clawed her way to the surface once again.

She began to swim knowing the six-foot Black Tip was circling back toward her.

The boat will explode, she thought, I just have to stay alive until it explodes.

Her eyes widened in terror as she saw the shark turn and move directly toward her. She dove beneath him.

A third shark was headed right toward her. She dove beneath him, too.

"Swim, pretty Sage," she heard Oz shout, "I want to see you die."

Sage surfaced and looked back at the boat. It was in flames.

Treading water she began to cough, the black smoke filling her lungs.

She heard Oz's malicious laugh one last time before an explosion ripped through the boat. She dove back into the water as a surge of water hit her.

Surfacing again to gasp some air, two pieces of flaming wood fell around her.

She turned to see Oz still teetering on the edge the boat. He screamed, twisted, and fell into the water.

Two sharks were immediately upon him. His scream shrieking across the water before his body was taken below.

There was nothing she could do for him now but save her own life.

The water was turning red in a feeding frenzy. Unnoticed, she floated still as several black tips swam past her toward the activity.

She would not go unnoticed for long, so with long strokes she began to swim toward shore, knowing she would never make it there alive.

Overhead she caught the sudden sound of a helicopter and the sound of a fast moving boat.

"Help, help," she screamed, swimming frantically toward the boat.

"Sage!" Jon screamed in a guttural cry filled with terror.

Swimming toward the sound of the motor, she heard him cut the engine and felt the roughness of a rope glide past her head to fall a foot behind her.

Still fighting the groggy effects of the drug, she grabbed for the rope.

With one seamless pull, she felt herself glide across the water, and felt Jon's powerful hands on her shoulder. He yanked her onto the Boston Whaler as a black tip shark dove under the boat.

The shark had been upon her.

Exhausted and dizzy from the drugs, Sage opened her eyes; her smile was sweet to his worried expression.

"It'll be all right, honey," he said bringing her into his arms. "Lay here, we have got to get away from that boat, it might explode again."

Sage nodded and lay back on the warm deck.

Jon wasted little time as he spun his boat toward the safety of the shore.

"I got her," Jon shouted into the mic.

"Can see that," a helicopter pilot said overhead. "Nice going, Chief. Better get out of there."

Overhead, Sage saw the helicopter dip and move instantly out of sight.

With his boat at full speed, she heard a massive explosion behind her but she didn't bother to rise to look. She couldn't.

As her eyes dropped in heaviness, she studied Jon's worried expression tight with a mixture of rage and worry.

How had he known where to find her?

René must have talked. Jon would have tried to contact her and when he called the set, Double K would have told him she had left with Oz.

She wanted to tell him she loved him. She wanted to hear that he loved her, and with a silent smile, she remembered his words spoken, now is not the time, this is not the place.

There would be another time, the right time.

As she closed her eyes, she no longer had to fight the sleep that was upon her. Then she slowly opened her eyes once more and lovingly looked at him.

She was with Jon. She was safe.

He had found her.

She knew he would never let her go.

The End

EPILOGUE

From his corporate office overlooking Sunset Boulevard, Jack McCall stood looking out his window toward the Los Angeles skyline. My city, he thought with a measure of pride, my town.

Walking across the room, he looked at the photos resting on top of his desk.

His beautiful wife Savannah was every bit as beautiful as the day he married her. After all these years, he still looked at Savannah the way Jon Maddux, his new son-in-law, looked at his daughter Sage. Jack shuddered remembering how close they had been to losing Sage at the hands of a mad man. He chuckled; at least, she stopped showing those damn scars left by a Black Tip Shark on her leg. Sage had escaped death twice that day and now she and Jon were overseeing security for a film being shot in Mexico. She looked happy in the photo. Hard to believe they had been married two months. Knowing Jon would always be there to protect her, he was no longer worried about Sage.

Reading the headlines, he dialed his youngest daughter's phone number. No answer again. He racked his hand through his thinning hair and leaned back in his chair. Fear and anxiety knotted inside him. He tried to brush away the disturbing thoughts but the chill within of him continued to grow.

"Where the hell are you?" He snapped glancing at Mallory's photo. Blond hair, blue eyes, she looked back at him from the picture, flanked on either side by her German Shepard, Scout, and her Golden Retriever, Hunter. In tight fitting jeans, her T-shirt read, K-9 Search and Rescue. She was smiling. She looked safe. She wasn't. She was in danger.

Anxious, Jack picked up the phone and dialed her cell phone. His mouth was dry and his hands were clammy. Still, no answer.

She must have seen the headlines. Surely, she knew, there was a serial killer roaming the tall woods of Cold River.

The McCall Mysteries continue as Mallory McCall's adventure begins in The Cold River Murders.

ABOUT THE AUTHOR

Since exploding into the world of suspense, Linn Random has achieved top reviews for her novels. Her name is linked to spine tingling suspense, action packed excitement and characters that sparkle with intensity and emotion. Her novels are fresh with multi-layered plots that that will leave you breathless.

Linn Random lives in Central Florida with her husband and son. Linn works with K-9 Search and Rescue in Central Florida and is a member of NASAR, National Search and Rescue. Her K-9 Partner, companion and friend is a golden retriever Hunter.

She has been featured in numerous interviews in print and radio and is a prominent national speaker.

Linn is a member of the Mystery Writers of American, International Thriller Writers, Sisters in Crime and the Romance Writers of America.

Lights. Camera. Murder! is first in a series involving the beautiful McCall sisters, each involved in some aspect of the movie industry. *Lights. Camera. Murder!* will be followed by *Cold River Murders* where Sage's sister. Mallory, has moved to Northern California to escape the glitz and glamour of LA. She is a screen writer and works with her K-9 Search and Rescue Team until she finds a killer's private graveyard along the banks of Cold River

Cold River Murders will be followed by Fallon McCall's book *Mourning Song.*

If you love heart pounding danger, cover to cover action, with beautiful resourceful heroines and street savvy men who will leave your pulses racing, you will enjoy Linn Random's romantic suspense novels available in print, ebook and audio format.

*For a **FREE** Chapter Reads, watch "Movie Trailer's",*
Complete Reviews, Audio Books and Contest Prizes visit
__www.LinnRandom.com__.

ALSO BY LINN RANDOM:
Your Cheatin' Hearts
A Lucille Ball Comedy with a Twist of Magnum P.I.
The Ecataromance 2005 Reviewers Choice of the Year in
Comedy
5 Stars, 5 Cupids, 5 Unicorns, Recommended Reads

Combine one hair brain undercover assignment with two bungling kidnappers and get the most eligible bachelor in town. It's a recipe for disaster for pretty PI Shelby MacGregor who always gets her man.

EXCERPT:

"Mrs. Colter," Shelby MacGregor said trying not to sound impatient, "on the phone you said this was urgent, a matter of life and death."

"Did I say that?" Maggie Colter stammered almost as if taken by surprise. The older woman leaned back in her chair. She seemed a bit confused and quiet as though she were contemplating her reply.

Shelby remained silent. Meeting a private investigator for the first time made a lot of people nervous. In three years of heading her own agency, *Your Cheatin Hearts*, she knew she could learn a lot by nervous chatter as well as gain valuable insight into a client's personality. This was crucial, for if their spouse was found cheating, it was imperative she know how her clients would react.

Maggie Colter was different, she had no spouse. She did, however, need her help. Her call came just this morning. It was a matter of life or death she had pleaded. Now Maggie Colter sat hesitant and unresponsive.

Moments passed. Shelby sat patiently. Maggie was hiding something. What? More important why?

Suddenly Maggie Colter's eyes widened, her round face lit with delight. "Yes! That's it! My son is in definite danger, Ms. MacGregor."

The image of Jack Colter flashed in Shelby's mind. The ruggedly handsome Jack Colter looked like a man who could take care of himself.

"You son is in danger?" Shelby repeated. She heard the doubt in her own voice and she had the nagging suspicion that Maggie Colter was making her story up as she went along.

**For a FREE Chapter Reads, watch "Movie Trailers",
Book Reviews, Audio Books
And Contests visit www.LinnRandom.com**

ALSO BY LINN RANDOM
Pirates In Paradise
Two—5 Angels, 5 Blue Ribbons, 5 Unicorns

On the run from Drug Traffickers, US Marshals and FBI, Haley Rollins assumes her twin sister's identity. Her only hope is a modern day Pirate but can she trust him with her secret or her heart?

Excerpt:

The Bronco made a hairpin turn coming to a full stop directly in front of them.

Haley glimpsed a silhouette of a broad shouldered man dominating the driver's side of the vehicle. The driver sat motionless. Time stopped. A frightening premonition swept over Haley; warning her with a fresh new fear she couldn't name. Somewhere deep inside her, she knew that from this moment forward, nothing would ever be same again.

The door opened. A tall man stepped out and headed toward them in a catlike stride. Dressed in a black T-shirt and black jeans, his skin glistened bronze in the moonlight, Haley caught her breath at the broad shoulders. He was menacing and she knew to be afraid. He made no attempt to conceal the restless energy in his muscular physique. Watching his approach, Haley said under her breath, "This is your friend?"

"That's him," Frank answered with a hard gasp of air.

Stepping under a streetlight, the stranger's short, dark cropped hair glistened in the yellow-white light. A light breeze ruffled one lock forward and he swept it back with a large hand.

Haley noted his classically handsome face, his aquiline nose and square jaw. Darkness obscured the color of his eyes. Small drops of moisture clung to his damp forehead and she saw an inherent strength that seemed vaguely familiar.

Hardly giving Haley a glance, he jumped without being asked into the boat. With the craggy look of an unfinished sculpture, he bent his head down to take a better look at Frank's arm. "You didn't tell me you were shot."

"Yeah, well, you can drop me off at the hospital then get out of town. By the way, this is Jenna Rollins. Jenna, this is the infamous Captain Jack Morgan."

With the moonlight against Jack's profile, he stood well over six foot, and possessed a sensuality that was almost frightening. He nodded at her. His generous lips parted to give her a dazzling display of straight white teeth.

Haley stood stupidly still, knowing she was the source of this night's evils. She looked down and away. Men had died because of Jenna's lies and her silence. They would never understand she had been trapped into assuming her twin sisters identity; now there was no way out.

**For a FREE Chapter Reads, watch "Movie Trailers",
Book Reviews, Audio Books
And Contests visit www.LinnRandom.com**

Enjoy more spine tingling action, adventure, and romantic suspense in 2006 with these exciting Romances from Linn Random.

Haunted Hearts—Summer 2006

Beautiful Psychic Medium Devin O'Shea must fight both a poltergeist and a handsome nonbeliever if she is to help the trapped spirit of a 1920's flapper girl. This scary-sexy romp is a laugh out loud adult comedy and a haunting romance.

Black Waters—Fall 2006

Black Waters is a psychological thriller set in Louisiana Bayou Country where Investigative Reporter Jet Williams is researching the resurgence of Voodoo in the old south. Brent Broussard is a Police Chief in over his head. Jet and Brent have their own private agendas for unmasking this terrifying cult. Into the Black Waters they search without realizing…they've become the next targets.

Cold River Murders-2007

Beautiful Mallory McCall has moved to Northern California to escape the glitz, the glamour and the crime in LA. Her life is confined to writing screenplays and working with her K-9 Search and Rescue Team whose searches are limited to missing hikers, lost hunters and an occasional Alzheimer's patient.…until one of her dogs finds a graveyard left by a serial killer along the banks of Cold River.

For a FREE Chapter Reads, watch "Movie Trailers", Book Reviews,
Audio Books And Contests visit www.LinnRandom.com

www.ingramcontent.com/pod-product-compliance
Lightning Source LLC
Chambersburg PA
CBHW071103260626
47162CB00012B/703